Jake McCarthy, Crosswind

Jake McCarthy, Crosswind

Jeffrey Baldwin

Authors Choice Press
San Jose New York Lincoln Shanghai

Jake McCarthy, Crosswind

Authors Choice Press
an imprint of iUniverse.com, Inc.

For information address:
iUniverse.com, Inc.
5220 S 16th, Ste. 200
Lincoln, NE 68512
www.iuniverse.com

This is a work of fiction. Crosswind, Oklahoma is a fictional place. The characters, places and incidents portrayed in this novel are entirely products of the author's imagination and are not to be considered real. Any resemblance to actual events, places, organizations or people is entirely coincidental.

Other books by Jeffrey Baldwin:

Jake McCarthy, Ironwood

ISBN: 0-595-19249-1

Printed in the United States of America

CHAPTER 1

A thick layer of dew coated the coarse, perennial rye grass, causing Jake McCarthy's leather boots instantly to become saturated as he walked from his new Ford Taurus station wagon onto the empty field. He had been preparing since the middle of March. His mind was focused on the next hour when his work would again be tested. He thought of the long hours, the early morning drills and the evening strategy sessions. Today would again demonstrate whether a total novice could take sixteen preadolescent girls and mold them into a winning soccer team. This was the day his girls would do battle with their archrival (or so his daughter, Kimberly, would have him believe). Today they squared off against the Oxford Orioles, a team from the neighboring village of Oxford that was allowed to play in the Rochester league because there weren't enough under-ten girls in Oxford to form a competitive league. Their goalie was good, and they had a fullback that feared no one. She wasn't big, but she was as tough as they come, and more than one of his girls had complained about her roughness in the last game of the fall season. The Orioles had beaten the Royals in the fall by a score of one to nil, and his girls were out to recover their honor.

Jake hadn't really focused on being a soccer coach. Until he had read a few books about the sport and attended a few training sessions run by the local Rochester Hills Soccer Club, he would not have known the difference between a touch line and a penalty box. He still wasn't one hundred percent sure of all the rules, but his girls seemed to know. Kimberly had been playing the game for six seasons and Ashley for four. They played together in the fall for the first time on a newly formed team, and were looking forward to a much-improved spring.

Jake and his wife, Maggie, had hosted the fall team party, and thus considered their responsibility to the team to have been met. The young coach was considered one of the best in the league, having played soccer in college. It came as a great shock to the parents when, at the end of the party, he announced that the General had transferred him back to its Electronic Data Systems Division in Dallas. He would not be able to coach in the spring.

These thoughts went quickly through Jake's mind as he walked to the middle of the wet, converted football field. It was 8:30 Saturday morning, and none of his team had arrived except his two daughters. Kimberly carried the team's ball bag, full of #4 soccer balls, and Ashley, his eight-year-old, carried the team clipboard with its diagrams and practice patterns clipped neatly under the team roster.

A smile came to his face as he remembered that Saturday in December when Maggie had received a letter from the Rochester Hills Youth Soccer League. It had been sent to all the parents of the sixteen girls on the Royals. "After numerous attempts to find a coach for the U-10 Rochester Royals, we must reluctantly report that we are unable to find any parent willing to take on the responsibility. Unless we can find a volunteer before the beginning of the season, we will be forced to disband the team. Of course, we will make every effort to place the girls on other teams in the league, but we cannot promise that they will stay together as a team or be on a team in the same neighborhood."

Maggie, Jake's wife of fourteen years, had read the letter over several times before she turned to Jake and said, "It's not fair. We get the two girls on a good team with all of their friends. They're happy. We're happy. But the league can't find a coach, and the team is disbanded.

There must be lots of dads out there who know about soccer and could coach. I'm going to raise a stink about this. Who do I call, Jake?"

Jake had been reading the Rochester edition of the Eccentric, a widely read suburban newspaper that focused on local events, and had not heard a word Maggie had said. "What, dear?" he asked in response to her question.

"Who do I call to complain about the league not having a coach for Kimberly's team?"

"Call the president, I guess," Jake responded as he returned to the paper. "I'm sure they'll find a coach sooner or later."

Ten minutes and several telephone calls later, Maggie sat down next to Jake on the leather, family-room sofa. He had switched to reading the sports page of the Detroit Free Press and was engrossed in a lengthy article by Mitch Albom explaining in graphic detail why the Detroit Lions could never be a Super Bowl contender. Maggie snuggled up next to Jake and started toying with the hair on the back of his neck. After a few minutes of this unusual attention, Jake put down the sports page. "That feels great! How about we call it a night and go crawl into bed?"

"Jake," Maggie responded softly, "I just spoke with the president of the soccer league, and he convinced me that you would make a marvelous coach for the Royals. I told him you would think about it and tell him tomorrow. I want you to do it. It will give you a chance to spend some time with your daughters and their friends. Please, please, please, Jake! John Martel said he has tried all the other parents and was just about to call you when I called. He said you don't need to know a thing about soccer because they will teach you in a series of Saturday clinics that start in January."

At first Jake resented Maggie's even thinking of volunteering his services without considering the consequences to his law practice. He worked almost every Saturday, and on weekdays he never got home before seven thirty or eight at night. "The commute from Detroit is too tedious if you leave before seven," he had rationalized to Maggie on many occasions. "I just don't have time for coaching, and you know it. You're the one who always complains about my hours. Why don't you volunteer to be the coach?"

Jake resented the pressure that Maggie put on him when he responded to her request with good, solid and very logical reasons why he could not be a coach. He was at a real crossroads in his career. Having made junior partner at the end of the firm's last fiscal year, he now had to show that he could not only do the work but also attract new clients and keep the two associates assigned to him profitably busy. How could he ever meet the required number of billable hours if he left early two or three times a week to conduct practices and never worked on Saturdays?

As much as he resented Maggie's urging, above all Jake really hated the fact that she had told the girls that he was thinking about coaching their team. Jake might have been able to use logic and devotion to his law practice to resist Maggie's pleas and pressures, but he was like soft butter in the warm hands of his two daughters. After his brush with death several months before in Michigan's Upper Peninsula, Jake had a new attitude toward life and his family. As he was led away to what he assumed would be his execution, he had focused on Maggie and his two daughters and realized that without them he really had nothing but a few tangible possessions and a demanding career that he had allowed to control his life. By noon the following day he had agreed to be the new coach.

Jake had started with indoor practices in March and had moved outside as soon as there was a field dry enough to use. Having missed most of Kimberly's games in the fall because they were always on Saturday morning, Jake was unfamiliar with the rules for full-field soccer. In the under-eight division the teams were smaller and the field was divided into zones to help teach the girls how to spread out and use the whole field. Under-tens used a full-size field and had to learn positions without benefit of pre-set zones. At the first coaches clinic Jake was lost, but after a while he began to see some of the logic in positioning, and by the third clinic he was beginning to understand how to run an effective practice.

The varsity coach of Oakland University's NCAA Class A soccer team ran the coaches' clinics. This small, four-year, private university located in Rochester, Michigan, did not have a football team and focused on soccer as its main fall sport. The clinics were well run, and in addition to learning about soccer, Jake found out that he was in terrible physical condition. What helped the most was the realization that none of the other volunteer coaches knew much about the game when they started, but their teams seemed to get along, and the players had fun competing. By the last training session Jake was enjoying the exercise, the camaraderie of the other coaches, and (although he hated to admit it) the game of soccer.

Jake's subconscious was still running through this series of events when the first of his team arrived. "Hi, Mr. McCarthy. Jill won't be here this morning. She has a sore throat," Cathy Perkins yelled as she ran by onto the soccer field kicking a pink and green soccer ball in front of her. Jake quickly adjusted his lineup for the morning. Jill was not one of his starters, and while her absence was unfortunate, it made the job of making sure everyone got enough playing time that much easier.

Jake had inherited a pretty good team to start with, and his aggressiveness and desire to win had elevated the quality and intensity of the game to the point where his girls were now contending for first place in the division. This game was critical to maintaining their standing in the division. Although the opposing team had won the fall season, it was not competitive this spring. Their goalie, who had stopped every shot in the fall, had quit the team to play softball, and her replacements hated the position. The Rochester Royals were victorious in a one-sided, 7-nil game. Kimberly scored three of the goals.

As Jake collected the soccer balls and his quintessential clipboard, he noticed his friend and senior associate, Bob Bringleson, walking toward him from the south end of the field. Bob had a daughter in the under-eight division and had questioned Jake on several occasions about coaching for the league, but there was no reason why Bob should be at the under-ten game field on this Saturday morning.

"Hey, Bob. What brings you out to the under-ten game field? Isn't Katie in the under-eights?" Jake asked.

"Hi, Jake. Great game. Your girls really are cranked. Yeah, Katie's only in under-eights. Parker asked me to come by and talk to you."

"Parker? Is he upset that I'm not down there on Saturday mornings like I used to be?"

"No," Bob responded. "He knew I lived out this way and asked if I was likely to run into you sometime this weekend. I took that as an order. He knows you're coaching your daughters, and he supports that one hundred percent. In fact, he asked how your team was doing and seemed genuinely interested. He asked me to ask you to see him first thing in the morning on Monday."

"Any idea what it's about, Bob?" Jake asked.

"Nope," Bob responded. "He had kind of a melancholy look on his face, but otherwise just asked me to convey the message."

"Thanks, Bob. I'll make a point of being there first thing. Last time he called me into his office, I was gone for two weeks to the Upper Peninsula and nearly got killed. Now I'm kind of gun shy about being summoned into the Chairman's office."

"Yeah, I heard about that. I also heard that your client paid a very substantial fee for your efforts and that you now represent his business interests in the U.P. Nice work. Well, see you on Monday. I sure wish my daughter's team could play like yours. How do you get them to pass so accurately?"

"Practice, practice, practice. And it helps to have a couple of really good young athletes. Katie will come along. You should get out and help coach. Thanks for bringing the message. Are you and Mary going to the Rochester Hills Memorial Day Fair? They asked my team to march in the parade, so we'll be there. Why don't you come out? Maggie would like to see Mary again."

By this time Jake had reached the parking lot and was throwing coaching paraphernalia and soccer balls into the back of his Taurus wagon.

"Take it easy," Jake called as Bob began walking toward his car.

CHAPTER 2

As usual, Jake was up and out of the house by 6:30 a.m. to miss the Monday morning rush into the city of Detroit. The thirty-mile commute from Rochester Hills was somewhat less enjoyable in Jake's new Taurus wagon. He had reluctantly turned in his Buick Riviera for the wagon at the end of his lease. There were too many kids and balls and dirty cleats for a Riviera. Nonetheless, the wagon was comfortable, and he had ordered the premium JBL sound system to compensate for the loss of his luxury automobile.

By 7:15 Jake was pulling his wagon into the Renaissance garage, and fifteen minutes later he had poured his first cup of coffee and was about to check his calendar for the upcoming week. He figured he had at least an hour and a half before Reginald Parker, the founder and managing partner of the firm, would be calling him into his office. On Sunday Jake had spoken with his assistant coach, Cindy Smith, and outlined a strategy for team coverage in the event that Parker wanted him in on Saturdays. Jake was at that point in his career when success or failure could rest squarely on whether the partners thought he was pulling his own weight. If Parker said be there, Jake would respond. At any rate, there were only two games left in the spring season.

As he opened the Romulus Asphalt file to review the deposition notes prepared by his paralegal, the intercom sprang to life with the unmistakable voice of Reginald Parker. "Jake, I just saw you pour a fresh cup of coffee. Bring it and yourself into my office. I have something I want to discuss with you."

Jake was stunned by the sudden interruption of the intercom and by hearing Parker's voice so early in the morning. He never was in the office before 9:00 a.m. Quickly reclaiming his suit coat and dutifully bringing his half filled coffee mug and a yellow legal pad, Jake walked past the empty desk normally occupied by Mrs. Woods, Parker's secretary for over twenty-five years, who had yet to make her appearance for the day. After knocking, Jake entered the wood-paneled office of the Chairman.

"Good morning, Jake. Thanks for coming in so early. Did you see Bob Bringleson this weekend?"

"Yes sir, he came by after my daughters' soccer game and said you wanted to see me first thing."

"Sit down, Jake. I want to tell you a little story. It won't take long."

Jake took a seat in one of the leather chairs opposite the Chairman's large, mahogany desk. "When I was a young man attending college," Parker began, "I wasn't sure that I wanted to follow in my father's footsteps and go into the law as a career. I used my summers to explore other opportunities. While some of my classmates worked in law offices as runners and file clerks, I tried to get out of town and see some of this great country of ours. My father always insisted that I have a job of some kind, but making money was not the only reason for working."

Parker leaned back in his high-backed leather senator's chair and looked up at the textured ceiling of his large office. He said nothing for a few long moments. Jake did not know whether to respond to this monologue, but decided to wait. He knew from prior experience that Parker often stopped to collect his thoughts before proceeding with his discussions, and Jake sensed that this was one of those times. Parker was looking for just the right words.

"The summer between college and law school was particularly memorable. Back in those days, law school did not begin until mid

September, and I graduated from Michigan in early May. I made it a challenge to see just how much money I could make that summer so that I would not have to work during the first year of law school. I figured if I didn't like the law I could leave and repay my father for the first semester. That way I wouldn't feel trapped, and I could always try something else. As it turned out, I loved law school and the law, so it didn't much matter.

"Back in those days, rumor had it that the best paying jobs were working on the oil rigs in Texas and Oklahoma. My father did not exactly approve, probably because of the risk. I think he figured I'd be climbing all over the rigs all the time and probably fall flat on my face. I was young and strong and fear was not in my vocabulary. I got a job with Standard Oil working in an oil field in the western part of Oklahoma and spent the entire summer in a small town called Crosswind."

Jake took a long swallow out of his cup of coffee, crossed and uncrossed his legs, and shifted his yellow legal pad as he watched Parker. He had stopped talking and was again staring intently at the ceiling of his office.

"Soon after I arrived in Crosswind, I met a young lady who was enrolled as a freshman at the University of Oklahoma. She was home for the summer vacation, and we struck up an acquaintance that, in its own way, was very special. By today's standards it would have been dismissed as nothing more than a shallow friendship, but for the mid fifties it was nothing less than a torrid summer romance. I can barely remember the work that I did on the oilrigs, but I have many precious memories of Molly Stewart and the fun that we had that summer in Crosswind, Oklahoma. She was striking in appearance with beautiful blue eyes that were as clear as a mountain stream, and her skin was soft and pure like new-fallen snow."

Jake again shifted in his chair, relieved that Parker had not mentioned his absence on Saturday mornings and just a little concerned that his senior partner was maybe becoming a little too senior. Jake remained quiet.

"Molly was my first love, and had I not chosen to stay in law school or been less disciplined to carry through with my education, I might have returned to Crosswind and married Molly Stewart. It was that kind of sudden and passionate relationship that one has, if they're lucky, when they're nineteen or twenty years old.

"When the summer was over, we continued our friendship for a number of years through letters and an occasional telephone call; but she was unwilling to wait while I finished law school, and I was unwilling to give up what now had become my chosen profession. Several weeks before graduation from law school, I received notice of her marriage to a hometown fellow by the name of Richard Allen. I was already dating Martha and thought nothing more of Molly for a number of years.

"About ten years ago I had business in Oklahoma City and decided on a whim to see if Molly Stewart, now Molly Allen, still lived in Crosswind and whether she remembered me. I rented a car and drove the 120 miles southwest of Oklahoma City to see if the wind still blew around the rocky escarpment that gave Crosswind its name, if they were still pumping oil out of the Ringo Wells that I had worked on, and if I could find Molly. As much as the world has changed, it is, I suppose, always comforting to find that some things don't change. Crosswind was much as I had remembered it. The Ringo Oil Wells still produced oil, the giant red rock that raises up out of the southern part of the City and gave Crosswind its name is still as impressive as ever, and Molly Allen was as strikingly beautiful as I remembered. Her blue eyes were still crystal clear, and her skin was fine as silk. To top it all off, she remembered me as if we had seen each other just yesterday."

With this, Parker refocused his gaze from the ceiling of his office and looked Jake squarely in the eyes. Jake noticed a glassiness in

Parker's eyes, which, after a few seconds, Jake realized were tears. Still Jake said nothing.

After clearing his throat, Parker continued. "Molly had married the only son of a prominent car dealer in Crosswind. He stood to inherit his father's Ford dealership, which appeared to be prospering. Molly took me down to visit with Richard in his office. His father still ran the place, but Richard was the sales manager. They lived in a lovely house on the north side of town and seemed to have all of the trappings of affluence. Molly had no children, and I sensed a slight sadness in her voice as she tried to put a positive twist on their inability to conceive. Molly and Richard showed me around Crosswind and their property, and I had an opportunity to see firsthand how a car dealership works. From what I could tell, they don't work very well, but at least the owners seem to make a very good living off selling cars.

"After that visit, we exchanged Christmas cards each year, and Molly promised that she and Richard would come visit us in Detroit. She never came, and maybe that was for the best, since I really never explained my connection with Molly to Martha."

Jake had been waiting for an opportunity to speak, and saw his chance as Parker again hesitated following this last admission.

"Did something happen to Mrs. Allen?" Jake asked.

Parker did not respond immediately, but again searched the ceiling of his office to find the appropriate words. After clearing his throat one more time, Parker continued, "Last Friday night I got a call from Molly Allen. Fortunately, Mrs. Woods had gone home for the day, and I was working late on the new baseball stadium proposal for the mayor. I think if Mrs. Woods had answered the phone, Molly never would have gotten through to me. But I was here, the phone rang and I answered. It's funny how you can remember voices that you haven't heard for years. I knew it was Molly the minute I heard her voice, even though it was not her usual way of talking. She kept saying, 'Reggie, I need help. I am all alone, I don't know where I am, and I need help.'"

Parker's eyes were again misty, and he sniffed a few times before continuing. "I asked her where she was calling from, but she seemed incapable of telling me even the basics of whether she was in Crosswind or Timbuktu. I finally asked her if there were any other people around, and soon I was speaking with a very kind woman who was on duty at the Salvation Army shelter for the homeless in Oklahoma City. She told me that Molly Allen had been brought to the shelter about a month ago with no money, no clothing other than what she had on her back, and no memory. The only name that she seemed to remember was 'Reggie Parker.' The woman explained that they had tried repeatedly to draw out more information, but the more questions they asked, the less she said. I guess she finally said something to one of the other residents about Detroit. They called up to the Salvation Army detachment here in Detroit and asked for help from Lt. Col. Clarence Harvey. You know him. He and I are in Rotary together. Clarence recognized the name 'Reggie Parker' and gave them my office phone number.

"I asked a lot more questions," Parker continued, "but they had no more answers. Jake, I am so deep into this baseball stadium project that it's impossible for me to go to her aid. I need to find out what happened to Molly and to respond to her cry for help. I know you have a busy litigation schedule, but I also know you are better able to handle this than most, and I'm sure I can trust your discretion."

The time had finally come to respond. "You were very fond of this lady. As soon as I get back to my desk, I will start making phone calls to sort out what happened to her. Do we know who brought her to the Salvation Army shelter? With your permission, I would like to use Carol Brooks to help me with these calls. She has a way with bureaucrats, and her hourly rate is substantially lower than mine. I take it that we are doing this pro bono without much hope of Molly Allen or anyone else picking up the cost of our time."

"Jake, I tried all weekend to get information over the phone. When the woman at the Salvation Army could not tell me anything, I called the dealership in Crosswind. All they would tell me was that Richard Allen was dead, the dealership had been sold at auction under the supervision of the bankruptcy court, and they had no idea where Richard's wife was.

"I must have tried ten different sources, including the church where Molly used to worship way back when I was out there working. They had never heard of her, so I guess she either stopped going to church or went to Richard's. Finally, a reporter from the small newspaper in Crosswind told me that Richard had committed suicide. He apparently put a gun to his head and left a terrible mess which poor Molly found when she returned home. The dealership, family home and the rest of Richard and Molly's assets were mortgaged to the hilt. When Molly couldn't make the payments, the probate estate was placed under the protection of the bankruptcy division of the County Court, and everyone foreclosed. She was evicted from her home about two months ago.

"Jake, I want you to get on a plane tomorrow morning and go to Oklahoma City to talk with Molly and get to the bottom of this. It bothers me that no one in Crosswind seems to remember her. They were well-to-do citizens of Crosswind. They must have had friends who can explain how this decent and loving woman ended up broke in a Salvation Army shelter. For purposes of billing your time, use my personal client identifier. I'll make sure that your time is counted as good, billable hours. I have worried all weekend about this matter. Molly is not a spendthrift, and there should have been something left over even if Richard were up to his neck in debt. Something doesn't add up, and Molly can't seem to remember enough to help herself.

"I will have Mrs. Woods handle the travel details," Parker continued, without giving Jake a chance to respond. "Take whatever time is necessary to find out what happened and report back. You will need to make arrangements to cover your caseload. Carol Brooks can help, and we have a number of new associates that can dig into the research. I know this is sudden, but we need to get out there quickly. She sounded so distant and weak. I don't know how much longer she can last. Good luck. I want daily reports."

Jake stood, shook hands with Parker, and assured him he would get to the bottom of it. As Jake left the wood-paneled office of the senior partner, Parker called from his desk, "and when you get to Crosswind be sure to spend some time down at Red Rock Park. It is an amazing landmark that was an important part of the history of the West. You can't miss it."

Mrs. Woods was sitting at her desk with her usual unpleasant scowl. "Good morning, Mr. McCarthy. How long has Mr. Parker been here? I have never seen him in this early. He never gets here before I do. How could he? What's going on? Do we need to open a new file? Will you be working on the new baseball stadium with Mr. Parker?"

Jake sensed immediately that Mrs. Woods knew nothing about Molly Allen. This was a surprise because Jake thought Mrs. Woods knew more about Parker than Parker knew about himself. Apparently this was a part of his life that he chose not to share with his wife or his "Executive Administrative Assistant." Jake recalled the discussion at the partners meeting held in January where Parker presented a request from Mrs. Woods that her title be changed from Executive Secretary to Executive Administrative Assistant. Jake chuckled when he heard the proposal, and assumed this was just an old woman trying to be more than she was. When he looked around the table he quickly realized that the rest of the partners took this seriously. He soon learned that personnel problems consumed most of the partnership meetings, and what you call somebody often dictated what you had to pay them. He learned that an Executive Administrative Assistant makes approximately $5,000 more a year than an Executive Secretary, who makes approximately $5,000 more than a Senior Secretary. Connie, who was better than the best of them at typing and keeping track of pleadings, was only a secretary, but even she made over $20,000 plus benefits.

"Jake, are you listening to me?" Mrs. Woods interrupted. "Do you have any information about this new client? Should we open a new client file with a billing number?"

"I'm sorry," Jake responded. "The identity of the client is to remain confidential at this time. Mr. Parker asked me to ask you to open a file using Mr. Parker's personal billing number. My time and expenses are to be charged against his billing number rather than opening a new client account. He asked me not to divulge any other information."

Mrs. Woods smiled and nodded in agreement. Jake knew that there was no way Parker could keep this a secret from her, and it was only a matter of time before she knew all about Molly Allen and whatever Parker may have done over half a century before.

As Jake walked past Mrs. Woods' desk, he asked her for a copy of the airline guide to see what flights were available. TWA had a flight out through St. Louis, that was scheduled to leave Detroit Metropolitan Airport at 8:35 the next morning. Jake thought for a moment, then a frown appeared on his face as he realized that he would miss Wednesday's all-important soccer practice in preparation for the biggest game of the regular season on the following Saturday. He made a mental note to be sure to call his assistant coach to warn her that she would be in charge of Wednesday's practice and maybe Saturday's game. Jake had been fortunate to find a decent assistant coach. Just like Jake, she had lacked fundamental understanding of the game, and tried to overcome this shortfall by overemphasizing aggressiveness instead of developing good skills and patience in handling the ball. Once Jake pointed this out to her, she switched to stressing skill development and team spirit. The team loved her, and she was the role model for each of his young players. Jake hoped he would be back for Saturday's game, but it was important that Cindy Smith know in advance that she might be the only coach for the last regular-season game. If the Royals won, they would be division champs and qualify for the Memorial Day weekend playoff game with the other under-ten division.

Jake walked slowly back to his office with mixed emotions. He had four important depositions scheduled over the next three days. He had looked forward to them because he knew the opposing counsel, who had an incredible ego and few ethics. Jake had what he thought to be a nearly airtight defense and looked forward to playing with this attorney if only to listen to his ranting and raving about meaningless trivia. A more junior lawyer might not appreciate the opportunity to put this airhead in his place.

Of equal concern to Jake was the thought of missing Isaac Stern at the Detroit Orchestra Hall on Thursday night. Stern was playing the Brahms Violin Concerto, which was one of Jake's favorites. Listening to it on his CD player would have to suffice.

"Take the Ajax Paving files down to Carol Brooks' office, Connie, she'll have to handle my depositions this week," Jake called to his secretary as he walked into his office.

"Where're you going, boss?"

Connie had been Jake's secretary for almost six months, and unlike most of the other secretaries in the firm who called their attorneys by their last names, Connie almost immediately starting calling Jake "boss." She was young, pretty, and could type 110 words per minute with almost no errors. Jake could overlook the lack of formality, and Connie knew it.

"I'm off to Oklahoma City to meet Molly Allen at a Salvation Army rescue mission. Don't ask me what I'm supposed to do when I find her. Do you have my Symphony ticket? I'll need to find an associate interested in absorbing some culture. Damn! I really wanted to hear Stern play the Brahms Concerto one more time, and this is a great seat."

"Here it is, boss, and if you're not going to use it, I'd like to go. I love Orchestra Hall, and I think they're playing a Mendelssohn piece after the Brahms."

Amazed that his secretary would know the program for the Detroit Symphony, but too professional to show it, Jake quickly responded, "It's all yours, enjoy!"

After dictating several letters and answering five calls that had been left on the newly installed Audiodex automatic voice mail system, Jake rang Mrs. Woods to see if his tickets had been delivered.

"Yes, Mr. McCarthy, your tickets are here as promised. We have reserved a Cadillac for you in Oklahoma City and have booked a room for you at the Hyatt Regency. Mr. Parker told me to book the room for two weeks, but you can extend the reservation if you need more time. Your flight leaves tomorrow morning at 8:30 from Metro and gets to Oklahoma City just before noon. Mr. Parker asked me to tell you that he expects regular reports on your findings concerning this client." She hung up before Jake had a chance to assure her that he would.

"Two weeks," Jake thought to himself. "Why did Parker book the hotel room for two weeks? I'm willing to miss the game Saturday, but I can't miss the playoff game against the Racers! Maybe I can fly back for the Memorial Day weekend. This shouldn't take very long. All Parker wants me to do is find out what's up with his old girlfriend and figure out a plan for how we might be able to help her. It must have been a powerful summer romance." Jake filled his briefcase with several clean legal pads, a variety of advance sheets, several files that he was working on, an article on commercial litigation, and a new paperback book that he had just purchased on the ten best strategies to winning soccer. There being no room left in his briefcase for the three Wall Street Journals that had piled up in his office from the prior week waiting for Jake to fulfill his promise to himself to read them, Jake ceremoniously retrieved the entire stack of papers from his credenza and placed them in the wastebasket.

Several minutes later Jake was on the elevator down from his 34th floor office in the northeast tower of the Renaissance Center. He never tired of looking out over the City as the elevator sped down through its glass tube to the office level, which led directly into the six-story parking garage. He noted with pride that the Detroit Medical Center was growing in stature and size, and that construction of the new Veterans Administration Hospital was scheduled to begin that summer. Located on the edge of the Detroit Medical Center and Wayne State University, the VA hospital would take advantage of the outstanding intellectual resources of the Wayne State University School of Medicine and the world-class facilities of the Detroit Medical Center. He thought to himself for the thousandth time, "Detroit has so much to offer, but so much has already been wasted." Jake could never forgive the insular politics of the former mayor, who drove white residents and businesses out of the City by making it into a Black fiefdom with 'Hishoner' as the feudal lord. Jake hoped that Detroit's new mayor would be able to reverse the decay and economic deterioration of the City that had followed in the wake of pervasive cronyism. So many businesses and families had already relocated out to the suburbs that it seemed improbable that Detroit would ever regain its stature as a decent place to live and work.

Later that afternoon Jake pulled into the driveway of his four-bedroom Colonial in prestigious Rochester Hills. His girls were waiting for him.

"Hurry, Daddy, or we'll be late for practice!" Kimberly chimed in as he walked into the living room. Jake hustled down to the large first-floor master bedroom and quickly changed into his coaching clothes. Ten minutes later, he and Kimberly and Ashley were at the field, and all thoughts of Romulus Asphalt, Ajax Paving, Molly Allen and the deplorable financial condition of the City of Detroit gave way to setting up cones and encouraging his girls to dribble and pass with their left foot and strike the ball with their foreheads instead of the top of their heads.

That evening, after the girls had been excused from the dinner table, he and Maggie enjoyed a leisurely cup of coffee in the family room. "I had a long meeting with Mr. Parker this morning, and he has asked me to take on another special assignment, this time in Oklahoma City."

"Oklahoma City! I didn't know the firm had any clients in Oklahoma City. Is it a trial?" Maggie inquired.

"I'm not really sure what I'm supposed to do, but I need to find an old lady by the name of Molly Allen and figure out why she is in a Salvation Army shelter. Parker knew her many years ago, and she called him for help, so he's sending me."

"How long will you be gone?" Maggie asked in a quiet voice, remembering the difficulties that Jake had encountered on his recent assignment to Ironwood.

"Parker's got me booked for two weeks at the Hyatt Regency in Oklahoma City, but I can't see why this assignment should take so long. Maybe he knows something I don't. In any event, it looks like I might not be home for the game this weekend with the Rochester Rockettes. I already warned Cindy that she will be in charge."

"Well then, we'll have to make tonight something special so that you don't forget your family while you're out in that old dust bowl trying to find your Molly Allen."

Jake looked over at Maggie and saw the face of his young bride as he remembered her during their first year of marriage. Her invitation left no doubt in his mind and body that tonight would be a treat.

CHAPTER 3

Jake had just finished proofreading his trial brief in the Adrian Land Development Company action against the Charter Township of Oak Grove when the announcement came over the public address system that TWA Flight 284 to Oklahoma City was ready for boarding. The plane had already been delayed for more than two hours, and Jake was exhausted from the extra concentration needed to complete the brief and avoid the drowsiness that beckoned him. He had been waiting in the Lambert Field airport since 10:30, when the first leg of his trip from Detroit had landed pretty much on time.

Once back on the plane, Jake dictated a short memorandum to his secretary, ordered several cups of coffee while waiting for lunch, and pulled out a yellow legal pad to map out a strategy for the next several days. His first stop would be at the Salvation Army shelter in Oklahoma City to meet Molly Allen. Jake noted on his yellow pad, "Get directions to Salvation Army. Meet MA."

Jake stared at his legal pad, noticed a young man across the aisle from him with a lap top computer who seemed intent on building some kind of financial model, and asked for another cup of coffee. In the margin of his legal pad he wrote, "Crosswind?" and underneath that, "date of death, place of death, cause of death." But these were all questions to ask and not strategies for how to unearth the chain of events that led to Molly's seeking shelter among the homeless.

Jake ate the roast beef sandwich lunch, enjoyed the fresh apple for dessert, pulled out an old Wall Street Journal, and then succumbed to an unsettled and uncomfortable sleep. It seemed to Jake that he had just dozed off when a high, nasal voice came over the loud speaker right over his head announcing that they were beginning their descent into Oklahoma City.

Jake rubbed his eyes and realized that he had been awakened out of a sound sleep that had done serious damage to his neck and right arm. After stretching both arms over his head and rotating his head in a clockwise motion to work out the kink that his nap had created, Jake reclaimed his legal pad from the pocket in front of him and started again to try to map out his approach to this assignment.

At 2:40 in the afternoon, central time, TWA flight 284 from St. Louis touched down at Oklahoma City's Will Rogers International Airport. The 727 had to wait several minutes to find an open gate, but by three o'clock Jake was standing before an attractive Hertz agent who was giving him directions to the Salvation Army shelter in downtown Oklahoma City. Jake had decided that if anyone asked why he was interested in the shelter, he would say that he represented Publisher's Clearing House and had a check for one of its residents. No one asked.

Jake was again amazed at how efficient Mrs. Woods was when it came to making travel plans. Hertz had reserved an almost new Cadillac Deville, and within minutes Jake was on Interstate 44 heading north into the heart of Oklahoma City. The attractive car rental agent had been able to give Jake pretty good directions to the only Salvation Army facility in Oklahoma City, and thirty minutes after leaving the airport he eased the large Cadillac into a parking space in front of a two-story brick building that announced to the world in large brass letters that it was the Salvation Army's Oklahoma Regional Shelter. The grounds around the building were well cared for, and the neighborhood, while not affluent, was by no means an inner city ghetto. Jake was impressed with the size, cleanliness and overall quality of the facility that now housed his newest client.

"I'm looking for a lady by the name of Molly Allen," Jake asked of a well-dressed young woman of African-American heritage who was standing behind a Formica counter in the main entrance area of the shelter. "Is she here?"

"She sure is. Are you her kin or someone from Social Services? She's been here over a month now. A real sweetie. We've been taking good care of her. What's your name?"

"Jake McCarthy. I am an attorney from Michigan. I have come here to find out how we might be able to help Mrs. Allen."

"Dat's good, dat's good," responded an elderly woman seated in a padded rocking chair to Jake's left. Her low, gravelly voice was intense but difficult to understand because of her raw Oklahoma accent. "We only wants the best for Miss Molly. She never has nothin' bad to say 'bout nobody, and she's real quiet when all them other women's a-wailin' and a-cryin' 'bout bein' beat up and all." The deeply wrinkled, apparently malnutritioned woman paused for a moment as if expecting a response from Jake or the young black woman.

Getting none, she picked up the pace of her rocking and continued. "She's a nice old lady. Kind of strange sometimes, but so's the whole dang world kind of strange sometimes, if you ask me. She don't mind talking to me none cause I'm her friend, see, and I don't ask her no questions 'bout who she is or where she been. She don't remember much, but she ain't crazy like some of them people back there."

Following the lead of the desk clerk, Jake tried to ignore the old woman and continued his questioning, but the clerk simply repeated for the third time, each time in a nicer and slightly different way, that neither she nor the shelter knew anything about Molly Allen other than her name, which they found on an envelope in her purse. Jake gave up on his first line of inquiry and asked, "May I see her now?"

With a quick, "Sure," the attractive desk clerk slid from behind the counter and extended her hand toward an internal door about twenty feet from the desk. On either side of the short hallway leading away from the reception area were appropriate signs denoting the bathroom and locker facilities for men and women. Jake and the young woman entered a large room filled with about forty metal cots, each with identical navy blue blankets. There were no people in the room and no furniture other than the cots.

"Not too bad, now. Mostly old men come in here to sleep. As long as the weather is OK they usually stay outside. Can't say as I blame them. Gets pretty depressing in here when we have a full house. Sometimes the smell can be positively overpowering."

"Men and women live together?" Jake asked as they headed toward the back of the room.

"No," the clerk responded. "We have another, smaller room for the transient women. Too much temptation letting them all stay together. Of course we encourage them to meet one another and socialize, but they don't much."

Leading Jake past the rows of empty cots, the clerk showed him through a second door leading into another hallway, which led into a smaller dormitory room with only a dozen cots. By each bed there were small piles of clothing.

"We use this room for the women who need to stay for an extended period of time. Unlike the men who tend to come and go without much thought, most of the women who seek out the shelter come because they are battered at home or were kicked out. Sometimes they stay for a week or a month. We don't force them out until they are ready, and we offer a great counseling program to help them get back on their feet. Most of them have jobs or are at least looking. We can usually help them the most. Molly Allen is in this area."

Sitting on a cot in the middle of the room and huddled beneath a white blanket was an elderly woman with snow white hair, a creamy soft and remarkably unwrinkled complexion, and downcast eyes staring at the floor of the dormitory room.

"Mrs. Allen, you have a visitor," the clerk called softly across the room.

Slowly, Molly Allen's head lifted and her deep blue eyes gazed absently past Jake as if staring into space. She said nothing.

"Mrs. Allen?" the clerk called again as if to rouse her out of a dream. "Mr. McCarthy has come all the way from Detroit to see you. He's from that Mr. Parker you know back in Detroit. He says he is here to help you."

At the sound of the word, "Parker," the dreamlike stare quickly focused on Jake and a slight smile appeared.

"Thank you," came the only response from Molly Allen.

The clerk left quietly as Jake cautiously made his way over to the middle of the room. Extending his hand he said, "Hello Mrs. Allen, my name is Jake McCarthy. I am an attorney from Detroit sent here by Mr. Parker to help you."

There was silence. Jake waited, not wishing to upset his new client. There was no place to sit in the dormitory room other than the small cot across from his client that would soon be occupied by another homeless woman. Jake sat on it and tried to be as non-threatening to this fragile old lady as possible.

Along one wall of the room there were individual wooden lockers, which served as closets for each of the residents of the shelter. A small table sat in the near corner, which Jake thought might be a suitable spot to interview his client, but there was only one chair. Otherwise, the room was devoid of furniture save for the twelve cots. The only light in the room came from a bank of fluorescent lights that produced a harsh glare made tolerable only because the furniture, for the most part, was wooden and old.

"You came to help me? Can you help me? Do I need help? Do you know Reggie Parker? My name is Mrs. Richard Allen, but you can call me Molly if you're a friend of Reggie's. Where are you from?" Throughout this burst of questions, Molly Allen's eyes remained fixed on Jake's briefcase, which sat on the floor by his side. Jake was uncertain whether her eyes were truly focused or simply staring blankly forward.

"I am from Detroit, and I know Mr. Parker very well. He is my partner in a law firm, and he sent me here to meet with you and see if I could help you out of this shelter. Would you like to go for a ride in the car?"

"Ride in the car? Oh my yes, I would like to go for a ride in the car. I have a car, I do, you know, I have a new car every year because my Richard always gives me a new car, every year." There was a long pause as Molly Allen seemed to catch her breath and let her mind catch up with the almost continuous flow of words.

Then in a very low, almost inaudible voice nearly devoid of any emotion, Molly said, "Richard is dead," and fell silent as she began to stare at the far wall of the room as if in a trance. She said no more despite Jake's efforts to reestablish his connection with Reginald Parker.

Leaving Molly sitting on the cot staring at the blank wall of the women's dormitory, Jake returned to the front desk to see if this were a normal reaction or something brought on by Jake's presence. He also wanted to know what the rules were for removing a person from the shelter. Parker had been quite specific that the first thing he needed to do was to get Molly into a safe and comfortable environment.

Approaching the desk clerk, Jake asked, "How long has she been like that?"

"Little over a month. The police brought her in here all dirty and without anything but the clothes on her back and a small purse without a wallet or any money. The police suspect that her wallet was stolen, but she had no recollection so it was difficult to follow up. We took a liking to her since she was so refined looking...after we got her cleaned up and all. She didn't say much to start with. Just kept staring out the window or at that old wall in there. I can't figure out what she's looking at. Every once in a while, maybe for a couple of minutes or so, she'll start talking a mile a minute about something, and then she'll stop all of a sudden. It's kind of as if she has all these things to say, but when she starts, something makes her stop. When she stops it is sometimes days before she will say anything else. We get a lot of people who don't exactly act normal, but she's a real strange one. Easy to take care of, though, and we figured sooner or later someone would come for her. She's too nice a person to have no one to look after her. So we decided to let her stay here as long as she wanted to, and we kind of made sure that she had what she needed. Salvation Army's good about that kind of stuff. Likes to try to preserve human dignity as much as possible under the circumstances."

"Do you recall ever hearing her talk about her hometown of Crosswind?" Jake asked, hoping for even a morsel of information.

"Well, sir, not as I can recall but then I don't see too much of her. I pretty much tend to the desk here and some of the bookkeeping. We have some orderlies that take care of the sleeping area, and they may have overheard something. Mostly, though, the residents here tend to talk to each other rather than the staff. I guess there is some comfort in being among others who are in need."

"Dat lady, she talk to me," came the raspy voice from the corner of the room followed by a hacking cough caused by years of heavy smoking. The disheveled old woman stopped rocking long enough to stare at Jake, and then resumed her rapid rocking as she continued speaking.

"She one confused old lady. One minute she a-talkin' 'bout the President of the United States his self as if she knows him real good, and the next she's off in some really nice place called White Sands. Don't know where that be, but she been there 'cause she done described it to me one day when nobody was around. Big houses with large pillars like in the old South, and golf courses and lakes and stuff. Says she's going to live there someday 'cause her Richard told her so. Said it was going to be their reward for workin' hard. Ain't nobody giving me no reward for workin' hard. All I gets is this here rocking chair, and I got to fight to get it. Anyway, she gets to a point and then she goes blank on me. So we sit and I rock, and eventually she'll say something' that don't make no sense like she'll ask me if I know where her mother is.

"Yes sir, I've been sitting with dat old lady for almost a month now trying to figure out what makes her tick. She a strange one. Don't say much. Husband killed his self. Bullet right in the head. It was in the newspapers. She don't talk about it though. That's her problem. She'd be better if she talked about it. 'Stead she don't talk much about nothing. You ask her about it, she don't say nothing. Keeps talking about her Richard."

Jake listened intently trying to absorb information through the heavy Oklahoma accent and slurred words. He couldn't decide whether the woman was drunk, suffering from the after effects of a stroke, or simply difficult to understand.

"Thanks for taking an interest in her," Jake said to the old lady as she finally finished her monologue. "You have been kind to spend time with Mrs. Allen, and now we will try to figure out what happened and how we can help her."

Jake's acknowledgment of the information made the old woman rock faster in her chair. She had a big smile on her face. This little bit of attention from Jake was the highlight of her day. She said no more, just kept rocking, her dark eyes fixed on Jake and her smile pasted permanently on her wrinkled face.

Turning to the clerk, Jake asked, "What do I need to take Mrs. Allen out of here? Are there papers that need to be signed or anything to verify that I am here to help her?"

"No, sir, it's a free country. She's here of her own free will, and she can come and go as she pleases. Of course the Salvation Army would appreciate a small donation to help out other unfortunate souls, but it is not mandatory. If she doesn't want to leave with you, then we may have a slight problem, but I trust your intentions and will help convince her that she should go with you."

Thirty minutes later, with the help of several of the female attendants at the shelter, Molly Allen, together with a small suitcase containing all of her worldly possessions, most of which she had acquired from the Salvation Army, left the shelter and climbed carefully and very slowly into the front seat of Jake's rented Cadillac.

After gently closing the front door on the passenger side, Jake thanked the several Salvation Army attendants who had helped Mrs. Allen and presented the desk clerk (who seemed to be in charge) with a firm check made out to the Salvation Army in the amount of $1,000.

"We very much appreciate all of the attention that you have given Mrs. Allen. She seems to have been well taken care of amidst what must at some times be a very confusing and desperate group of people," Jake said with sincerity as he handed over the check.

After checking himself into the Hyatt Regency, where Mrs. Woods had booked him a VIP suite, Jake negotiated a senior citizen's discount for his client in a corner room overlooking the city. She was quiet as they made their way to her room. Jake wondered in the elevator whether it was a wise idea to take her out of the Salvation Army environment that she apparently had grown to trust and put her in this high-rise hotel. He had no real sense that she was capable of taking care of her own needs, but somehow she had survived in the shelter, and he hoped that she would be able to survive in a luxury hotel. He was pleased to see her eyes light up upon entering the corner suite.

"This is lovely. Can I stay here?" she asked in an almost childlike voice.

"Yes, Molly, for the time being this is your room, and you can stay here. First, you and I are going to have a decent meal in the restaurant downstairs, then I want you to come back up here and get a really good night's sleep before we start the process of finding out how you ended up in that shelter. Does that sound like a good plan?"

"Oh yes, but I must get dressed for dinner. It wouldn't be right to go to dinner in these clothes. I must unpack and put on a proper dress for dinner. Richard would never approve…." Suddenly Molly went silent, and her eyes lost contact with reality as she stared out the widow of the hotel room as if there were something out there of infinite complexity.

Jake waited several minutes, and then said, "I will be back in an hour. Stay here, get your clothes unpacked, and get ready for dinner. I don't care what you wear, but try to be ready in an hour. I'm working on Eastern Daylight time, and I'm hungry."

There was no reaction from Molly, but as Jake left the room she meekly asked, "Will I see you again?"

"Yes," Jake said, "in about an hour. I will come here to get you and take you downstairs to dinner."

"Oh, I would like that," she said.

CHAPTER 4

As Jake made his way up to his room on the 27th floor of the Hyatt Regency, he looked forward to a hot shower and cold drink, but before indulging in these personal comforts, he decided to check in with Mr. Parker. It was nearly six o'clock in Oklahoma City, so Jake placed his call to Parker's home in Grosse Pointe Shores. Mrs. Parker answered the telephone, recognized Jake's voice, inquired about Maggie and the girls, and then put Parker on. Jake was unsure whether Mr. Parker had confided in his wife about his summer in the Oklahoma oil fields, but was relieved when Parker's first question was, "Well, how is my old girlfriend, Molly Allen?"

Jake carefully described the conditions in the Salvation Army shelter, his first encounter with Molly Allen and the steps he had taken, including providing the corner suite at the Hyatt Regency for this confused lady from Crosswind, Oklahoma.

"I have done nothing, so far, to inquire about her circumstances or how she ended up in the shelter," Jake said to his senior partner. "She is very frail and preoccupied to the extent that her responses are not entirely consistent," Jake said delicately.

"You mean she's loony?" Parker responded.

"My guess is she hasn't had much to eat in the last few weeks, and she seemed not to understand where she was when I picked her up. Maybe, with some wholesome food and a couple of nights of uninterrupted sleep, she may be a lot more responsive. I think she kind of went into a state of hibernation or self-preservation that allowed her to ignore her surroundings and block out her life until it was safe. When she entered her hotel room, her eyes lit up, and she suddenly seemed to be coming out of her shell. Then she began staring out the window again, and I lost touch."

"Take whatever time is necessary, Jake, and keep me informed. It seems impossible that two years ago she was the wife of a very successful automobile dealer, and now she is destitute and alone. I don't know what we can do for her other than give her some short-term shelter from the world, but we must try. You have the firm credit card, and I will have Mrs. Woods wire additional cash to the hotel in case you need it. Keep me posted on what you find out."

"Yes sir. Goodbye."

After a hot shower and a Jack Daniels from the complimentary mini bar (which, as far as Jake could tell, was about all you got for the additional cost of being on the concierge level), Jake kicked off his shoes and fell back on the king-size bed as he waited for his client to get dressed for dinner. Jake could only guess at the kind and condition of the clothes in Molly Allen's small suitcase. Jake's eyes closed as he allowed his body the luxury of a catnap to shrug off the twelve hours of travel.

At precisely seven o'clock Jake knocked on Molly Allen's door. There was no answer. He knocked again. "Mrs. Allen. It's me, Jake McCarthy. It's time to go to dinner. Are you ready?"

Still there was no answer. Suddenly Jake became worried that the excitement or the malnutrition or age or whatever had overcome this frail lady. Quickly he returned to the elevator and descended to the first floor to seek help. He had forgotten to get an extra key to her room.

Jake immediately went to the bellhop's desk. "I need your help. I'm here with an older lady, and I'm afraid she may have hurt herself. She doesn't answer when I knock at her door."

The bellman gave Jake a strange kind of look and said, "maybe she just doesn't want to see you tonight."

"No, no, no, you don't understand. She is in her sixties and very frail. She has snow white hair and blue eyes, and looks like anybody's grandmother."

"Oh, you mean Mrs. Allen. She was here only a few minutes ago looking for Mr. Parker. We looked over the entire hotel guest list, but there is no Mr. Parker here. Are you Mr. Parker?"

"No, but it's close. Do you know where she is now?"

"Last time I saw her she was heading off toward the gift shop. You might check there."

A minute later, as Jake entered the small gift shop off the main lobby, he heard the sales clerk say, "and shall we charge this to your room, ma'am? The total cost is $127.33."

Molly nodded, and then showed the key to her room and said, "Yes, I'm Mrs. Richard Allen. We live in Crosswind and are here for the weekend."

Jake walked up to Molly and said, "Bought yourself some nice things there, Molly. I know you're going to enjoy them. Are you ready for dinner?"

Molly looked at Jake with the same blank stare that had bothered Jake at the Salvation Army shelter and again in her hotel room, but after several seconds, responded, "Yes, thank you, I am quite ready for dinner. Will Reggie be joining us?"

Jake's first dinner with Molly Allen was difficult. Although her manners were refined, she ate slowly and seemed always to have a mouth full of food, making any meaningful conversation impossible. To almost every question asked, Molly Allen responded with a nod of her head and either an "OK" or a "no." If the question couldn't be answered by a simple response, then there was no response. At one point about half way through dinner, Jake carefully worded a non-threatening question about Richard Allen and was met with the now all-too-familiar blank stare that seemed to look straight through Jake at some unknown object on the far wall of the restaurant. Once she went into this state it took almost fifteen minutes to bring her back. She stopped eating and just sat, nearly motionless, and sealed off from the world. After this abortive attempt at gathering a few facts, Jake decided to let her eat and not try to cross-examine her tonight. He hoped that rest and some good nutrition would restore her memory and her willingness to talk about her past. Without information from her, Jake knew it would be very difficult to help her out of her present predicament.

Jake was still on Eastern Standard Time when he awoke the next morning at five o'clock. Typically on any assignment, he would prepare an outline or strategy for reaching the ultimate goal, which in most cases meant either a no cause or a substantial monetary verdict, depending on whether he was defending or prosecuting. He was restless this morning because he had no plan in mind. Without information from his client, it was difficult even to start putting the few bits of information together, much less make them fit into any kind of pattern. If Molly Allen continued to suppress the recent past, either subconsciously or because she had suffered a stroke that wiped out part of her memory, then Jake would be forced into a fishing expedition in Crosswind to try to pick up any leads that might help his client. Jake wasn't quite sure what helping his client really meant, other than trying to restore some of her assets (if there were any) and finding a suitable and safe place for her to live.

In dictating his thoughts into a memorandum that would eventually get back to Parker via the Internet, he commented to his secretary, "I'm not quite sure what this has to do with being a lawyer. It seems more like a caretaker or housemother. She's a nice old lady, but I really don't know what to do with her."

After finishing dictating the memorandum, Jake pulled on some jogging shorts and a Detroit Pistons T-shirt and took to the early morning streets of Oklahoma City. It was already warm.

As he walked into his room after the hour-long run, the phone in the sitting room of his suite rang. Jake answered quickly, "McCarthy."

"Hi, Jake, this is Suzanne Woods. Mr. Parker would like to speak with you." Without asking or seeking consent, Mrs. Woods immediately transferred the call into Mr. Parker.

Jake related his experience with Molly the night before, and then summarized his observations so far. "Molly has been through a lot in the last two months. I mean, she has gone from being a successful member of Crosswind society to a street lady with no money and no family. She doesn't even know where her mother is or if she is still alive. She knows that her husband is dead, but when I try to find out how or why, she clams up, sometimes for hours."

"I am sure this has affected her more than any of us can possibly imagine," Parker responded sympathetically. "You have the lead on this, Jake, but I suggest maybe that you should try to find a psychiatrist who might be able to work on the reasons for her blocking this information. Or you might try a hypnotist. I think you're right that reintroducing her to normal living with decent food, comfortable lodging and intelligent people around her may restore her memory, but who knows how long that might take."

"Sir, I have a funny feeling that she's going to run up a pretty high bill here at the hotel. Should I worry about that? She dropped over a hundred bucks yesterday at the little store here in the hotel and charged everything."

"It's okay for now," Parker replied. "I have already asked Mrs. Woods to locate an assisted living apartment outside of Oklahoma City, and based on what you told me this morning, I will ask her to retain a home health agency to provide periodic care for Molly until we can make other arrangements for her. I don't want you to be bothered with being a nursemaid for her. You have more important work to do in Crosswind and wherever the investigation may take you. I'll let you know when the apartment is ready. Keep me informed."

"Thanks," Jake replied. "I plan to stay around here for a couple of days to see whether I can coax any more of the facts out of her. If I continue to hit a dead end on that score, I will take off for Crosswind and see what I can find out there."

Jake spent a long and frustrating breakfast trying to communicate with his client, but if anything, the food and good night's sleep seemed to make her less communicative. She was withdrawn and unresponsive even to simple comments that the night before had at least provoked a nod or an occasional "OK."

After several unsuccessful hours with Molly, Jake decided to take his senior partner's advice and begin the process of locating a psychiatrist specializing in adult senility and dementia. His first call was to the Oklahoma Regional Medical Center, a large teaching facility affiliated with the University of Oklahoma. He was pleased to find it had a comprehensive referral service that was quickly able to give him the names of several psychiatrists who might be able to deal with the problems of adult psychiatric disorders. He also learned that adult senility was not considered a psychiatric disorder, but when he had finished describing Molly to the referral nurse, she suggested that this might be something more than simple dementia.

Of the three names, two were men and the third a female. On the assumption that it might be less threatening for Molly to meet with a female psychiatrist, Jake placed a call to Dr. Martinique Glasseur and arranged to have a consultation with her that afternoon.

CHAPTER 5

Dr. Glasseur's office was on the fourth floor of a professional office building connected to the Oklahoma Regional Medical Center and, through a series of underground tunnels, to the Oklahoma University School of Medicine. The waiting room was functional with the appropriate number of outdated Psychology Today magazines and enough chairs for half a dozen patients.

"Hello, my name is Jake McCarthy. I have an appointment with Dr. Glasseur for one thirty," Jake said as he approached the receptionist.

The neatly dressed nurse behind the office counter responded, "Do you have health insurance?"

"No, this is not a treatment session. This is simply a meeting with the doctor. I have an appointment."

"Okay, I'll let her know you're here."

Several minutes later Jake was ushered through the waiting room door into a small office furnished with contemporary, bleached oak furniture and displaying a number of diplomas and certificates attesting to Dr. Glasseur's competence as a psychiatrist. Behind the desk there was a matching credenza on which sat an open laptop computer with a screen saver full of fish making strange noises. Otherwise, both the desk and the credenza were bare.

Jake was trying to interpret the Latin inscription on one of the diplomas when Dr. Glasseur entered the small office. "Hello, I'm Martinique

Glasseur, and you must be Jake McCarthy. I was intrigued with your description of the problem and hope that I can be of some assistance."

Jake hadn't thought much about what Dr. Glasseur might look like, and was completely taken aback by the strikingly beautiful young physician that presented herself to him. Her jet-black hair was combed neatly to hang just off of her shoulders. Unlike many in the southwest who have abused their skin through exposure to the driving desert sun, Dr. Glasseur's skin was soft, white and radiant. Although slight of stature, her breasts were full, and she made no attempt to hide them behind a physician's white lab coat.

"Thank you for seeing me on such short notice, Dr. Glasseur," Jake said after she had invited him to sit. "I and my client really appreciate your ability to look into this matter so quickly."

"You can call me Marty if I can call you Jake," Dr. Glasseur quickly responded. "Tell me what you know, and I'll tell you what I think I might be able to do for you."

Jake briefly related what little he knew about Molly Allen's last six months—the violent suicide of her husband, loss of all of their assets, and ending up in a shelter in Oklahoma City. "Sometimes she seems to be responsive, especially to food and memories of her childhood. She apparently remembered Mr. Parker from somewhere way back in her memory, and once she asked whether her mother was at home. She was able to tell us that her Mother's name was Agnes Stewart, and I tried directory assistance for Crosswind to see if her mother or father were still alive. There was one Stewart, but unrelated and unaware of any other Stewarts in the area. When I try to discuss any of this with Molly or ask her about her family or Crosswind or her husband, she retreats into an almost trance-like state and stares, usually at a blank wall, out a window or at nothing."

"What would you like me to do?" Dr. Glasseur asked after noting these observations in a spiral pad. "It is not uncommon for people to suffer emotional problems following a crisis. In all likelihood she will regain much of her sensibilities—assuming this is a stress-provoked phenomenon—just through time and maintenance in a healthy environment."

"I need to know what happened following the death of her husband, why there was no property left from his estate, and how Molly ended up in Oklahoma City. I have absolutely nothing to go on other than her appearance in the Salvation Army shelter. I had hoped to start my investigation with her, but so far I have drawn a complete blank."

"From your description, it sounds like post-traumatic stress disorder, or PTSD. This is not the most common manifestation, but there appears to have been a significant emotional change arising out of a very traumatic condition, and that usually is a strong indication of PTSD. She is manifesting a form of escapism that is in many ways consistent with other forms of psychotic behavior that we often see occurring following major trauma, such as the loss of a loved one, but her condition seems far more severe and long lasting. Time is a great healer, and most forms of PTSD are improved through patience and preservation of a safe environment, but it can take years to cure. In some cases PTSD never really goes away, but with counseling and direct psychiatric care, people can work around this disorder and lead a completely normal life. On the other hand, if it's dementia, and she simply can't remember near term events, there is not a whole lot we can do other than try some of the new medications that provide short term relief from the affects of dementia.

"Can you bring her in to see me tomorrow morning, say around ten, after I finish my rounds? I was scheduled to deliver a speech on alternative therapies tomorrow, but the series of lectures has been postponed pending the return of our chief of staff, who happens to be traveling in Turkey this week. My day is open, and so is my evening. Why don't we plan to have dinner tomorrow night, and we can discus my findings in a less clinical environment. There is a nice French bistro up near the Hyatt called the Metro."

"It's a deal," Jake responded, welcoming the opportunity to have dinner with someone other than Molly Allen, especially someone as attractive as Dr. Glasseur.

When Jake returned to the Hyatt, Molly Allen was sitting in the spacious lobby of the hotel in one of the overstuffed chairs near the entrance to the dining room. She appeared to be reading a news magazine and was completely preoccupied. She looked up only after Jake announced his presence. He noticed that she had been staring at a full-page advertisement for Ford cars.

"I know you, you're from Reggie? Reggie sent you here to help me? He was in Crosswind, you know, not too long ago. He met with my Richard. My Richard is dead, you know. I am hungry, are you? This is a nice hotel, isn't it? Reggie sent you here, didn't he? Do you know Reggie?"

"Yes, Molly, I know Reggie and he sent me here. It's time for dinner, and then I want you to get another good night's sleep. Tomorrow I will take you for a short car ride over to the University to meet a friend of mine that may be able to help us. How does that sound to you?"

"Yes, I would like that," Molly said. "Richard loves cars. I get a new car every year from Richard." Then, in an abstract voice that signaled the end to any responsive conversation, Molly said, "Richard shot himself and there was blood everywhere." After reciting those facts, Molly became quiet and did not say another word as Jake took her hand and led her into the hotel's main restaurant, which, at five o'clock in the afternoon, was nearly empty.

At ten o'clock the next morning, Jake McCarthy and Molly Allen walked into Dr. Glasseur's office. Molly had a slight smile on her lips, but otherwise was hollow in appearance. Her blue eyes and white hair contrasted noticeably with Dr. Glasseur's black hair and green eyes. There was no hostility; indeed, even the staff at the Salvation Army had reported that Molly was never mad or upset, just unresponsive.

"Hello Molly, my name is Dr. Martinique Glasseur. I want to help you and be your friend. You can call me Marty or Doctor as you please. Mr. McCarthy asked me to spend some time with you to see if I could help you recall some of the events of the last several months. Is that okay with you?"

Molly, who had been reasonably relaxed in the car driving out to the University of Oklahoma Medical Center, suddenly stiffened and her eyes fixed on the small window behind Dr. Glasseur's credenza. She said nothing.

Dr. Glasseur gently ushered her into a much more spacious setting than the small office. "Molly, would you like to lie on this couch and get a little rest? I want you to be comfortable and know that you are safe and secure here with me. Mr. McCarthy and I want to help you and protect you from other people. You can relax here with me or I will ask Mr. McCarthy to come and join us."

Molly agreed to rest on the couch, and slowly the process began of trying to unravel her life over the last six months. While Dr. Glasseur conducted her first interview of Molly Allen, Jake sat patiently in the waiting room with a legal pad and Cross pen trying to develop a strategy for moving forward with this investigation. He pulled out his map of Oklahoma and tried to estimate the time it would take to drive to Crosswind, which was situated in the southwest corner of Oklahoma near the Texas border. The city was just large enough to rate a small inset in the state map, giving details of the city streets. The AAA road map (efficiently provided by Mrs. Woods when she gave Jake the airline ticket) also contained demographic data indicating a population in Crosswind of between 50,000 and 75,000 and that it was the county seat for Broken Bow County. A small picture of an oilrig adjacent to the circle on the map indicated that oil was a significant part of the economy of Crosswind. The mileage chart showed a distance of 117 miles from Oklahoma City.

Jake started to make a list of the people he might contact in Crosswind. Richard Allen had owned the Ford dealership in Crosswind. First on Jake's list was a stop at the dealership to see if there were any employees who could give him more information than his client. The Crosswind newspaper, if there was one, must have carried a news story about the suicide, so that would be his next stop.

As Jake jotted down his thoughts, his mind clicked into gear, leaving behind the ill formed and shifting thoughts that had plagued him ever since meeting Molly Allen. Already he was beginning to think up questions to ask of the citizens of Crosswind.

Before long, Jake had filled three pages on his legal pad and was about to start on his fourth when the interior door to the waiting room opened. With a blank stare that was all too familiar, Molly Allen emerged from the doorway and moved toward Jake. Dr. Glasseur was right behind her and speaking softly. "You don't need to be afraid, Molly, we can help you and we want to help you. Mr. McCarthy, here, has come to help you."

A small smile appeared on Molly Allen's face when she looked at Jake. She said, "You know Reggie don't you? Did Reggie send you here? I talked to Reggie last week, or was it last month? I'm really tired. Can we go now?"

Jake assured her that they would be leaving shortly, and then moved across the small waiting room to speak with Dr. Glasseur privately. "Are you still up for dinner tonight?"

"Yes, I have much to tell you about Mrs. Allen's condition and would love to have dinner with you. I hope you like French? I forgot to ask. The Metro is on 14th Street just off of Cheyenne Boulevard where the Hyatt is located. Say seven o'clock?"

"Fine, that will give me a chance to get Mrs. Allen fed and tucked in for the night. See you then. Thanks."

Molly Allen was quiet as she and Jake left Dr. Glasseur's office and headed for the elevator that would take them to the parking garage. Jake did not provoke a conversation and gently led his ward through the garage to his car. Pushing the button for keyless entry, the lights quickly came on as the locks popped up, and Jake gently eased Molly Allen into the front seat of the car.

Two blocks from the hotel, Molly finally spoke. "That woman was nice to me. Can I go back? Do you know who she is?"

"What did you talk about?" Jake gently asked in response to Molly's questions.

"We talked about oil wells, I think. Then we talked about my mother and Richard. She didn't know him. He was a fine man. Do you know Richard? Richard is dead. Richard is dead!"

At the sound of these chilling words, Jake looked over at Molly only to find her staring abstractly out at the hotel entrance. They said no more until they were in the elevator. Molly finally said, "I am so tired, all I want to do is go to sleep right now. Tomorrow I would like to go for another ride in your fancy car. We always drove Fords. Fords are the best cars made. My Richard says so, and he is right. I'm too tired to dine with you this evening."

"Would you like me to order some food brought to your room?" Jake asked as he checked to see that Molly's room was clean and ready for her. But the question went unanswered. Molly Allen's eyes were focused on the far wall of the hotel room, and Jake could tell that her mind was consumed in subconscious thought that excluded reality. Quietly Jake left the room.

It was now almost two o'clock. On returning to his room, Jake called to the concierge desk and arranged for one of the hotel staff to look in on Mrs. Allen to see that she was resting peacefully in her room. He also ordered a small tray of cheese and crackers with some fresh fruit to be brought to her room around dinnertime.

After checking to see if he had any messages, Jake pulled back the covers of his king-size bed and placed his tired body on the clean sheets for a much-needed catnap. In law school, Jake had learned how to discipline his body and his internal clock in such a way that he could doze off for fifteen minutes or half an hour or longer, depending on how much time he had. Although not quite sure how his biological clock worked, it did, and he could count on waking up within seconds of the prescribed time that he had set aside for the nap.

Several hours later, after a long, hot shower, a shave to scrape off the beginnings of a five o'clock shadow, and a cold beer from the mini-bar, Jake put on a fresh shirt, khaki slacks and a blue blazer, and left for dinner with Dr. Glasseur. He arrived at precisely seven o'clock and found Dr. Glasseur waiting for him just inside the Metro. A short maitre d' with a French accent (Jake couldn't tell for sure whether it was acquired at acting school or in France) showed them to a nicely set table in a quiet part of the small bistro.

CHAPTER 6

With the tip of his salad fork, Jake began toying with the leaves of spinach and Romaine lettuce in his salad, then looked at Dr. Glasseur and asked the question that they both knew would change the relaxed atmosphere that so far had been the hallmark of this fine restaurant. “Any ideas on what’s wrong with Mrs. Allen? Will she always be as spacey as she seems most of the time? Will she ever be able to tell me what happened in Crosswind?”

“I wouldn’t go so far as to say that she is a classic case of anything,” Marty Glasseur said as she took a small sip of her merlot and thought for a moment before proceeding. “From what you have described of her recent past, she has undergone a severe traumatic experience. You should not underestimate the shock of finding your spouse fatally shot in the head. Just the sight of blood can sometimes be enough to cause severe shock that can last for months. From what little you have told me, it sounds like it was pretty messy. A pistol shot to the head will do that. I assume she has no family to fall back on. Usually there is enough family to support a person in post-trauma shock. It’s part of the whole healing process that starts with the wake or visitation, extends through the funeral service and last farewells, then daily or weekly check-ins by family and friends to help with the adjustment. She obviously had none of that support, and the death of her husband was followed by a series of bad things that landed her here in Oklahoma City with nothing, not even her mind.

"The human mind copes with disaster in various ways, some of which are predictable and some not. One defense is to escape by drawing within and blocking out reality. Like an ostrich, Molly Allen has hidden herself from the world by shutting out all that is around her and blotting out all of the recent past. Her defense has allowed her to recall only a few memories of happy times when she felt secure. She remembered your partner because he made her happy and offered a sense of security, possibly because he represented an outside force that was bigger than Crosswind. He must have made her happy and secure, and that's what she is willing to remember. Although the relationship with him was many, many years ago, it was undoubtedly a high point in her life. Likewise, she has called for her mother, a common result of her desire for stability. She mentioned a few other things to me that make me think that her mind is capable of absorbing information; therefore, I don't think this is simple dementia. She has just commanded her mind to forget what is unpleasant, which, for the most part, has been everything in the past six months. I suspect with some coaching we will be able to get her to pull her head out of the sand long enough to see that there are people here to help her, but that process may take time, and even then I doubt whether she will be able to tell a coherent story about what happened to her husband. She may not know, and until she has undergone some fairly extensive therapy we will not know for sure whether she is repressing or really does not know."

"How long do you think that will take?" Jake asked.

"I really do not know. Sometimes these post-traumatic stress disorders resolve themselves quickly, and in other cases it takes years. Our Vietnam veterans are classic examples of what can go wrong when you are exposed to high stress without a lot of preparation and no family support. It was nearly criminal of our government to put those boys over there in an unknown culture riddled with drugs and prostitutes, expose them to an ugly war that they did not understand, ask them to fight to protect a tiny piece of real estate that we had no claim to, and expect them to come back normal after a year of watching their buddies die. Some of those guys are still suffering from PTSD."

"What do you recommend for Molly?" Jake asked, sensing that the Vietnam War was a sore subject.

"First, I decided not to do a complete history and physical on Mrs. Allen this morning. I lack the equipment in my faculty office, and it's hard to do a history on someone who can't remember anything. It is my impression, however, that Mrs. Allen is somewhat undernourished and possibly suffering from deficiencies in vitamins and minerals. There are no obvious physical problems that a good diet, vitamin supplements and exercise won't cure. How does she eat?"

"Slowly," Jake quickly responded. "Every meal so far she eats well and seems hungry, but it takes forever. She loves candy and cleaned out the little shop in the Hotel."

"Does she complain about any physical ailments?" Dr. Glasseur asked.

"No, not that I can recall. She is pretty docile and doesn't say much unless I ask, and then I get only partial responses."

"I suggest that we put Mrs. Allen in the hospital under my care. Medicare will cover the cost of hospitalization, although there will probably be a substantial deductible that will need to be paid. Will your partner cover that cost?"

"Yes," Jake responded.

"Once we have her in the hospital, we can perform a complete history and physical on her—or at least a complete physical, and a semi-complete history depending on her ability to provide information to us. I will also contact the hospitals in Crosswind to determine whether she has any medical records from which we might gather data. The hospital records should tell us whom she saw as her family physician or gynecologist. After we have a pretty good picture of her physical condition, then we can start working with her mind to try to bring her back to reality. If she feels safe, she may be willing to confide in me or one of the social workers that will be working with her. We are testing some new ways of treating these kinds of disorders and have received a grant from the Robert Wood Johnson Foundation to pursue alternative therapies. Molly might be a candidate. It's all very gentle. We don't want to use shock treatments unless it is absolutely necessary to keep her from hurting herself or others. How was she after our visit this morning?"

"Molly said almost nothing in the car as we drove back to the hotel, but she did say that she wanted to see you again. So I guess you two hit it off pretty well even though you may not have known it."

"It makes sense that she would wait until she got back to the hotel. She is beginning to feel safe there. It is a comfortable refuge for her. We will try to make the hospital as warm and cozy as we can so she will feel safe.

"I'm glad she remembered the visit," Dr. Glasseur continued. "Several times in our discussion, I pushed her a little harder than might have been prudent, since I knew that you were in need of specific information. Apparently I didn't push too hard, or at least she didn't take offense. It is significant that she remembered our interview. Short term memory sometimes is the most difficult to penetrate."

Jake had just finished the last piece of asparagus in his salad when the young, dark-haired waiter brought the evening's entree, a full rack of lamb that the two of them had agreed to split.

"Let's enjoy dinner for now, Jake," Dr. Glasseur said. "We can talk more about Molly Allen later on tonight. This lamb is too good, and I am too hungry. Tell me about Detroit."

True to their agreement, Molly Allen did not complicate the enjoyment of a very fine rack of lamb, a light but tasty flan for dessert, and a special blend of French espresso and Kenyan coffee that was a specialty of the restaurant.

"I like this restaurant for its outstanding food," Dr. Glasseur commented, "but I love it for its coffee. This comes as close as I can find to the great coffee that we enjoy when we go back to France." The waiter poured a second cup for both of them and left a silver-plated coffee pot on the table.

"Before we get back to business," Marty enquired, "are you up for a little late entertainment tonight? It's been a while since I've been to some of the night spots in Oklahoma City—not that there are a lot of them—but this is an interesting case and you're an interesting date, so how about it?"

"Sure, but let's finish our work before we give into the vices of the night."

"Here's what I propose. I want to admit Molly Allen to the Adult Behavioral Health Floor of the Oklahoma University Medical School. She'll be in a special unit reserved for elderly patients suffering from dementia, Alzheimer's and similar, non-violent diseases afflicting the elderly. It's very safe, was recently redecorated to provide a more home-like and friendly atmosphere, and is well staffed with professionals who are required to wear street clothes instead of white uniforms. I want her to have a roommate and will be very selective in whom I choose. She needs socialization with someone she can trust. I'm the Medical Director for the unit and have the ability to make those kinds of decisions.

"I would like her for at least ten days because I think it will take that long to restore her body to physical good health, and that's assuming she has no underlying chronic or acute illness. While we work to restore her physical health, we will present her with a variety of social workers, behavioral health psychologists, and, of course, I will spend a good deal of time with her trying to get through her post-trauma stress. At the end of ten days we will re-evaluate, but I doubt whether we can justify keeping her longer unless she has some other physical condition. Do you have a place for her to stay after she leaves the hospital?"

"We are making arrangements for a supervised living facility just south of town. It should be available before she is through with her stay in the hospital. I will finalize those arrangements tomorrow. What if this doesn't bring her out of this condition?"

"Jake, I want you to understand that this is not a simple disorder. She has entered a near catatonic state where all of her faculties are focused on literally obliterating from her mind all memory of the recent events that caused this tremendous stress in her life. Sometimes the strongest people are the most difficult to deal with once they have crossed over the boundary into post-trauma distress. If therapy is unable to release this incredibly strong and focused obliteration of recent events, we may suggest a mild form of shock therapy that would help unfocus this determination on her part to forget. When she starts to stare at the opposite wall or out a window at a distant object, her mind is actually focusing on a specific spot as a method of ignoring or blocking out all other senses. She doesn't hear. She doesn't smell. She doesn't taste. All she can do and all her mind will let her do is focus on that point on the wall and thereby put every other aspect of her life out of focus and out of mind. Unfortunately, the very information that you are interested in triggers this reaction, and until we can reverse that effect I'm afraid you will not be able to learn much more about what happened to Molly Allen, at least not from her."

"Will you need me to work with you and Molly while she's in the hospital?" Jake asked.

"No, I don't see how you could be of much help other than perhaps reminding her of your partner and their relationship. We should keep in touch so that I can report on any changes and you can give directions on how we should proceed. We will need to get her consent to admit her to the hospital. She will not be in a locked ward or anything like that, and she will be able to leave whenever she chooses. I think she will choose to stay because it is safe and will make her feel better. If she leaves, she will need somebody to keep track of her and help her stay out of trouble. But we can keep her here for 72 hours without her consent, so if she decides to leave I will have time to find you and have you put plan B into effect."

"In that case," Jake responded, "I think I'll drive down to Crosswind to see what I can find out if happened to the Allens and how Molly found her was to a Salvation Army shelter."

CHAPTER 7

Jake eased the metallic gray Cadillac Deville onto Interstate 40 heading south and west out of Oklahoma City towards the Texas border. The morning was bright, without a cloud in the sky, although a small haze was beginning to build over the city, indicating a possible ozone alert day. It was Saturday morning, and there was almost no traffic at seven o'clock. Jake was aggressive in his acceleration onto the expressway. He had looked forward to testing the responsiveness of the NorthStar engine that now came as standard equipment on the Cadillac Deville. He smiled as the large car jumped forward, responding to the 300 horses that had propelled the Cadillac Division of General Motors from its former status as the mark of excellence for anybody over the age of fifty to an American luxury car with European design and Detroit muscle.

As he maneuvered the large car into the passing lane, Jake retrieved his hand-held dictating machine and began dictating a memorandum to the Molly Allen file summarizing the events of the last several days, including an incomplete report of his late-night consultation with Dr. Glasseur. He stuck to the clinical details, omitting discussion of his after-hours odyssey around Oklahoma City as Dr. Glasseur demonstrated that her education at the University of Oklahoma School of Medicine was not entirely devoted to textbooks and cadavers. Among other interesting facets of her life, Jake quickly ascertained that she was single, had never been married, and had no plans for marriage. Her profession was her life, and she had little time to spend outside of the hospital and her office. Her invitation to Jake was out of impulse, mostly because she knew he was from out of town and that she would not be opening herself to a relationship.

Jake reported that since her first meeting with Dr. Glasseur, Molly had returned for one more office consultation followed by an order for admission to the hospital on the following day. Meanwhile Jake had found a place for Molly to live in a suburban assisted-living complex fairly close to the Oklahoma University campus.

Jake included in his memorandum a description of the facilities and the living arrangements that had been made. This included a taxi service that would pick up residents every day at a pre-set time, deliver them to their physician or the hospital, and wait while they received treatment. The drivers were instructed to take their passengers wherever they wished to go in Oklahoma City, but under no circumstances were they to leave their passengers alone, even if they insisted. Jake was fortunate in finding an elderly driver whose mother had suffered from dementia and was equally undependable when left to her own devices. He was sympathetic, and Mr. Parker, who spoke personally with the driver, was generous. The apartment would be available in two weeks, which was about how long Dr. Glasseur thought Molly should be hospitalized while she and the hospital staff performed physical and psychological tests on her.

With Molly safely in University Hospital and her living accommodations arranged for, Jake felt comfortable leaving Oklahoma City to check out Crosswind and see where his investigation might lead.

By the time he had finished his dictation, Jake had moved well beyond the outskirts of suburban Oklahoma City and was on a long stretch of flat superhighway leading eventually to Crosswind. Jake eased down on the accelerator of his Deville, and the car immediately responded. There was almost no wind noise or other distraction from the Delco premium digital sound system until the car hit 95 miles per hour. At that speed the aerodynamics of the luxury car produced a noticeable wind noise that increased significantly as the speedometer inched past the 120-mph mark. Jake had never treated his Taurus wagon this way. Somehow the NorthStar engine, the steel gray car and the open road beckoned him to push on. At 135 mph he came to his senses and eased back to a cruising speed of 90 mph. The car and engine met his every expectation but for the wind noise which, he assumed, came with any car going over 100 miles per hour.

Crosswind is, by Oklahoma standards, a medium-sized city with a population of just over 70,000. It is, and since the early twenties had been, an oil town. Its fortunes rose and fell with the fortunes of the oil producers and wildcatters. International oil prices had been low since the end of the 1973 oil crisis, and Crosswind had suffered by low production of crude and no interest in new wells. It looked tired, but not depressed. Jake approached the outskirts of Crosswind from the northeast, and in the morning light it seemed relatively clean as the sun's rays began to bake the reddish clay that made for a sharp contrast from the lush green and rich black soil of Michigan.

As Jake proceeded from the outskirts into the middle of the small city, he noted an absence of the strip malls and movie multiplexes that had appeared throughout the country as urban centers expanded into the suburbs. Many of the shops looked like they needed paint, and store windows were often coated with a fine red dust, giving the glass a pinkish tint. It was just after nine o'clock when Jake rolled into the central business district. He needed a strong cup of coffee and a sweet roll. As usual, he had skipped breakfast at the hotel, relying instead on two cups of room-brewed coffee and a few breath mints that he had taken the night before from the large silver bowl decorating the registration desk of the Hyatt.

Although lacking in strip malls, Crosswind had not avoided the usual array of Burger Kings and McDonalds, but Jake avoided fast-food restaurants whenever he could. With two young girls in the family, he had memorized most of the meals offered by the fast-food chains, and had little appetite for any. As he approached what he guessed was about the center of town based on the presence of the Federal Courthouse, he pulled in front of the Wildcat Café and parked his now reddish-gray Cadillac next to a red Ford F150 pickup truck. Compared to the Ford, his Cadillac looked like it had just had a wash and wax. Outside the café in a metal box were copies of the Crosswind Gazette, which Jake assumed was the local newspaper. He deposited two quarters into the appropriate slot, pulled the metal handle forward and retrieved a copy of the Gazette for the week of May 15th.

While sipping on a cup of black coffee and waiting for his sweet roll, Jake scanned the weekly tabloid, looking in particular for the address of the newspaper office. He had decided that he would use the local newspaper to do research on Richard Allen's death. While there, he could search for editorial comment or news that might provide background information or explain why Molly Allen was homeless and broke.

"Is this the only paper in town?" Jake asked the waitress as she brought his roll and a fresh cup of coffee.

"Yep. No need for a daily paper since we get USA Today and the Oklahoma City papers. Most folks don't even read that one 'cause it's only weekly. It gives the movies and local scores for the high schools, but it isn't much of a paper. Where you from?"

"I'm from Detroit, here on some business. Any good hotels in town?"

"Well, it depends on what you call good. We got a motel that's good for getting laid, and we got a Motel 6 out by the highway that's good and cheap. I guess it's clean and all that, and they say they leave the lights on. But if you're looking for a good bed and a decent motel without too many frills, I would try the Best Western Suites Motel out on Route 23. 'Course if you want some action, the Cavalier Motel over there on Second Street has plenty of action, but hide your wallet and don't drink the drinks. The sex is cheap, but the hangover ain't worth it, far's I'm concerned, and you never know what kind of bugs are crawling around them beds."

Jake asked for directions to the Best Western, and then asked where he could find the offices of the Crosswind Gazette.

Thirty minutes later Jake sat in the small, sparsely furnished waiting room of the Crosswind Gazette while the office clerk attempted to locate John Chambers, the owner, editor and lead reporter. Within seconds of the attractive blond clerk's sending out a digital message to his PageNet beeper, John Chambers called into the office and was notified of Jake's presence.

"Mr. Chambers said he would be back in about an hour if you would care to stay, but he has another appointment at that time so he won't have much time. He will be free around 3:30 this afternoon if you can come back later."

"I think I'll drive around town to get my bearings, maybe go out and check in at the motel. Tell Mr. Chambers I'll be back this afternoon around 3:30."

"Okay."

Pulling the shriveled-up piece of napkin with directions to the motel out of his jacket pocket, Jake started out to find the Best Western Suites Motel that the talkative waitress at the Wildcat Café had recommended. On the way he passed by a large Ford dealership, which Jake guessed at one time had been Allen Ford, but now the large blue and white sign read "Crosswind Ford." Jake decided to stop.

"Nice-looking car you're driving. You looking for something for the missus?" a poorly dressed middle-aged salesman said between puffs on his cigarette. "Lots of women are driving the Explorer these days, and we are running a special this month that could put your wife behind the wheel of an Eddie Bauer Limited Edition for only $369 a month with a couple of grand down."

"No, I am not looking for a car right now. I represent the wife of the former owner of this dealership, and I'm trying to find someone who can tell me what happened to her husband, Richard Allen."

"Blew his head off, he did, about four or five months ago. Just before Christmas. It was in all the papers. Real mess. I guess he lost a lot of money on some bad investments or something, seems like all his assets were used up to pay creditors. Sure you don't want to look at one of our special Explorers?"

"No thanks. Did you work for Richard Allen?" Jake asked.

"For both of them. No finer man than Senior. Always fair, always concerned about his employees. Good businessman, too. The whole town shopped here. Junior wasn't the same. Or maybe I should say Junior tried to be like his old man, but he just wasn't as good. Wasn't quite as fair or quite as concerned about his employees, and he wasn't much of a businessman. Didn't spend any time or money fixing up the place or running special programs. You know, the kind of things that promote traffic through the dealership. He loved cars, but mostly the old ones. Used to spend days at a time out in that old shed back behind the used car lot. Had a mint condition Model T that he restored and a couple of younger cars that he would drive in the parades and stuff. I liked the old '48 Ford wagon that had the real wood panels. He'd drive that in the Labor Day Parade down Main Street. Did it every year for as long as I can remember. Always had an 'Allen Ford' sign hanging off the tailgate. It was kind of sad when he up and sold all of his antique cars back in the spring of '94. Guess he was having money trouble way back then. After that he used to come to work and go through the routine, then he'd wander on back to that old shed. Guess he was living off his memories of those cars he loved. People here think he killed himself 'cause he ran out of money and didn't know any other way to pay the bills. Funny how people get themselves in trouble, although Junior didn't really seem like the type. Wasn't real flashy or nothing. Had a nice house and all, but didn't throw cash around like some of his contemporaries in town. Business was pretty good, too. We were selling about the same number of cars as usual even without the specials. Lot of customer loyalty, especially to the old man."

Throughout the flow of words the salesman interspersed his comments with long drags on his cigarette and emphasized his response with exaggerated facial movements that included an annoying distortion of his mouth and a rather incredible ability to raise his bushy eyebrows until they seemed to touch his even bushier hair. "New owner's putting some money into the place. Making it look a lot cleaner and brighter. Still selling about the same number of cars. He seems to be making money, though. Hangs out a lot at the country club with his pals, goes on long vacations and kind of lets us do our thing. Hard to figure why Junior couldn't make it."

"Anybody else here that might have known more about the financial condition of the dealership—a sales manager or accountant or chief financial officer?" Jake asked.

"I'm kind of the old hand around here. Name's Ralph Tyson. Mr. O'Connor, the new owner, brought in the rest of the bunch. By the time Junior punched out, most of the staff had either retired or quit anyway. Don't know who was looking after the books and all. I figure Junior was in to the bank for a pile of money. About a year ago we started getting our paychecks from the bank rather than from the company. Then he up and killed himself, and we lost two whole months of pay because of the bankruptcy. But I guess Mrs. Allen has it even worse. Understand she lost her house and all. You say you represent her. How is she? Does she still live here in Crosswind?"

"No," Jake responded without elaboration. "Thanks for your help. Do you have any idea whether any of Mr. Allen's records or files might have been left behind? Maybe in a file cabinet or desk?"

"Doubt it. They came in here and just cleaned the place out. All the books and that sort of stuff went to the bank or to the court or somewhere. I never saw people move so quickly following a death. It was like vultures picking over the carcass of a dead steer. I was kind of surprised that they were able to sell the dealership out of bankruptcy so fast. O'Connor was in here within a month after Mr. Allen killed himself, and they closed on the sale two weeks later with the blessing of the bankruptcy court. I don't even know how he found out about the place. He comes from Boston or someplace like that. Big city guy. Brought the new manager with him. Kind of a city slicker type. Tight pants and gold rings. That kind of stuff. Doesn't go over too well with us country folk."

"You say the bank was doing the payroll for the last year or so, was that the First State Bank of Crosswind?"

"Yes sir," Tyson responded. "I understand Mr. Allen had to factor the receivables. Bank had already loaned him a pile of money, or so I was told. Don't know how much. We used to floor plan through Ford Motor Credit, but the bank took over the floor plan about three years ago. I'm sure it cost Junior a bundle. Ford Credit was always a point to a point and a half under the banks. The old man used to tell me how important it was to keep Ford Credit happy so as not to lose the floor plan. Don't know why Junior switched to the bank. Maybe had something to do with that savings and loan they were always working on. I guess they had a good plan, but it sure went sour in a hurry. Say, you sure I can't show you a new Crown Vic or maybe a little Mustang?"

"No thanks," Jake responded with a big smile on his face. "You have been helpful, and if you think of anything that might help me piece together what caused Mr. Allen to commit suicide, please let me know. I will be staying at the Best Western Suites."

"OK, but here's my card. If you change your mind and want to dump that Caddy, you come see me. I'll give you a great deal, for Molly and for the old man."

It was almost one o'clock in the afternoon when Jake left Ralph Tyson and the former Allen Ford dealership. Since the editor of the newspaper was not due back until 3:30, Jake decided to check in at the motel, check in with his office, and then see what he could find at the Crosswind Gazette.

To his surprise, the Best Western Motel recommended by the waitress at the Wildcat Café was clean, modern and well equipped. The bedroom suite had a large sitting area with a writing table and kitchenette, and the queen-size bed only half-filled the separate bedroom area. Jake decided to check in with his office and report his findings to Mr. Parker.

"Mr. Parker's office," came the acerbic response from Mrs. Woods.

"This is Jake McCarthy, is Mr. Parker in?" Jake asked.

Jake noted just a hint of warmth in Mrs. Woods' response as she reported that Mr. Parker was at lunch and was not expected back until after four o'clock. "So how is Mrs. Allen doing, anyway?" Mrs. Woods inquired. "What does she look like?"

"She is a very nice lady. Tell Mr. Parker I will call him later tonight to report on my findings so far. Would you please switch me to Carol Brooks." With a defeated sigh, Mrs. Woods begrudgingly transferred Jake to his associate, who quickly filled him in on the status of various cases that Jake had been working on.

Next, Jake placed a call to Dr. Glasseur to check on his client.

"Hi, Jake, glad you called in. Molly is comfortable but very confused. I think she appreciates the safety and comfort of her room in the east wing, but we are having little luck in trying to pierce through the mental block caused by her trauma. We are working on a combined program of nutrition and gentle exercise to build up her stamina. Sometimes restoring health to the body will also restore emotional strength."

"Have you come to any final diagnosis on her condition?" Jake asked.

"She shows all the symptoms of post-traumatic stress disorder, just as we had originally suspected. It is sometimes hard to tell whether a single triggering event will cause this problem or whether it is the culmination of a series of events ending with a single, overwhelming event. It's a tricky condition that we are only just beginning to recognize.

"I would like to try a new procedure on her that we have been working on now for several months. It is totally safe and involves a form of therapy that attempts to heal the body through a combination of modalities. Do I have your permission? Molly has already said yes, but we can't rely on that entirely."

"Sure," Jake replied. "I know you will take good care of her. No shock therapy yet, right?"

"Right!" was the quick response. "Have you found out anything?"

"I haven't confirmed it yet with the newspaper accounts, but I'm reasonably confident that Molly was the first person on the scene of her husband's suicide. Apparently he put a gun to his head, and the result was not pretty—blood and bone and brains. Her husband's assets must have been mortgaged to the hilt, and when he died his creditors came after everything in a hurry. I met a fellow at the dealership who confirmed that the new owner bought the dealership and property out of the bankrupt estate. It happened awfully fast, and I'm going to try to find out how and why. Bankruptcy courts normally are slow and very deliberate, but in this case the dealership was sold within two months after the death. Say hi to Molly. She has been through a very rough period. I'll call you back tomorrow to find out how she's doing."

"Okay, Jake. When do you think you'll be returning to Oklahoma City? I've got another restaurant that I think you will like."

CHAPTER 8

After tending to strategy questions from several of the new associates assigned to his cases, Jake decided to get his bearings around the small city while waiting for the editor of the newspaper to return. The news clipping that Molly had tucked into her purse about the tragic suicide of her husband reported that Richard was on the Board of Directors of the First State Bank of Crosswind, so Jake decided to find it in anticipation of a thorough review of the Allen's accounts. It took less that ten minutes to find the main office of the Bank, which was located within two blocks of the Gazette.

The First State Bank of Crosswind occupied an old but apparently well built and respectable building about two miles from the former Allen Ford dealership. Although much of the financial information would be contained in the bankruptcy file, Jake knew that a friendly banker would be a lot more understanding than a bankruptcy clerk, and the information maintained by a bank on the financial condition of a corporate customer should be a lot more reliable. He had time to kill, so Jake decided to check out this possible source of information.

The front door to the bank was made from solid oak, with a beautiful frosted glass panel covering the upper two-thirds of the door. In old but untarnished gold leaf paint and centered in the frosted glass was inscribed:

FIRST STATE BANK OF CROSSWIND
Founded in 1917
By
Hon. William C. Hathaway, Sr. (1898–1979)

Jake entered the building not knowing what to expect other than old oak and green eyeshades. He was not surprised to find the interior not unlike the interior of many older banks throughout the country: functional, uncluttered and uninteresting. Rather than go directly to one of the three young tellers standing behind the oak counter, Jake sought out and found an elderly floor manager who beckoned him to sit in the straight-backed chair next to her modest desk.

"Welcome to First State. My name is Judy Falsworth. What can I do to help you? We have a special running right now that will give you free checking if you maintain a minimum balance of $500 in your savings account."

"No thanks," Jake responded to this sincere but rehearsed sales pitch. "I am looking for information about the financial affairs of a former customer of your bank, Richard Allen, and his wife, Molly, who is my client. I'm sure you recall his recent death. Is there a person here that I could speak with?"

At mention of the name "Richard Allen" the woman's face went pale, and she appeared distracted. She did not respond immediately to Jake's question but seemed to be fumbling for the right words. After several awkward moments Jake continued with, "You do know who I am talking about, don't you?"

At this the woman seemed to come back to her senses. "Why yes, of course, I knew Mr. Allen personally, and his father before him. He was a regular customer and was on our Board of Directors until…until his death. How is Molly? I did not know her well, but she always seemed to be such a fine person. Please convey our sincere condolences."

"Is there someone here I can talk with about Mr. Allen?" Jake asked again but in a softer tone. This poor woman had suddenly gone into mourning over a death that had occurred over four months previous.

"Mr. Hathaway should be in his office. He is the president now that his father passed away. Hathaway Senior, the founder of the bank, was here until the day of his death, God rest his soul. Hathaway Junior, the son of the founder, was chairman of the bank for just over ten years before he died in a tragic automobile accident about five years ago. When Junior died the board had little choice but to elect the current and last of the Hathaways to the presidency of the bank. In addition to being the founder's only grandson, Mr. Hathaway and his mother control almost all of the Bank's stock. Senior put all of his stock in trust for his son and daughter-in-law, and when Junior died his share of the trust passed on to our current president, Hathaway the third.

"Senior was a tough old coot, but those of us who have been here for a while got to understand his stubbornness and insistence on details. 'The Devil's in the detail' he used to say, over and over until we were thoroughly sick of it. But even today when I go to do a closing or put the papers together for a major loan proposal for the loan committee, I always remember his saying and thank him for it. Junior was a bit slow, but honest as the day is long and kind to his staff. The bank did well under his chairmanship, mostly because we all liked working for him. We pretty well knew the business, and he let us do our thing."

"Molly and Richard Allen?" Jake reminded her after this burst of unrelated information. "I have a power of attorney from Mrs. Allen to look into their accounts. Can you help me or is there someone else?"

"Oh yes, of course, I have been prattling on, haven't I? I don't usually take floor duty, but the bank has been short of staff lately, and we have had to use our management staff. I will see if Mr. Hathaway can see you. What is your name?"

"Jake McCarthy. I'm from Detroit."

Several moments later Mrs. Falsworth returned with word that Mr. Hathaway could see him in twenty minutes if he would care to wait, otherwise he should come back at ten-thirty Tuesday morning since Mr. Hathaway would be out of town on Monday. Jake decided to wait. It was too early for the appointment with the Gazette and too late to track down any other information. He pulled his legal pad out of the slim-line briefcase that he carried to meetings where documentation was not as important as face-to-face negotiation, and began to piece together the few bits of information that he had gained from his half day in Crosswind.

After twenty-five minutes Jake became slightly fidgety, but decided to be patient. It was nearly three o'clock before a rotund man in his mid-fifties (or at least looking like he was in his mid-fifties but perhaps hiding his youth behind layers of fat) approached Jake and introduced himself as William C. Hathaway, III, president of the bank, namesake and grandson of the founder, William C. Hathaway, Senior. Jake followed him back behind the solid oak teller's counter to a well appointed office complete with computer, facsimile machine and a fancy bookcase that contained leather-bound volumes of the Oklahoma statutes relating to the banking industry.

Jake began the conversation. "I represent Molly Allen, who has asked for our help in straightening out her financial affairs."

"Where is Molly?" Hathaway asked.

"She's safe in Oklahoma City under medical supervision. She's OK, but badly undernourished and in need of a safe, comfortable environment. Did you know the Allens?" Jake asked.

"Yes, of course. My father was Richard's godfather. Although Richard was several years older than I, we were very best friends. We were shocked and horrified at his sudden and tragically violent death.

"My Granddaddy, William C. Hathaway Sr., founded this bank back in 1917 when he moved here and fell in love with the rock. Have you been down to see our one and only landmark? It is pretty impressive in its own, rugged, way—especially during the sunrise and sunset.

"That's Senior's picture over there on the wall. He died about fifteen years ago from a blood clot in his lung following hip surgery. He was getting on in years, and we warned him about climbing around on that old rock. He called it "his" rock because he and it were the oldest things in town. Fell one day and broke his hip, had to have surgery, threw a clot, and the rest is history. My daddy never really ran the bank. Had no mind for numbers. Some folks thought he was a little slow, if you know what I mean. Father entrusted the bank to me although he was chairman of the board. I guess that was only fair since he and my mother owned most of the stock in the bank following my grandfather's death.

"My father died in a car crash in '89. He and my mother were divorced at the time, and I was the only child. Mom remarried about ten years before my father's death. She lives back on the east coast. She didn't want to run the bank, so she and the trust elected me.

"Now that you know who I am, who are you and what do you wish to know about Richard Allen?"

Taking a moment to catch up after this spontaneous outpouring of information about the Hathaway clan, Jake responded. "Well, my name is Jake McCarthy. I'm an attorney from Detroit, and my firm has been retained by Molly Allen, the widow of Richard Allen, to look into her financial and legal affairs following his death. Thank you for seeing me on short notice. I believe Richard Allen was a member of the board of directors of this bank."

"It was such a tragic suicide. Richard had been a member of our board for several years, and his family was a pillar of Crosswind society. We had no idea that he was so despondent over his financial condition. We were working with the dealership to help it out of a financial crisis. You're from Detroit, so you know the auto industry. Very cyclical. Ups and downs. Allen Ford was in a down, but we were sure it would return."

William C. Hathaway III suffered from a skin condition that turned his face crimson and caused him to perspire when under any kind of pressure. He was bright red, and sweat was already running down the sides of his face. He wiped at it with a large white handkerchief. Although short of stature, Jake guessed that he probably weighed 280 pounds. A disproportionate amount of that weight was centered in his double chin, which hung from the tip of his chin proper down to the bottom of his neck. His heavily pleated trousers were held up by braided leather suspenders, which also helped to keep his shirttails tucked inside of his trousers, but only just barely. The pants, which Jake guessed had at least a 56-inch waist, were loose around his massive girth.

"Do you have a power of attorney from Molly Allen authorizing you to inquire on her behalf?" Hathaway asked.

"Yes sir, I have obtained this comprehensive power of attorney authorizing me to pursue whatever financial information pertaining to the Allens that I consider important, whether or not it might be considered confidential. Mrs. Allen has signed it in front of two witnesses and a notary." Jake did not tell Hathaway that the witnesses were Dr. Glasseur and her receptionist, and that the notary was a friend of the receptionist who worked for the University. Even though Molly was not entirely lucid, they knew Jake was trying to help her, so they were willing to help.

"Last time I saw Molly, she wasn't capable of signing such a document. Are you sure she was mentally alert?" Hathaway asked.

"I explained to Molly what I intended to do, and she appeared to understand fully. The document was properly executed and notarized. Are you questioning its authenticity?" Jake asked.

"Well, it is highly unusual. The power is not prepared in accordance with the bank's usual format, and we insist that individuals seeking confidential information use the Bank's form. I'm afraid we will need to discuss this with our corporate counsel to see whether this document is adequate to allow you to inquire into this personal information about Richard and Molly's accounts. After all, he is dead."

"How long will that take?" Jake quickly responded, having not anticipated resistance from the Allens' longtime friend and banker. But, he rationalized, this was a bank, and this is the way bankers behave.

"Well, I think Howard is out of town right now. If I'm not mistaken, he will be gone for the entire weekend and is not due back until late Monday. He should be back in his office on Tuesday. Are you in a hurry?"

Jake was about to respond sarcastically to the person causing this unnecessary delay, which was costing him and his client both time and money (although it was highly unlikely that Molly could pay even a fraction of the firm's fee). Jake decided not to appear overly aggressive at this point. Something about the way this corpulent bank president responded gave Jake an uneasy feeling, but now was not the time to exert pressure. The power of attorney was short but all encompassing, and there should have been no resistance to his access to the Allen account information. Richard was dead, and Molly had no money. Unless the bank had actual knowledge that the power of attorney was not authentic, it had the absolute right to rely on it as permission for Molly Allen's attorney to see the documents. Jake sensed that Hathaway was hiding something, but pressure now might make it even more difficult to sort out what happened.

Instead, Jake asked, "What's Howard's last name? Maybe our firm has had some dealings with him or his firm."

"Howard W. Stern, Esq. He's with the firm of Stern, Foster and Smith. I'll get this power of attorney over to him this afternoon and tell his secretary to give it to him as soon as he gets back from his trip."

"Thank you, Mr. Hathaway, I will check back with you on Tuesday around two o'clock. I would like to look over the bank records of the Allens for the last three years if they are available, and I will need to look at the loan transactions and the factoring arrangement between the bank and Allen Ford. This bank did provide the floor plan financing for the dealership, didn't it?"

"I'm afraid that will have to wait until Tuesday," Hathaway answered. "If Howard says the power of attorney is OK, then we can discuss whatever you want about the Allens and Allen Ford."

Standing up, Jake offered his hand to Mr. Hathaway and quickly left the office and the bank. The Crosswinds Gazette was only a few blocks away, so he began walking along First Street toward what appeared to be the center of town. At the corner of First and Main was a five-story building that dominated the Crosswind cityscape. On the front of the building there were a dozen or so brass plates denoting legal firms, accounting firms and a small deli that occupied part of the first floor of the office building. The law offices of Stern, Foster and Smith were on the top floor.

Jake had almost half an hour to kill before his meeting with Chambers at the Gazette, so he entered the building, walked briskly to the open elevator and rode to the fifth floor. On the solid walnut, oversized door immediately opposite the elevator appeared the words "Stern, Foster and Smith, Attorneys and Counselors, specializing in real estate, banking and commercial transactions."

Jake entered the office and approached the receptionist.

"Can I help you, sir?" the attractive young lady asked, looking up from a thick paperback book that she had been reading. She had a freckled face with bright red hair, an aquiline nose that matched perfectly with her sharp features, and narrow-set eyes. Her expression was healthy and innocent, and her voice clearly demonstrated a desire to please. She quickly removed the paperback book from the top of her desk, but not before Jake saw the erotic cover depicting two scantily clad adults—Jake couldn't decide for sure whether a man and a woman or two men—wrapped around each other.

"Hello, my name is Jake McCarthy," Jake responded, trying not to smile at the signs of embarrassment showing through the young lady's crimson face. “I’m here from Michigan and would like to talk with Mr. Stern. Mr. Hathaway at the bank recommended him to me. Is he in?”

“Do you have an appointment?” she asked, trying to regain her composure.

“No, I just got into town. I would like to make an appointment with him, but thought if he were available I could meet him and arrange for an appointment tomorrow.”

As she pushed several buttons on the console in front of her, the receptionist replied, “Let me check with his secretary.”

“Sally, this is Louise up at the front desk. There is a Mr. McCarthy here to see Mr. Stern. Is he available?”

Jake could not hear the answer to that question but expected a report that he was out of town and would be back the following Tuesday.

Instead, the redheaded receptionist responded, “Mr. Stern is unavailable right now, but Sally, his secretary, said he has an opening this afternoon and could meet with you at 5:30 for half an hour. Can you come back then?”

“I’m most appreciative,” Jake responded. “I will be back at 5:30.”

CHAPTER 9

Jake left the thick carpeting and highly polished mahogany furniture of the law offices of Stern, Foster and Smith and walked three more blocks to the town's only newspaper. He arrived at the small, sparsely furnished office of the Crosswinds Gazette five minutes early for his 3:30 appointment with its owner, editor and seemingly only reporter, John Chambers. Jake had been forced to search through newspaper files once before in his legal career and didn't relish the thought of plowing through volumes of old newsprint. Modern newspaper offices were completely computerized, and searching old files was often no more difficult than doing legal research through Lexus or Westlaw. In fact, many newspapers were online with Lexus, Westlaw and other internet-based legal research browsers. Jake was certain that the Gazette was not one of those newspapers.

Jake was pleasantly surprised when Chambers immediately came into the small waiting area and greeted him personally. There was only one word that adequately described this newspaper person: huge! William Hathaway was corpulent with layers of fat over a sedentary body, but Chambers was massive in girth while not appearing to be soft or flabby. His handshake was strong, and he gave the impression of being an energetic person trapped in a grossly oversized body.

After greeting Jake with a friendly smile and confirming that Jake was interested in viewing past copies of the paper, Chambers ushered him back into the working part of the paper to a computer terminal, which, Chambers boasted, was connected to the newspaper's central computer and the repository of old copy.

"I'm impressed," Jake said as he viewed the array of modern equipment. "This looks like first-rate equipment."

With obvious pride in his computerized data storage system, Chambers quickly responded to Jake's compliment. "It's all IBM equipment networked into a mainframe computer that stores all of the data, allows for electronic layouts, edits for typographic or grammatical errors, operates the printing presses and performs a number of other functions that only a newspaper editor could truly appreciate. I picked up the system about four years ago after my father died. He did nothing to modernize this paper during his thirty-five years running it, and we were sorely in need of a new system."

Pulling up a chair next to the one that Jake now occupied, Chambers deposited his ponderous bulk on and around the metal seat as he proceeded to lead Jake through a series of commands that would awaken the data retrieval process. If Jake needed hard copy of a specific article, he need only click on the title of the article, then on the "print" icon, and the computer would automatically print the entire piece, even though portions of it might be on later pages of the newspaper.

Searching the files was relatively easy if you had the exact date. If not, you could feed in parameters such as April 30, 1992–October 31, 1993, then give the computer key words such as "Richard Allen" and "death." The computer would search for that combination of words within the dates specified. Jake found the logic so similar to legal research that within minutes he was able to sort through the entire database and retrieve the information he was looking for.

Soon he was reading a lengthy article describing the tragic suicide of Richard Allen on December 19, 1994. Jake quickly scanned the article, and then printed out a copy on the Hewlett-Packard laser printer that sat conveniently beside the computer terminal. He then scanned through the months of January and February of 1995 to see if there were any other articles concerning Richard Allen or the Allen Ford dealership. The computer found half a dozen notices involving the sale of assets of Richard and Molly Allen, the estate's filing for bankruptcy, and notices to creditors. There was a real estate listing for the Allen home for $550,000. On the day after Richard Allen committed suicide the newspaper ran a lengthy article about the man, his contributions to Crosswind, his membership in the Crosswind Country Club, and his wife, Molly (Stewart) Allen. After that article, but for the notices and formal obituary, the names Richard Allen and Molly Allen did not appear in the Crosswind Gazette.

Jake then changed the parameters to the period from January 1, 1989 through December 18, 1994. He again typed in the name Richard Allen coupled with "death" to see whether there were articles concerning the death of Richard Allen Sr. When he hit the enter key, the computer quickly responded, "You have chosen a quantity that is outside of the database of the computer. The earliest entry is June 26, 1989. Do you wish to change this quantity?" The computer then offered two answers, yes and no. Jake used the mouse to click on the word "yes," and the computer promptly responded by posting a lengthy article about the death of Richard Allen Sr.

Jake was so impressed with the speed and efficiency of the computerized retrieval system installed at the Crosswind Gazette that he began requesting information on some of the other individuals that he had met. First he asked the computer to search for articles on William Hathaway. The computer indicated thirty-seven articles referencing the name William Hathaway. Jake began at the first.

Four articles into the search, Jake came across the obituary of William C. Hathaway Jr., the son of the founder of First State Bank of Crosswind. Jake read the article in its entirety:

> The Wm. Hathaway family reported the death of its senior member today. After heroic efforts to survive the crippling effects of a tragic automobile accident six weeks ago (see Crosswind Gazette article dated April 4, 1989), Bill Hathaway finally gave up the fight, dying peacefully in his sleep at home. He never regained consciousness following the terrible automobile accident, which broke his neck and severed his spinal cord. The Underhill Funeral Home is handling the arrangements. There will be a memorial service on October 15 at 2:00 p.m. at St. Francis Catholic Church. Donations can be made to the Crosswind Community Hospital Foundation.

After scanning the rest of the thirty-plus articles for anything of interest about the bank, Jake looked for articles on Red Rock Savings and Loan or its founders. He found several dozen articles about Red Rock and began scanning them for information about the rise and fall of this small savings and loan. Most of the articles were written during the first six months of its existence and portrayed the new venture as a great opportunity for Crosswind and for interested investors. Only one article reported the bankruptcy of Red Rock, and it focused on high interest rates as the reason for its demise. While the earlier stories routinely mentioned the founders of Red Rock Savings and Loan, such references were noticeably lacking as its fortunes fell.

Although interested in gathering as much background information as he could, Jake did not want to miss his appointment with Stern and was running out of time. Thanking Chambers for access to the fine computer data bank and requesting another session in front of the IBM terminals when he had more time, Jake left the Gazette and walked back to the offices of Howard Stern, arriving several minutes before the 5:30 appointment. The fancy decor of the law offices of Stern, Foster and Smith contrasted greatly with the Spartan furnishings and gray drabness of the Gazette. The desk and chairs sparkled with the high gloss of freshly polished fine furniture. The spacious waiting area adjacent to the receptionist's desk contained several upholstered wingback chairs and three sofas covered in a tightly woven wool. The furnishings looked out of place for a small law office in southwest Oklahoma. Everything appeared to be of very high quality. Someone had spent a lot of time and money decorating the waiting area, and Jake was curious to see whether the rest of the suite was similarly decorated. The mahogany desk behind which the young receptionist sat was large and devoid of papers or equipment except for a small computer terminal that kept track of the firm's telephone system and allowed the receptionist to direct incoming calls to the right attorney or paralegal. Track lighting focused intense halogen spotlights on several large paintings of Indians racing across the plains, and on a table against one of the walls was what Jake thought to be an authentic Remington brass sculpture of three cowboys trying to rope a calf. Not being an expert, Jake couldn't tell for sure whether it was an original or one of the many copies that were available even through discount houses. Based on the rest of the office furnishings, Jake guessed that it was real.

At the invitation of the receptionist, Jake sat on one of the sofas and instinctively reached for something to read. On the end table were a dozen or so copies of a professionally published firm brochure. Jake was immediately impressed by the gold leaf letters embossed into the cover of the brochure and the engraved lettering on the title page.

Stern, Foster and Smith was the oldest firm in Crosswind. Malcolm H. Stern had formed it in 1893. The short biography on Howard Stern Jr. indicated that he was the great grandson of the founder and the only Stern currently active in the firm. His father, Judge Howard Stern Sr., was listed as counsel to the firm. His extended biography described a distinguished career, specializing in oil and gas. He had been president of the Oklahoma Bar Association and the Southwest Council of Circuit Court Judges. In 1987 Judge Stern was appointed to the United States

District Court for the Southern District of Oklahoma sitting at Crosswind. At the end of the biography there was a brief explanation of the Judge's current condition:

> Following a tragic fall from his horse in April of 1989, Judge Stern suffered a compound fracture of his neck and back that resulted in the severing of a substantial portion of his spinal cord. He has retired from the Federal Bench and the practice of law.

Jake was leafing through the rest of the firm brochure when an attractive middle-aged woman entered the waiting area and approached him. "Are you Mr. McCarthy?"

Jake rose from the overstuffed sofa and responded, "Yes, I'm here to see Mr. Stern."

"I made the appointment for this afternoon thinking that Mr. Stern would return after his afternoon meeting, but he called in to say that he was getting a jump on his weekend trip and would not be back. We did not know how to contact you to let you know he would be unavailable this afternoon. He asked me to convey his sincere apologies for any inconvenience that this may have caused you. Mr. Stern will be back Tuesday afternoon, and he asked me to inquire whether you would be available to meet with him at that time. If not, perhaps there is another attorney in the firm that you would like to consult concerning your real estate matters."

"I'll be in town for several days. Mr. Stern was specifically recommended, therefore I would like to meet him and determine whether he can provide the necessary services. Perhaps we can make an appointment now, say two o'clock Tuesday afternoon?"

"That will be fine. I will post it in his calendar. Where are you staying so that we can contact you if there is another interruption?"

"I'm staying at the Best Western Suites Motel on Route 23. I'm in room 206, and the desk clerk indicated there is voice mail on the motel's phone system. If I'm not there, just leave word. Here's my card. I look forward to meeting with Mr. Stern."

CHAPTER 10

Like an emerald stuck in the middle of a rusting crown, the Crosswind Country Club occupies nearly 1,200 acres of land on the northeast side of the city. Built in the mid-1920s, the country club facility boasted the only neogothic architecture in the entire area. It was the architectural creation of Jonas Seabring, a fellow of the American Academy of Architects. He had done his undergraduate work at Yale University in New Haven, Connecticut, and his postgraduate architectural work at the Princeton University School of Architecture. Drawing on his Ivy League experience and a nearly unlimited supply of money flowing from newly discovered oil wells, Mr. Seabring created a clubhouse and golf facility for the Crosswind Country Club that equaled any private club in the East or Midwest of similar vintage. Surrounding the clubhouse were the immaculately maintained fairways and greens of two championship eighteen-hole courses designed by Donald Ross and a separate nine-hole "executive" course that had been built to provide the older members of the club with a less challenging and shorter course with larger, more friendly greens.

Through an iron-clad contract drafted by Malcolm Stern, the Crosswind Country Club was guaranteed riparian rights to a sufficient volume of water diverted from the north fork of the Red River that it could irrigate the entire 1,200 acres and fill the twelve water hazards sprinkled throughout the two courses in perpetuity.

In addition to the grand dining room that hosted almost every major social event in Crosswind, the club had four smaller dining rooms that could be reserved for private parties. Even after Prohibition Crosswind had remained a "dry" city where alcohol was forbidden. Although the country club had agreed to observe the city ordinance prohibiting the sale or use of alcoholic beverages, the board of directors of the club had constructed a separate dining room that permitted a privileged few to enjoy a cocktail or two without fear of discovery by the more pious members of the club or by the law. Now that very private dining room was reserved for current and former board members and their guests, and liquor was served freely throughout the club and the city of Crosswind.

Clad with solid oak paneling and furnished with beautifully upholstered chairs around a large hand-finished oak dining table, the inner dining room was a sanctuary for those who wanted privacy.

By design the room was completely isolated from the rest of the club, although it occupied space near the center of the massive clubhouse. It had double-thick walls made of poured concrete and western sandstone. Although it was physically located within the four walls of the main building, it had been built like a fortress. Its heavy oak doors could be locked from the inside so that not even the club's manager could enter. Until 1994 no female had ever entered the room (or so the club's older members would explain to newcomers, usually over a glass of brandy). They were still not welcome, but the wife of a young board member had pushed the issue and forced the club to allow her access to the room. Once the tradition had been broken, several of the board members who routinely used this special dining room requested that female waitresses be allowed to serve meals, partly because the few remaining male waiters were not performing as well as they should and several members had complained about their personal hygiene. As a result the club had recently hired some young, physically attractive waitresses to service this special dining area. They were instructed to be particularly friendly to the middle-aged male members.

On this evening the single large oak table sat in the middle of the private dining room, surrounded by five of the club's more distinguished members. The dinner meeting had been called by William Hathaway and included Howard Stern, James O'Connor, the new owner of Crosswind Ford, John Chambers, and Eric Beamer, CPA and managing partner of the firm of Beamer and Associates.

"Gentlemen," Hathaway said as he attempted to bring the meeting to order. Cocktails had been served, and the general discussion had ranged from concerns about the early heat wave that had scorched Crosswind for the last fortnight to details of an extended weekend trip that they had planned as a reward for successfully responding to the recent inquiry into Red Rock Savings and Loan by the FDIC and Resolution Trust.

After bringing the group to order, Hathaway continued. "I think you all know by now that Molly Allen has hired an attorney to look into the circumstances surrounding Richard's death. When I called Eric to warn him of the possible inquiry, he suggested that before we leave on our trip to Dozier Creek Ranch we make sure that we all are singing out of the same hymnal and that we have covered every possible base so that this McCarthy fellow from Michigan will find everything in order. Howard, are you absolutely sure that the probate documents and bankruptcy papers are in order?"

"Yes, Bill, you know they are. How about the bank records? My documents are all based on the records you and Eric sent over to me."

"Eric, any second thoughts? Our records are what you put together. I just hope you weren't so hard on Molly that she has gone and hired herself some self-righteous somebody who will put a monkey wrench in our plan. He's going to want to see documents, and the power of attorney that he gave me pretty clearly gives him that right, although I told him that Howard had to give his legal opinion to that effect. Howard, have you had a chance to render your legal opinion?"

"It doesn't take a genius to authorize someone to look at bank records," Stern responded. "Yeah that power of attorney is fine, and we really have no reason to challenge its validity. If we tried to stonewall it at this point, it would only cause more suspicions. This will be another good test of just how good you are, Eric."

At that point a young woman with dark skin and Mexican features entered the room carrying a small tray. She wore a very short skirt and white cotton blouse that adequately displayed her large breasts. The top two buttons were intentionally left unbuttoned, and although both Hathaway and Chambers tried hard not to stare as she walked by, they were both intent on checking to see if the waitress wore any undergarment.

"Would you like another round, or are you ready to order dinner?" she asked in nearly flawless English.

Chambers, who had been silent throughout the discussion of Richard and Molly Allen, quickly piped up and said, "we'll have another round and another bowl of those mixed nuts." John Chambers was big, some would say morbidly obese, and he made no effort to change his appearance. Under his management the Crosswind Gazette had not grown even at the modest rate that the town of Crosswind had grown. Conversely, the newspaper editor had grown in size and weight following the death of his father in 1989. John Chambers had been smoking since his mid teens and already had a hacking cough easily identifiable as the beginning signs of chronic emphysema. Weighing over 300 pounds, Chambers often explained to anyone who would listen, "When you weigh three times as much as anyone else, you need to drink at least three times as much as the rest of the folks just to get a buzz on." In keeping with this profound insight he had already ordered another double bourbon and water.

"I think you all know the importance of continuing to respond appropriately to inquiries concerning Red Rock and our recently departed partner," Hathaway began after the waitress had distributed the second round of drinks and left the room. "Eric, if I were to send this McCarthy guy over to you tomorrow, would you have the dealership books and records in order, as well as Dick and Molly's personal accounts?"

"Yeah, they're just like they were after the Feds came in. Everything balances nicely and consistently comes to less than zero. I've been doing those books ever since Dickey's old man had his unfortunate accident. They are consistent from year to year, and it would be virtually impossible for anyone to dig behind the numbers. We have Dickey's signature all over the Red Rock documents. Poor bastard never did take the time to read them. Send this McCarthy fellow over. I'm not the slightest bit concerned. I'll open the books for him or anyone else."

Hathaway turned to Howard Stern, who was sitting uncomfortably in one of the green leather chairs fussing with a Corona cigar that had not cooperated when he tried to clip its end with the club's cigar cutter. "Howard, what did McCarthy tell your receptionist when he came up to your office?"

"He said he was interested in some kind of land deal. Don't know what he had in mind. After you called, I put him off until next Tuesday afternoon like you said. I don't much like that. We could use the work. Damned overhead is killing us. At any rate, the probate files are all in order, and once the court accepted Eric's financials, there wasn't much left to fight over. Besides, Molly wasn't in any condition to question anything, and she just told me to go ahead and take care of it for her. Signed all the documents before we even typed them up. Richard's will came out of the Farley office that his old man used, so it was in perfect shape. Judge Evans used to be a member of that firm. Probably could have recited the language without even reading the document. Don't know what else he could want from me except for those probate documents and the results of the bankruptcy proceedings."

The conversation was interrupted again by the waitress, who carefully placed salads in front of each of the five gentlemen, delaying slightly as she leaned over to place the salads on the table. As she leaned forward the shape of each breast came clearly into view. She never really understood the enjoyment that these middle-aged men seemed to get from this simple act, but she knew that her tip would reflect the care with which she had removed her bra and left the top buttons on her blouse open. She departed without a word, satisfied that she would go home a few dollars richer.

"I'm going to get me some of that woman before the end of the year if it's the last thing I do," O'Connor boasted as the heavy oak door closed behind her. "I get a hard on every time she's our waitress. Something about that smell or the way she moves or something."

"Ah, quit bragging. Some of us have forgotten what a hard on feels like," Chambers said, taking another mouthful of bourbon to wash down the fistful of nuts that he had just poured into his willing mouth.

"Yeah, it's been a while since we took our last field trip over to White Sands on our way to Dozier Creek. I am looking forward to our field trip next weekend so that we can detour down over the Texas border and taste some of that sweet West Texas pussy," O'Connor replied. "Too bad that property turned out to be sterile. I was convinced that your diviner knew what he was doing, Howard. He sure convinced me with all of his so-called successes. You even checked him out, John, and his references backed up his story that those willow branches can detect water below the surface. Sure fooled me, but more importantly it fooled Richard into thinking we could build a whole community on that worthless patch of desert and scrubland. But all was not lost, was it guys? Instead of an underground river, we found Dozier Creek and the ranch that bears its name; and that discovery made up for the lack of water in White Sands. After putting up with those federal investigators,

I'm ready for a long, Memorial Day weekend at the ranch. It's been too long, and I'm going to be horny all week long in anticipation."

"Gentlemen," Eric Beamer said, trying to divert the conversation away from the upcoming trip to the Ranch and back to the purpose for the meeting. "We've made it through one major investigation by the Feds, and it is appropriate that we take off a few days to celebrate. But, we need to prepare for another inquiry from this Detroit attorney. You all know what to say, right? You remember who found Dick's body, and be sure to say how shocked we all were to find how deeply in debt he was. Bill, and you, Howard, need to emphasize that Richard had shown you a list of his multi-million-dollar investment portfolio for purposes of his estate plan and in support of the substantial loans, which the bank had extended to him over the last few years. As his friends you never questioned the veracity of the investment account and were shocked and betrayed when you discovered that it was a hoax. Out of respect for your friend you, of course, did not advertise his misrepresentation since there was no way of recovering any more from his estate. Any questions? Anything the federal investigators may have asked that caused concern or may present a problem responding to McCarthy?"

"Oh, come on Eric, you worry too much," O'Connor said. "From what Bill here says, this attorney is just here doing a friend a favor. This ain't no inquisition. And, besides, we've been through this a couple of times already. If we can fool the federal regulators who get paid to find stuff, we should be able to take care of this dude who's got no chance in hell of getting paid for his work. We know Molly can't pay him anything, so he's going to lose interest real quick. Right? That's the way all attorneys are. No money, no service. And if he gets too nosy, we'll treat him the same way we did Richard. That's the way we do it up in Boston. Just because I got shipped down here to this hellhole doesn't mean I've got to forget my entire upbringing. Now let's focus on next weekend instead of some punk from Detroit." O'Connor finished with a coarse laugh followed by a hacking cough caused by years of smoking Pall Mall cigarettes and drinking cheap whisky in Boston bars. The others did not respond.

"You are right, Jim, let's focus on Dozier Creek Ranch," Stern finally interjected. "For now we are in the free and clear, and we deserve to celebrate. We can deal with McCarthy when we come back all refreshed and relaxed after our weekend in the wild."

CHAPTER 11

It was Sunday in Crosswind, and Jake decided to use the morning to catch up on some sleep, review the stack of memoranda that his associates had E-mailed him during the week, and devote the afternoon to exploring the area that had given the city its name. Stern wasn't due back until the following Tuesday, and Jake had been going pretty much full out for the entire week. He slept in, took a long shower, ate a full breakfast, and started working through the messages and memoranda that filled his computer inbox.

In the distance Jake heard the clarion tones of a carillon calling its parishioners to Sunday mass. On impulse, Jake closed his laptop computer, slipped into a clean shirt and slacks, and headed for the Catholic Church that he had seen on his way into Crosswind. Ever since his brush with death in the wilderness of Michigan's Upper Peninsula, Jake had experienced a new interest in church and an awareness that as much as he might think he had control over his live and career, there was a force greater than he could comprehend. Perhaps it was that force that drew him to church on a sultry Sunday in Crosswind, Oklahoma, or perhaps he was just looking for an excuse for avoiding the chore of reading memoranda written by inarticulate associates. Whatever the reason for his deciding to go to church in the first place, after the service and experiencing the ritual common to all Catholic Churches, Jake felt a sense of renewal and confidence in himself that helped prepare him for the week ahead. The service at St. Mary's Church of the Immaculate Conception in Crosswind was unremarkable, yet upon leaving the Church Jake felt a new determination to help his destitute client. But first he would follow the directions of his senior partner and check out the giant red rock that stood as an ever-present landmark.

Located to the west and south of the small business district, the towering peak of wind-worn rock that was the central feature of Red Rock Park dominated the landscape for miles. Jake estimated the giant escarpment was probably 1,000 or 1,200 feet high and a quarter of a mile in length. In the morning and afternoon sun, it glowed a brilliant red, and from a distance appeared to be devoid of vegetation. As he drove through the park entrance, Jake noticed that footpaths criss-crossed through and around the giant rock. Along the trails there were cactus and other vegetation typically found on the high plains and semi-arid deserts of the southwest. The westerly face of the rock was, however, remarkably smooth along its entire length, most likely because of the hundreds of centuries of wind-driven sand that had blasted it clean of any growth.

Jake parked near a small bronze monument and read the inscription attesting to the significance of this rock in the history of the town of Crosswind:

> This giant rock growing out of the southwestern Oklahoma prairie was the sacred meeting place of the Five Civilized Tribes that inhabited what was known as the Indian Territory. The tribes included the Cheyenne, Arapaho, Comanche, Kiowa and Apache Nations. Until disrupted by the westward movement in the mid nineteenth century, the Five Civilized Tribes lived peacefully, each respecting the territory occupied by the other and sharing the abundant buffalo and deer that inhabited the Indian Territory. Each year as the days grew shorter and the scorching summer heat gave way to cool breezes, the chiefs of

the Five Civilized Tribes would meet in the shadow of the red rock to discuss common problems and resolve any disputes. These tribal meetings occurred after the summer harvest and were regarded as the signal to each of the tribal hunters that it was time to prepare for winter. Following the ceremonial meeting of tribes, the hunters would join in an organized buffalo hunt that would feed the nations throughout the winter.

All of this changed in 1830 when President Andrew Jackson signed into law the Indian Removal Act, which authorized the systematic relocation of these once-peaceful tribes to more remote locations so that the early settlers to the Indian Territory could take their prime hunting, fishing and grazing lands.

In 1832 the first major migration of settlers saw this giant rock growing out of the flat plains from nearly 100 miles away as they crossed out of the foothills of what is now eastern Oklahoma and onto the great prairie. It shone in the bright sun as a red beacon for the weary travelers as they fought their way west. Some of these travelers continued on into Texas and New Mexico. Many kept going until they reached the Pacific Ocean, where the smell of gold was beginning to rot the minds of men looking for instant wealth. A few decided to stay near the ceremonial rock, and soon a small town grew to the north of the rock along the Red River.

Red Rock Park received its name because of the intensity of red color, especially in the morning as the sun reflects off the great rocks northeasterly face, and in the evening as the sun sets on the westward side. It continues even today as a landmark for travelers to the western plains of Oklahoma. The flat face of Red Rock lies at a 90-degree angle to the prevailing westerly winds, which cross the flat prairie. Because of the length of the rock and its smooth surface, the prevailing wind deflects off the rock and heads almost due north. Standing in the center of town,

> people are amazed at the wind turbulence caused by the crossing of wind as it comes from both the west and the south at the same time. The name Crosswind was formally adopted by the Town Council in 1854 as the official name of this new frontier community.

A small building located at the eastern end of Red Rock Park announced to the public its mission in life. The sign over the door into the building said in large block letters, "INFORMATION." Although the morning sun beat down hard on Jake, the dryness of the air made the heat bearable. He decided to walk the several hundred yards to the information center. Collecting souvenirs of travel, no matter where they were from or why they were selected, was an absolute necessity with two young daughters full of questions, waiting for his return and the gifts that he always had for them.

The building was small, clean and appropriate for the limited tourist traffic of this small city. A woman possibly in her early sixties sat behind a small counter covered with books about Oklahoma and the significance of the Indian Territory. Jake nodded to the woman as he entered the main room of the building and began a random check of the merchandise for sale. Historical photographs hung on every wall depicting, for the most part, the Indian heritage and the development of Crosswind as a frontier town. Occasionally a picture of an oil well would appear as a reminder that oil had changed the very fiber of this town, but there were no cans of WD-40 as souvenirs.

As he studied the weathered face of an ancient wooden Indian sitting cross-legged with a long pipe held in his right hand, Jake heard the woman say in a dialect unique to Oklahoma, "Apache. You know much about Indians? That piece was hand-carved out on the reservation. We can ship it anywhere in the world. It's a great piece that will only grow in value. Would you like it? Can't gift wrap it for you, but we'll throw in the cost of shipping."

Jake responded without turning around to address the woman. "No, I'm just here on business and thought I would check out the city's landmark so that I could report back to my two girls in Michigan."

The elderly woman continued, "What kind of business you got here in Crosswind? You some kind of government investigator? There was a bunch of people from Washington in here a couple of months ago looking into that Red Rock Savings and Loan thing. You one of them guys?"

"No," Jake said. "I'm here on behalf of Molly Allen, who used to live in Crosswind. Maybe you knew her."

"Oh shucks, I don't get to know them kind of folks unless they come here to the shop with their out-of-town touristy type friends. She lived up on the north side of town where all the fancy folks live. I did read in the newspaper that her husband up and killed his self. Don't know why. Seemed like he had a lot to live for. Did she die or something?"

Jake thought for a moment before responding, then answered truthfully that she had not died, but did not provide any other details.

"Do you know about this Red Rock Savings and Loan that was being investigated?" Jake asked, trying not to act like an attorney cross-examining a witness.

"Well, you see, some people think I am a gossip, and some people think I'm just an old busy nobody that isn't smart enough to know that I could make more on welfare than I make in this place. But I like to work, and sometimes I get a chance to talk to people like you and those out-of-town investigators that were here back in February. Not much to do in Crosswind unless you're into whoring up at the Cavalier Motel or shooting tin cans down in the dry river bed."

"I understand Red Rock Savings and Loan went out of business and is now part of the federal program to bail out these savings and loans. Is that what those guys were down here for?" Jake asked.

"Yeah, I guess so, and not just guys. There was that one FBI agent that was as pretty as they get. For the most part they seemed to be really pissed off because they couldn't find out much about the savings and loan or the fine citizens of Crosswind who put it together in the first place." Although the Oklahoma accent continued to play havoc with Jake's ears and create a challenge to understand what was being said, the disdain and contempt in the woman's voice when she referred to the "fine citizens of Crosswind" came through clearly.

"I take it that you're not a fan of the bankers in town?"

"I ain't no saint, and I don't pretend that I haven't done some things that I'm not real proud of, but those jerks do things that they shouldn't be proud of, and they get away with it, and they're not only proud that they did something wrong, but they're proud that they got away with it. Now I don't always do what's right, and I don't always know what's wrong, but it seems to me that some of them fellows must have made a lot of money off that there savings and loan and yet depositors and the government lost a whole bundle. Don't seem right to me. Didn't seem right to them fellows from Washington, neither."

"How long have you lived in Crosswind?" Jake asked, trying to defuse the rising volatility of her remarks.

"All my life, and I'm not going to tell you how many years that is. I've seen people come and I've seen people die, but most folks that come to Crosswind don't leave unless they get married or go off to university somewhere, and we don't never see them again. Come to think of it, that Molly Allen you talked about has been here a long time. I think she used to be a Stewart. Saw her name up on the high school honors list as valedictorian of the class, I think. She was a little before my time. Her husband owned the Ford dealership in town, didn't he? I'll bet she's sitting pretty with the money from the sale of that place. Are you here to help her collect her money?"

"No," Jake responded, "but I am here to help sort out her husband's affairs."

"Don't know much about that. Wasn't too much in the paper other than that he killed himself. He put a gun to his head or something. Happened about four months ago, I think, just before Christmas. Bad time of year. People get depressed about what they don't have instead of being happy for what they do have. See anything you like?"

Jake picked out a few postcards featuring the large red rock from a number of angles with the sun rising in some and setting in others. "This sure is a pretty landmark. Does the park have trails that go up into the rock?" Jake asked.

"Oh my, yes. The city owns the park and the Boy Scout Council is responsible for maintaining the trails and cleaning up after the slovenly few who'd mess up their own mother's grave rather than spend a few seconds picking up a gum wrapper or snuffing out their butts and scattering the tobacco. You can walk right up to the top if you have enough time. The trail crisscrosses back and forth. 'Course there's a whole lot of crazy folks that try to climb right up the face of the rock just for fun. Had a bad accident a few years back. In fact, it was the father of that Richard Allen guy who blew his head off. He loved to hike up into Red Rock Park. I saw him down here a lot. He'd come down on a Saturday morning, hike up into the park all day, and get back to his truck just about dusk. Used to come in here to buy a candy bar or a cup of coffee. Said he liked the view from the top of Red Rock."

"What happened?" Jake asked.

"Don't know. He came down here one day—I was working but I didn't notice his truck. He'd park way down by the entrance to the park. When he didn't come home that night his son sent out a search party. Found him at the bottom of the main face of the rock. Neck was broken. He was a good man. Bought my first car from him. A used Ford Fairlane. I thought I was something special in that car. It was real sad when he died. In the prime of health, too. They figured he got too close to the edge and slipped on some loose gravel. There's a lot of that up there. Say he died instantly. Funny, with all the crazies climbing up that face with ropes and all, they don't get hurt, and poor old Mr. Allen who just loved to walk up through the park slips and falls."

Behind Jake the door to the small information building opened and a young man in his early thirties with his wife, two small children and their dog came trooping into the building. Jake picked out one of several picture books on the town of Crosswind, paid the informative woman $18.95 for the book and another $5 for the post cards, thanked her for her information, and left the building. As he left, he saw the two small children trying on handmade Indian moccasins undoubtedly another product of the local Indian reservation.

The shock of stepping out of the air-conditioned building into the noonday sun momentarily stunned Jake, and by the time he had walked back to his car, he was beginning to think that Michigan weather was not too bad. A black Toyota sedan was parked several spaces away from the rented Cadillac. At the end of the parking area closest to the information hut was a Ford Aerostar van, presumably owned by the family currently seeking mementoes of their visit to Crosswind and its only tourist attraction. Whoever owned the black sedan was not in sight.

Jake climbed back into his Cadillac, quickly adjusted the air conditioner to maximum output, and headed back to the Best Western Motel. He made a mental note to check back copies of the Crosswind Gazette for more information about the death of Richard Allen Sr. and maybe even check in with the County Coroner to see if an autopsy was done to establish actual cause of death. Experienced climbers don't just slip and fall to their deaths, but an elderly climber may have suffered any number of maladies that could have contributed to the fall.

CHAPTER 12

After a four-mile run to clear out the Monday-morning cobwebs and get his blood pumping, Jake had treated himself to a leisurely shower to wash off the sweat and dust that seemed to be a part of the southern Oklahoma landscape. He had poured his second cup of coffee from the in-room coffeemaker and was about to call the local police department to see if he could set up an appointment to review the official investigative record of Richard's death. As he was looking up the number, the phone rang.

"Jake," came Parker's familiar voice, "I got your memo. Amazing what these machines can do. I sense that you're having trouble getting straight information from the very people that were the closest to the Allens. Sounds fishy."

"Yes sir," Jake responded, surprised that the chairman would be calling directly. "Molly and Richard Allen were good friends with the Hathaways. He's the banker, and Howard Stern was their lawyer. They have both avoided me either by not letting me see bank records or by claiming to be out of town. I'm not ready to make a judgment, but I get the impression that Hathaway and Stern are trying to hide something. They sure didn't want to talk to me. I don't think it's time to get nasty, so I'm trying to temper the litigator in me and continue with the line that I'm here to try and help an old friend."

"Excellent. Until we know why they're being so defensive, we should not push them into a corner. What's your next move?"

"This afternoon I'm going to see whether there were any official police reports on the deaths of Richard Allen Sr. and Richard Allen Jr. Then I'm going to check to see whether autopsies were done on either. Next I plan to check the court records of the bankruptcy proceedings under which all of Richard Allen's assets were sold. Oklahoma is a community property state, and theoretically Molly was entitled to half of those assets. I assume she signed the mortgage notes and that foreclosure was on her assets also. I just want to check out all those details to make sure that I understand how and why she is in the financial condition that she is in."

"You need somebody there you can trust," Parker responded. "One of my law school classmates, Larry Nicholson, is the managing partner of one of the largest firms in Oklahoma City. I thought about asking him to step into this matter rather than send you, but I decided that Molly deserved more personal attention. I called him last night to see if he could connect me with a trustworthy person in Crosswind. He referred me to his long-time friend that lives in Crosswind and owns a large cattle ranch about fifty miles east of the rock."

Parker rambled on for several minutes about all the money made off the oil and gas business and how successful his classmate had been (even though he was in the bottom quarter of his class), then suggested a strategy for Jake. "I want you to contact Larry's friend if only as a matter of courtesy to Larry and me. He's been around there for a long time and may be able to shed some light on Richard Allen and his group of friends. Larry tells me his friend is well connected in Crosswind, but because he lives way outside of town he never became part of the social elite. He's kind of the rugged individual type that would rather ride horseback than play golf. Check him out. See if he can help. At least you might get a nice meal out of it and have someone friendly to talk to other than your computer. He's waiting for your call."

Jake chuckled as he said goodbye and hung up the phone.

An hour later Jake was sitting across the desk from Police Detective Randall asking questions about the two Allen deaths. Police reports had been prepared on both incidents, but the details in the reports were sketchy. Randall helped to explain some of the report.

"According to this report on the accident out to the big rock, we received a telephone call from Richard Allen Jr.–see here where it says RAJR–reporting that his father had not returned from a day trip up into Red Rock Park. The park goes all the way around Red Rock, and you can climb up into the rock itself and get an absolutely beautiful view of the city and of the western plains. You can see clear over into Texas, only there's not much to see."

"Did you investigate?" Jake asked.

"Yes, we sent a patrol car down to the park and found a brand new Ford Explorer with a dealer plate on it and assumed it belonged to Mr. Allen. According to the report, the patrol officer found the vehicle at 5:47 p.m. and reported back to the desk officer after making a quick search of the area for Mr. Allen."

"What's the date on the report?" Jake asked.

"The call came in at around 5:20 p.m. on Sunday, September 27, 1990. It was treated as a routine missing person and not given high priority, but seeing as how it was Mr. Allen and all, we responded pretty promptly. Many of us bought our first truck from that man, and he always made a big thing out of it. You know, made sure it was all sparkling and clean, even though most of the time we were buying used pickups. Ain't nothing like your first truck, and most of us made a point of going down to Allen Ford as soon as we turned sixteen.

"Well, as I recall, It was getting pretty dark. That time of year the nights come on quickly and it gets cold out there on the plains. We wanted to check out the area before it got too dark to see, so when the patrolman reported back that the car was there and Mr. Allen was missing, I and several other patrolmen responded immediately to Red Rock Park and began a search on foot."

"Was Richard Allen Jr. down there helping?" Jake asked.

"I can't recall. Wait a minute, now I remember. We found Allen's body around 6:30 that night thanks in part to some tracking dogs that we use, and I remember we called his son at home to report having found his father. He and his wife came down to the park to identify the body and authorize removal to the funeral home. Mr. Allen Sr.'s wife passed away a few years before. Young Mr. Allen—we always called him that—was badly shaken by it all. He was very close to his father."

"What happened?" Jake asked. "The police report says he was dead when the officers found him, but it does not seem to indicate how he may have died. Was an autopsy done?"

"Unless we know for sure the cause of death, we don't include it in the police report. From the way his body was bruised and battered, it seemed pretty clear that he had fallen from fairly high up on the rock. He was a pretty experienced hiker and had walked through the trails many times up in Red Rock Park, but that sandstone is pretty soft and he may have broken loose a piece and lost his footing. We don't really know. They did an autopsy—have to any time there's a death other than by old age—which confirmed that he had broken his neck in the fall."

"So the cause of death was accidental?" Jake asked.

"Yep. We don't have a lot of accidents out in the park, mostly because the trails are pretty well laid out and people don't tend to wander off the trails. Allen was in his eighties when he fell from the rock. He loved it up there and probably was investigating some unique formation or a new form of cactus growing on the side of the rock. We figure he just lost his footing. The sides of that rock are pretty steep, and once you lose your footing, there's not much left to grab on to. He was a major force in this community, well liked by everyone. He was honest and respected for the way he ran his dealership. His wife died of cancer, and it really tore him up. Maybe he wasn't quite as careful after her death. I don't know. Anything else you need from this report?"

"What about Richard Jr.?" Jake asked as Detective Randall closed the slim file on Allen Sr. and appeared preoccupied with other thoughts.

Detective Randall pulled out another police report and a much thicker file folder full of official-looking documents and photographs. He handed Jake the police report.

"Crosswind only has two police detectives, and both of us worked this case. Not too many shootings in Crosswind, and when there is one, we respond in force. As you can see from the report, we received a call from Mrs. Allen at approximately 4:10 in the afternoon of December 19, 1994, just a little over five months ago. She was really upset and could barely speak. The desk sergeant thought he heard the word 'shot' and was able to get the address from the caller i.d. system that we have built into our emergency 911 network. He immediately dispatched one of the cruisers to the Allen house on Country Club Drive. As you can see from the report, the patrol officer found Richard Allen on the floor of the office in his home with a large portion of his head missing. The patrolman immediately called for assistance, and the coroner and EMS were dispatched to the house."

"Was the gun still in his hand or close by? Was it pretty obvious that it was a suicide? Was it his pistol?"

"Yeah, he had bought a .357 magnum pistol two weeks earlier at the local gun shop. All the records were in order. Sid, the guy who runs the gun shop, remembered selling him the pistol. Apparently it was the first firearm young Richard had ever owned. Paid a lot of money for it, too. Over $1,000. Real nice pistol. Went for just under $200 at the auction. Thought about buying it myself, but the wife wouldn't let me. Said it was too much like work."

"Any note?" Jake asked.

"Yes, sir. In fact we made several copies of the note, and since the case is closed, I can give you one of these copies if you like."

Jake took the copy of the neatly typed suicide note from Detective Randall and read it slowly.

> My dearest Molly, you are the one bright light in my life of mediocrity. I regret that I could not give you children. Even in that I was a failure. Now I am a failure in business. I have lost everything. The financial strain is more than I can handle. I see no other way out. Forgive me. Your loving husband,
>
> Richard

"Pretty convincing evidence, isn't it?" Jake said. "Was any official investigation started into the cause of death, or were the circumstances so compelling that no further investigation was considered necessary?"

"The coroner's office came out and scraped up the pieces of flesh, took them back to the morgue where they did a very basic autopsy to comply with the state requirements, and we closed the case. Subsequent events demonstrated clearly how seriously in debt the Allens were, and, well, quite frankly, we don't have too many murders here in Crosswind. This is a pretty law-abiding community. We haven't had even a second degree murder case in over five years. We have an occasional B&E, and sometimes the migrant workers get in trouble, but for the most part people are pretty honest around here."

Jake thanked the police detective, then walked across the street to Broken Bow County Courthouse to undertake the task of searching through probate and bankruptcy files for Richard and Molly Allen. Jake was not an expert in either probate or bankruptcy, but he had put this chore down on his list of necessary tasks. Rather than try to come to some conclusion as he studied the documents, Jake took notes and used his hand-held recorder to capture his observations concerning the adequacy of fees and settlements with creditors. None of the probate files was thick, and the short inventory of assets disclosed nothing out of the ordinary other than a listing for 200,000 shares of Red Rock Savings and Loan, valued as worthless, and a membership interest in White Sands Development Company, likewise valued as worthless. Noticeably absent from the files was an independent appraisal of the value of the dealership, but the two-page petition for sale without appraisal drafted by Howard Stern claimed that the mortgage debt on the facility far exceeded any possible appraisal value.

The bankruptcy files were unusual in that the proceedings were before the State Circuit Court rather than the Federal Bankruptcy Court. They matched closely the probate files, and petitions to sell or otherwise dispose of property that were filed in the Probate Court were duplicated but for a different court and cause and filed in the Bankruptcy Court. While this was undoubtedly efficient, Jake noted it in his dictated comments and would ask other members of his firm who routinely dealt in these areas.

When Jake questioned the bankruptcy clerk about this practice and the speed with which the estate was both probated and disposed of through the Bankruptcy Court, the clerk responded, "We don't get much bankruptcy around here. Folks pretty much watch out for each other, but this here case was a real sad one. Young Mr. Allen really sunk himself deep, and nobody knew. State courts don't do much bankruptcy, but lawyer Stern, I guess he decided to do it here instead of the federal court. Judge Foster used to be with the Stern firm, and he was willing to expedite things to help out poor Mrs. Allen. It went pretty fast, too. That fellow from out east was a real help. He just sort of came out of nowhere and offered to buy up the dealership for the amount of the loans that had caused the problem. Pretty good deal for him, if you ask me. Sure them buildings were getting pretty old, and property around here ain't worth much unless it's out near the country club. But them dealerships must be worth something all by themselves, and I don't recall anybody putting a value on the franchise, only the real estate. I mentioned it to Mr. Stern, but he told me to mind my own business, and I guess he was right."

"Were there any other bidders on the dealership?" Jake asked.

"Not as I recall," the clerk responded. "Stern kind of forced the case through, and I don't recall any effort to advertise other than in the Legal News. I guess he figured he found a guy who would pick up the debt, basically paying off the bank, so he jumped on it. I doubt whether there would have been any other buyers, what with the suicide and all. At any rate, the whole case was completed within a couple of months after Mr. Allen's death. Mrs. Allen came down here and signed all the papers. It was kind of spooky. She had this kind of a look that made you wonder if she was really alive or not, but when Mr. Stern asked her if she understood, she spoke right out loud and said she did. She was here to sign the papers. I saw it myself."

Jake thanked the clerk and dictated notes to himself to pursue this issue at the up-coming meting with Howard Stern.

It was approaching four o'clock when Jake left the courthouse. He decided to call Thomas Mobley, the cattle ranching friend of Parker's law school classmate, to see if he could arrange a meeting. Mobley was in, had been expecting Jake's call, and had already arranged for a dinner meeting that evening at the Crosswind Country Club.

CHAPTER 13

Following the brief set of directions given to him by Thomas Mobley, Jake easily found his way to the Crosswind Country Club and parked his car in the large parking lot which, on this Monday evening, was less than a quarter full. He was too busy reading directions and taking in the beauty of the architecture of the club facilities to notice the black Toyota that had followed him all the way from the motel out to the country club or the tall, athletically built man that followed him at a discreet distance into the country club.

Thomas Mobley was waiting for Jake at the front door of the club, and, after introducing themselves, the two proceeded to a small table in the Men's Grill overlooking the eighteenth hole of the championship north course. A foursome was on the green as Jake and Mobley sat down for cocktails and dinner.

"So old Larry Nicholson gave you my name, did he? That old son-of-a-gun. How is he? I haven't seen him for four or five years. Dolores and I visited with him and his lovely wife, Polly, when we were in the city for a big cattlemen's convention back in 1991. Last one I ever went to. Bunch of people talking about the cattle business whose only credentials were an MBA from Texas A&M and a new Stetson. The way I see it, it's pretty simple. You deal honestly with folks. Pay a good wage for work done, give the men good horses and ample food, make sure when they go off to have some fun that they don't hurt themselves or anybody else, and don't get greedy. Most business decisions don't require an MBA. If you know the facts and don't try to outsmart anybody, and kind of do what makes good sense, business just takes care of itself."

Jake hadn't said a word as he listened to Thomas Mobley describe his business philosophy. Mobley looked fit enough to be in his early sixties, but from what Parker had told him, Jake knew he was over seventy. He had a full head of wavy white hair, his skin showed signs of years under the bright Oklahoma sun, and he walked with a slight limp which Jake later learned was caused by an overzealous effort to rope and hog-tie a young calf in celebration of his sixty-fifth birthday. Mobley spent a good fifteen minutes describing his efforts to prove to his family that he could still hog-tie a calf and was not about to retire from the cattle business. He blamed the calf for not responding when he grabbed the horns to wrestle it to the ground. Instead of dropping on its side, the calf surprised him by falling on top of Mobley's left leg, tearing the cruciate ligaments around his knee. Another ten minutes were consumed by a blow-by-blow account of his stay in the Crosswind Community Hospital and the surgeon flown in from Houston to reattach his torn ligament.

"My father, God rest his soul, started the Bar M Ranch back in 1885 when Crosswind was just getting started as a town. There were a dozen or so came around here about the same time. The Hathaways, the Sterns, the Chambers and my dad. He staked out a piece of property just east of town and bought himself a couple of head of cattle from a ranch down in Texas. Drove them all the way up here by himself. Made sure he had a good bull, and he just kind of let nature take its course. Started with about a dozen cows and one bull, and soon he had a herd big enough to warrant picking up a few more acres of land. He died in 1947 and left the ranch to me. Of course I've been working it all my life. When he died, we had about 27,000 acres of grazing land and over 2,000 head of cattle. Me and my four boys have kind of kept up the tradition, and now we're up over 100,000 acres and have over 10,000 head of cattle. Biggest ranch around here, maybe in the whole state. The boys pretty much run the operation now. Gives me time to come out here and play cards with my friends or just sit and watch people chase after that damn little white ball. Waste of time if you ask me.

"It was different five years ago. Nineteen eighty-nine and 1990 were bad years for Crosswinds. We lost four of our most prominent citizens and my very best friends. The five of us were all semi-retired having pretty much turned the business over to our sons or, in the case of old Howard Stern Sr., taking on the duties of a U.S. District Court Judge. He was the best. Some people thought he was too tough, but he was always fair and believed that people should be held accountable for their actions. Honest as the day is long, and now he sits out there in that wheelchair in the nursing home barely able to talk. I try to get out to see him once or twice a month, but it's hard to see an old friend all crippled up like that."

Mobley had been talking for twenty minutes straight about ranching, Crosswind, politics and his family. Jake had neither the opportunity nor the inclination to respond. It was as if Mobley had all of this information stored up waiting for the opportunity to talk to the right person. After describing Judge Stern in the wheelchair in the nursing home, Mobley fell strangely silent. It was Jake's opportunity to respond.

"I read about Judge Stern in the firm brochure while I was waiting to see his son. What happened to him?" Jake asked, trying to keep the information flowing.

"Damn fool was out horseback riding by himself one lovely spring morning four, maybe five years ago. Howie was a great horseman and knew his way around Crosswind as well as anyone. No one really knows what happened, but his horse came back to his ranch without him. Horse must have spooked at something. Maybe a snake. At any rate, they found Howie up in the foothills at the base of a small ravine. He was all but dead. Doc Andrews had a hell of a time keeping him alive. He was on the ventilator for over a week. Spinal cord all but severed in half. Doc was able to keep him alive long enough to air evac him to Oklahoma City. Suffered a broken neck and back, and now he just sits in that wheelchair in the Overlook Nursing Home paralyzed from the neck down. Apparently suffered major damage to his vocal chords, and can't speak except in grunts. He seems to recognize me, and in the last six months or so, I think he has improved mentally. The doctors say he'll never be able to regain any use of his limbs, but they are a little more optimistic about his ability to talk. Last time I was up there one of the nursing home staff suggested that he might be able to communicate better through one of those computerized gadgets. It's ironic. He never did like using computers when he was on he bench. Now it may be his only way of meaningful communication. Seems to enjoy having company. Must be real lonely living life without being able to talk or move."

At that point a neatly groomed young waiter delivered the main courses, and the discussion stopped while each began the age-old ritual of devouring the evening's meal. Jake had just taken his first bite out of the massive T-bone steak carefully placed before him when Mobley restarted his dissertation without prompting and without expecting a response.

"You probably know about my good friend Dick Allen. He was the father-in-law of your client and a really successful businessman in Crosswind. Although he was somewhat older than I, we both enjoyed being outdoors together in these vast wind-swept plains of southwest Oklahoma. There is such majesty in just feeling nature's relentless power. When we were younger, Dick and I used to take one of his trucks out onto the plains so that we could get a 360-degree view of the incredible lightning storms that rumble through this area starting about now and continuing all summer long. He loved cars almost as much as I love horses, but above all we both loved being successful in our businesses. He was always fair, and people who lived in these parts knew and respected that. He died shortly after Judge Stern had his terrible accident."

Jake interrupted just long enough to mention his conversation with the woman at the Crosswind information booth, but Mobley wasn't deterred by Jake's comments and kept right on telling his version of how his friend had fallen off the great Red Rock and broken his neck.

"Dick knew his way around that old rock pretty well, but sometimes you see a special animal or wildflower that takes your mind off of what you're doing or where you're going. He loved nature and all of its creatures. Sometimes he would get so engrossed in watching a small Gila monster devour its prey that he would forget I was even around. I figure his mind was focused on something other than where he was or how close he had come to the edge of that rock. I guess if you look at it philosophically, it was a great way for him to go. Shame, though. His son never did understand the business, quickly became known for being gone a lot. He allowed the dealership to become a bit shabby if you ask me. We got a new Saturn dealership in town, and I guess maybe the Ford dealership was losing market share. People out here are pretty loyal, but they occasionally like to try out new things. I guess that's why he was losing money."

As Mobley paused to take a few bites of his steak, Jake took the brief intermission to sneak in a few questions about Richard Allen's finances. Mobley was busy trying to catch up with Jake, who had nearly finished his 22-ounce T-bone, so Jake kept on asking questions without waiting for any response from Mobley. He finished his one-way conversation with a more general question. "What do you know about the Red Rock Savings and Loan Association that Richard Allen was involved with?"

The reaction from Mobley was instantaneous. He stopped chewing the julienne carrots that had followed his last slice of steak and stared angrily at Jake. After several seconds, he finished chewing his carrots, washed down the mouthful with a long swig of his Kendall Jackson Merlot, and in a low but intense voice, responded.

"My boys were supposed to be part of that group that invested in Red Rock. My oldest went to school with Bill Hathaway, and I guess Bill kind of put the squeeze on a lot of his friends to invest in the S&L. Fortunately they came to me with some of the early proposals and pro forma business plans. I don't know a whole lot about banking. My father taught me not to borrow except in emergencies, and fortunately we have never had any emergencies that couldn't be dealt with through our personal holdings. But I do know something about land values, and it appeared to me that the investments being touted by the promoters of Red Rock didn't have anywhere near the value that they projected. Oh, some of the land was on the edge of some potentially rich oil fields, but nobody's drilling right now since the price of crude overseas is so low. Maybe they might have been able to entice some folks to move out to that west Texas development at White Sands, but only if they struck water, which they didn't. You'd think they would have checked that out before they went and invested in all that land, but not those boys. They figured they knew it all. Damn fools believed in a diviner using a willow branch who said there was plenty of water down there rather than spend the money on a real survey and drilling. Oh, they had a grand plan for large residential areas, golf courses, office buildings and an airport, but the way I looked at it, it was just more sand and more prairie, and I didn't think it had much of a chance. Fortunately my boys had more confidence in me than that fat ass Hathaway and his number-crunching accountant, Eric Beamer. We declined the invitation to invest, and instead my sons and I bought another 10,000 acres of grazing land and expanded our herd. Best decision we ever made."

While the waitress poured each of them a fresh cup of Colombian coffee, Jake finally turned to personal questions concerning his client.

"Did you know Molly Allen very well?"

"Not well. She was married to my best friend's son, so I saw her occasionally. She is attractive, always well dressed and personable, and she has the most striking blue eyes I've ever seen. After Dick's death back in 1990, we didn't see much of her or Richard except maybe at the County Fair. I saw her at Richard's funeral, and she looked terrible. It looked like

Richard's cronies were taking pretty good care of her, so I paid my respects and left without really inquiring into her personal situation. I assumed that there would be adequate life insurance and other assets from Dick's estate that would take care of her. She is a real fine lady, and I would like to do whatever I can to help, including giving her some money to get her back on her feet, if that's what it will take. Hell, she can come out to the ranch and live with us. Dick would have done that for one of my daughters-in-law, and it's the least I can offer her."

"Thanks, Tom. That's a very generous offer, and we may have to take you up on it somewhere down the road. For the time being, Mr. Parker is helping her out back in Oklahoma City, where she can get some very personalized care to try to overcome her mental condition. You have already provided me with all kinds of interesting information that I need to go back and digest. Can we do this again sometime soon? I would like to come out and see your ranch. Maybe we could meet there next time."

"Consider it done. Let me know when you're ready. We'll have dinner, and I'll introduce you to my boys and their families. I have fourteen grandchildren. Each of them has a trust holding 3,000 acres of the ranch for their benefit when they turn twenty-five."

After a brief tour of the country club, including several plaques on the wall of the Men's Grill attesting to the golf prowess of several club members and the low scores achieved by Arnold Palmer when he played the course in 1958, Jake and Tom Mobley departed, promising to continue the discussion when Jake next returned to Crosswind.

Jake drove the twelve miles back to his motel feeling both uncomfortably full from the huge portion of western T-bone steak and unsettled by the cacophony of information now spinning through his mind. He was in no hurry to sort and categorize it all, and, lowering the window of his Cadillac, enjoyed the cool night air of the southern Oklahoma plains.

Jake hadn't thought to bring a legal pad with him to dinner. Parker had suggested calling on Thomas Mobley as a friendly contact in a town that, so far, had been singularly unwilling to disclose any meaningful information about his client and the death of her husband. Once again Jake marveled at the ability of his senior partner to sense that something was lacking and, even from a remote location, find a source for filling that gap. At least now Jake had a contact that could relay information apparently without bias and help decipher the difference between reality and fiction.

As he drove back to the motel, Jake tried to recall each of the major points as a mental exercise to help him organize his thoughts. Once back at the motel he would assemble the information in the form of a memorandum that would both retain the information for later analysis and provide a report back to Parker. He was too wrapped up in his thoughts to notice the black Toyota sedan that had followed him out to dinner and was now following him back to the motel. Likewise, had he been less focused on Mobley's comments at dinner, he might have noticed the tall, muscular driver sitting behind the wheel of the black sedan watching as Jake unlocked the door to his motel room.

Once inside, Jake opened his laptop computer and began entering notes about the day's activities and the evening's meeting with Thomas Mobley. When finished he e-mailed the memo to Parker through the inboard modem on his computer and the telephone provided by the motel, which had a connection made precisely for this purpose.

Next he wrote a short note to Carol Brooks, his bright young associate who, hopefully, was managing his cases back in the office.

> Monday, May 14, 1995. 10:22 p.m. mountain time. Carol, I need a favor. Please find out all you can about Red Rock Savings and Loan, a federally chartered savings and loan located in Crosswind, Oklahoma. I need to know when it was started, what happened to it, why it went bankrupt, whether the Resolution

Trust took over its assets, etc., etc., etc. See if you can find out the names of the principals, whether any criminal or civil actions were or will be filed against it or its principals, and anything else that sounds interesting. Charge your time to Mr. Parker's personal account (999999) and call me as soon as you have some information. Mrs. Woods has the phone and fax number here, or you can leave it on my e-mail. I need the information as soon as possible. Parker will give it high priority. Thanks. How's the weather? It's really hot here during the day and cool at night. Jake.

Almost forgot. Would you call Jim Evans at Ford Legal and ask him to do a favor for me and run down the financials on Allen Ford in Crosswind for 1988 through 1994? I have done a few favors for him, so he shouldn't give you any grief. If he does, let me know and I'll call him. As soon as you get those financials, fax them to the Hyatt in Oklahoma City. I'll pick them up there. JMc

After transmitting his documents, Jake pulled out his pad and began drawing boxes. In the first box he wrote, "RRS&L." To the left of this in a smaller box he wrote "White Sands Land Development Company." That was as far as he got. Sleep and a full stomach overcame him, and within minutes he was sound asleep on his queen-size bed, still in the clothes that he had worn to dinner.

CHAPTER 14

It was exactly 2:00 p.m. on Tuesday afternoon when Jake entered the offices of Stern, Foster & Smith for his appointment with Howard Stern Jr. He was not kept waiting. The same attractively dressed secretary that he had spoken with three days earlier ushered him back to a well-appointed conference room overlooking the massive escarpment that had given Crosswind its name. The brilliant mid-day sunshine enhanced the beauty of the giant rock. As Jake marveled at the stark beauty of this natural wonder jutting up from the Oklahoma plains, a casually dressed gentleman with shoulder-length hair pulled back into a neat-ponytail, and wearing a large gold medallion attached to a leather thong around his neck, entered the conference room.

"Hello, Mr. McCarthy. My name is Howard Stern. I understand that you represent Molly Allen and are here at the direction of our client, the First State Bank of Crosswind."

Jake took a few seconds to absorb the unexpected presentation of the senior partner of the largest firm in Crosswind. Although Jake had learned over the past few years not to expect any particular style of dress, Stern was a bit more eccentric than any other senior attorney that Jake had come across in his legal career, especially one representing a bank. He wore an open-collared silk shirt with American Indian designs embroidered on the sleeves and across the shoulders. The gold medallion around his neck hung outside of the shirt and also had an Indian motif, although it was difficult to decipher without staring at it. He wore neatly pressed blue jeans and cowboy boots that looked uncomfortably authentic.

"I assume you have spoken with Mr. Hathaway concerning the power of attorney granted to me by Molly Allen that allows for my inspection of her bank records," Jake responded. "I have a duplicate original in my briefcase if you care to see it, although I assume Hathaway has faxed a copy over here for your review."

"Richard was my client. He was a wonderful person, God rest his soul, but he was not shrewd about business matters and had a weakness for bad investments. He was always looking to make a quick buck and figured his capital resources were unlimited. Unfortunately, he did not confer with me on all of his investments, and after his tragic suicide, we found through probate of his estate that he was millions of dollars in debt. Like the rest of us who invested in Red Rock Savings & Loan, Richard lost all of his investment in that ill-conceived venture, but without my knowledge he had pledged all of his assets to participate in other investment schemes. Unfortunately, he had convinced poor Molly to sign over her rights to the homestead and all of their community assets, including the dealership, to support those bad deals. Within days after his suicide, creditors were banging on our doors demanding payment and filing notices of foreclosure on the dealership and their home."

"Did you handle probate of the estate?" Jake asked.

"Out of respect for the deceased and because I knew that we would not get paid for our services, I personally handled the probate of his estate and the bankruptcy petition filed by his creditors. The firm did not charge a fee for these services. Richard was a very decent person and a close personal friend. No one knew the extent of his financial problems. It was even a greater blow when it turned out that he had recently cashed in several whole-life insurance policies that his father had purchased for him and replaced them with two, million-dollar term life insurance policies that contained clauses voiding liability if the policy holder committed suicide within two years of taking out the policies. We went round and round with the insurance companies on this issue. They refused to pay off, and we determined, given the obvious fact of his horrible suicide, that the likelihood of successful legal attack was negligible. I have copies of the policies in my files if you would care to read them."

"No thanks. I hate reading insurance policies, but I respect your conclusion that filing a lawsuit to avoid the effect of a clear exclusion did not make much sense. I looked through the probate files on the Allen estate this morning, and I could tell that they were very deeply in debt."

"Yes," Stern replied. There wasn't anything I could do to stop the complete liquidation of all their assets."

"Can I assume that you approve of this power of attorney for me to review the bank records for Richard Allen, Molly Allen and the Allen dealership, and that the authority extends to records that may be in Mr. Beamer's files?" Jake asked.

Stern reached for the copy of the power of attorney that Jake had offered to him, briefly read the several paragraphs, and responded, "It looks fine to me. I will give Hathaway a call to let him know that you have her permission to review those records. When would you like to see them?"

"Tell him that I will be over within the hour."

"Is there anything else that I can do for you this afternoon, Mr. McCarthy?" Stern asked as he arose from the conference table.

"I noted in the probate files that the dealership was sold without an appraisal. Isn't that somewhat unusual?"

"We did not consider it necessary. The property had a book value of only $900,000 but Richard had first and second mortgages totaling over two million dollars. We were lucky to find a buyer without incurring substantial additional expenses for advertising and running the place at a loss waiting for an appraisal. The court agreed with me and granted the petition to sell without going through that formality."

"What about the value of the dealership license? Back in Detroit they are usually worth several million in their own right. I didn't see any accounting for that asset."

"We were told that the dealership is personal to the individual, and when he dies there is no value that is inheritable or transferable, so we did not pursue it."

Not wanting to pick a fight and willing to give Stern the benefit of the doubt at least until he had done some research on the inheritability of dealerships, Jake decided not to go any further. He gathered the power of attorney from the conference table, placed it in his briefcase, got up as if to leave the conference room, then asked Stern a final question. "Did you also probate the estate of Richard's father?"

As Stern was heading for the door of the conference room, Jake noticed a slight hesitation to respond to the question. Slowly, Stern turned around and faced Jake. "Yes, we did probate his estate following his tragic accident out in Red Rock Park. Our firm did not represent the dealership or Richard's father, but Richard asked us to handle his father's probate matters, and we also took over the legal work for the dealership once it was transferred over into Richard's name. Why do you ask?"

"I had trouble finding the probate file of Allen Sr. I guess they keep older probate files somewhere other than at the courthouse, so I thought if you had probated the estate you might have the files available in case I needed some further information."

"We may have put those into storage, but if they're here, you're welcome to see them. I will have my secretary find them for you. Anything else we can do?"

"Not right now. I guess I'll go make an appointment with Mr. Beamer. Nice meeting you," Jake said as he walked out of the conference room.

Five minutes later Jake entered the offices of Eric Beamer, C.P.A., and was greeted by a smiling young receptionist who appeared to be of high school age. She looked up as Jake approached the reception counter and politely asked, "Can I help you?"

"My name is Jake McCarthy. Is Mr. Beamer in?"

"Do you have an appointment with him?"

"No, I'm here representing one of his former clients, Molly Allen, and would like to ask him a few questions if I may."

"Mr. Beamer has clients in his office right now, and will not be available to speak with you. Would you like to make an appointment?"

"Will he be available later this afternoon?"

"No, he will be leaving the office around four o'clock this afternoon and will be out of town through the Memorial Day weekend. He will be back next week. He has an opening in his schedule at ten o'clock on Tuesday or later that afternoon at three o'clock. Would you like one of those appointments?"

"I guess not. Perhaps you could give me one of Mr. Beamer's cards, and I will call to make an appointment in a couple of weeks."

CHAPTER 15

Jake left the offices of Eric Beamer & Associates and quickly drove the few blocks back to the First State Bank of Crosswind armed with the approval of Howard Stern to inspect the bank records of Richard and Molly Allen and the Allen Ford Dealership.

Pausing momentarily to rub his hand along the aged oak of the massive front door of the bank, Jake stepped into its cool lobby and proceed directly to the floor manager, Judy Falsworth, who sat behind a well worn but solid oak desk.

"Mr. Hathaway, please," Jake stated as he approached the desk. "Jake McCarthy here to review bank records. Mr. Hathaway should be expecting me."

"Oh yes, Mr. McCarthy. Mr. Hathaway said that you would be coming in this afternoon and asked me to provide you with whatever you need. We have cleared space in one of our unused offices so that you can have privacy in reviewing these records. What is it you're looking for?"

"I would like to see the bank statements for Richard Allen and Molly Allen, and for Allen Ford, and I need to see all of their accounts—whatever different accounts the Allens may have had with this bank, including the mortgage on their home and any security arrangements that may have existed for the dealership."

"We keep only one year of hard copy. Anything over a year old is stored on microfiche for ten years, and then destroyed. If you need more than a year's worth of account information, you will need to go down to the microfiche office in the basement where there are machines that you can use to read the accounts."

"Are the accounts computerized?" Jake asked. "I mean, are the balances, debits and credits maintained on a computer file that goes back more than a year?"

"Yes," Ms. Falsworth said. "But all you will see are the daily totals, not each transaction. The computer numbers won't tell you anything about the payee, or, in the case of the Allens' joint account, who wrote the check or withdrew the money."

"I would like to see the hard copy for the last year, then if I still have time, perhaps you could show me to the microfiche room and point me to the right films. I would like to see the bank records for Allen Ford for at least the last five years. Is that possible?"

"Actually, for corporate accounts, we keep the records indefinitely. We could go back twenty-five years if the account has been with us that long. We've had the Allen Ford account since it was founded."

The attractive floor manager appeared to be in her mid fifties and, from her familiarity with the bank, Jake assumed she had been employed there for many years. She was thin with grayish-brown hair and a pleasant although unremarkable face. She moved with the grace of a dancer and the confidence of a corporate executive.

"Would you like to start now, Mr. McCarthy, or should we get the necessary documents ready for you tomorrow?" she asked in a friendly but professional voice.

"You can call me Jake, if it's not uncomfortable for you. And we may as well get started now."

"OK," Judy Falsworth responded, "and you can call me Judy. Most of my customers do. I've been with the bank for thirty-five years, started here right out of high school as a teller. Worked my way up to Senior Loan Officer with responsibilities for all commercial and residential loans and sat as a member of the Executive Committee of the Board.

Then Mr. Hathaway Junior, the only son of the founder, died about five years ago and his only son Billy—Hathaway the third—took over. Mind you, he has not had the courage to cut my salary, but instead of Vice President and Senior Loan Officer sitting on the Executive Committee, I am now the floor manager for the retail customers looking to open accounts with us. Not that I really mind. Much less stress out here taking care of the small fry and not worrying whether or not loans will be paid off by the dreamers coming in looking for million-dollar loans to build chicken farms for feather pillows."

"Were you the loan officer for the loans to Richard Allen?" Jake enquired.

"No sir," she quickly responded. "Mr. Hathaway always handled him personally. I have a pretty good idea how much he had borrowed over the last few years, and I doubt very much whether I would have approved the loans had I been the loan officer. The poor man was in way over his head, and I guess he could see only one way out."

As she finished these remarks, Judy Falsworth gracefully ushered Jake back to a well appointed office that was vacant of any furnishings save a well polished walnut desk and black leather upholstered chair. As he walked back to the office, Jake noticed two other similarly empty offices.

"If you'll wait in here, ah…Jake, I'll bring you the files as I find them. We'll start with the joint accounts of Richard and Molly Allen, then I'll see if they had any individual accounts."

"Check to see if you have the mortgage documents on their house—I don't know the address—and on the dealership."

"Okay," Judy replied over her shoulder as she walked out of the office and moved briskly to the bank of file cabinets lining the interior wall of the back office. Within minutes she returned with files containing a year's worth of monthly bank reconciliation forms. The account listed Richard and Molly Allen, jointly.

Jake began the tedious job of comparing the monthly income and disbursements from the account to help determine why Richard Allen died bankrupt. Jake started with the most recent statement for the month of February, 1995. At the top of the form in inch-high bold red letters was stamped "CLOSED." Attached to the report was a copy of an order from the Circuit Court for Broken Bow County attesting to the determination of bankruptcy and ordering the bank to transfer all assets of the joint account to the trustee in bankruptcy. The order was carried out on February 4. At the time there was $827.32 in the account.

January's statement was not much better. On December 31 there was a deposit to the joint account in the amount of $8,330, and that was the last deposit into the account. Jake began a month-by-month review of the income and expenses of the Allens and found an almost boring regularity about the income and disbursements. The only noteworthy payments occurred usually within several days after the middle of the month, including the month of December 1994, when Richard wrote a check for $14,723.64 to the First State Bank of Crosswind. Going back for the full year, he confirmed payments of around $15,000 to the bank each month.

As Jake was noting his findings and looking for other unusual payments in the monthly accounts, Judy Falsworth re-entered the office with another, much larger file. "These are the corporate bank records for Allen Ford. They cover all of calendar year 1994 and the beginning of 1995 through sale of the dealership. I was really saddened to see the big "Allen Ford" on the dealership marquis come down and be replaced by the generic "Crosswind Ford" that the new owners placed on the front of the building. Old Mr. Allen was a friend to all of us. I'll never forget my first Ford that I bought from Richard's father. 1963 Ford Falcon. Car ran like a top. We had it for nearly 10 years. He took good care of us over there at the dealership, and Richard followed in his footsteps, only he never seemed to be around when we would go over to the dealership to shop. They never gouged us on service and never pressured us to buy a new car. They both knew that when the time was right we would buy from them, and we did. I had just been promoted to Assistant Vice President, and we celebrated by turning in the old Falcon and getting a Ford Country Squire Wagon.

"Listen to me rambling on about cars and all. I'm going to look now for mortgages and savings accounts. I already checked, and there were no separate checking accounts under the names of Richard Allen or Molly Allen. Just the one joint account."

"I think maybe we should push this off until tomorrow," Jake responded. There is no way I can get through all of this by quitting time, and I assume you don't want me in here all alone. Do you have any idea what drove Richard Allen to borrow so much money? Was he a gambler, or did he have other expensive hobbies or habits that would require so much money?"

The office manager responded after a slight hesitation, "No, sir, I have no idea what caused him to take on such large amounts of debt." As she was speaking, Ms. Falsworth carefully pulled Jake's legal pad over in front of her and printed the following note:

> Cannot speak freely here. Meet me tonight for dinner at Casa Del Toro at 7:30.

Jake watched with amazement as Ms. Falsworth continued to speak and write simultaneously.

"Well, I guess that's that," Jake said as he returned the last of the corporate files to its pile and carefully tucked his legal pad into his briefcase. As she stood to leave, Jake gave Judy Falsworth a thumbs up sign and nodded his head yes. He wondered if she really thought the room had been bugged, but lost the train of thought as she left the room and William Hathaway entered.

"We're about to close up around here, Mr. McCarthy. I'd like to say that you can stay and work until you're finished, but my Board of Directors probably wouldn't approve. Did you finish?"

"No, not quite," Jake answered. "I only just started looking into the bank records for the dealership, but quite frankly I'm ready for a break. These numbers are dancing in front of my eyes, and I never was much good at numbers. I'll be back around nine tomorrow."

"Did you find anything interesting in the bank records?" Hathaway asked, trying to be as casual as possible.

"No," Jake responded quickly. "Everything seems to be in order. I will know more after I finish my review of these dealership records; however, my plan is to go back to Oklahoma City day after tomorrow, and I may not be back here until next week or the week after. If I am unable to get through all the records tomorrow, I may need to come back again. Is that all right?"

"Sure," Hathaway answered, letting out an imperceptible sigh of relief. "They aren't going anywhere, and your power of attorney will take care of you until you're finished."

Jake threw his legal pad into his briefcase, stood and shook hands with Hathaway and walked to the front door of the bank. Glancing at his watch, Jake realized that it was nearly five o'clock. His eyes were tired, and he welcomed the break from the monotony of reviewing columns of numbers in bank records. As he stepped out of the bank, he was again hit by the wall of oppressive heat that, even more than the giant red rock, would remain his most lasting memory of the western Oklahoma town of Crosswind.

CHAPTER 16

As Jake pulled into the parking lot of the Best Western Suites Motel, he focused on a tall, muscular man crossing the lawn in front of the section of motel in which his room was located and moving briskly toward a black Toyota sedan. Sometimes the subconscious mind will store data that the conscious mind overlooks. Whether it was recognizing the black Toyota that had been parked near the information building at Red Rock Park or the muscular build of the tall man wearing clothing that seemed not to fit in Crosswind, something about this seemingly unimportant event caused Jake to stop as he climbed out of his Cadillac and stare at the man as he got into his Toyota and pulled the door shut.

After changing out of his blue pinstriped suit and into more casual clothes, Jake opened a can of beer from the mini-bar and chewed on a Snickers as he opened his laptop computer to see whether there were any messages waiting for him. As he reached to press the power button that would return his laptop to life, he noticed the green light that indicated that the computer was already turned on. It was flashing to warn the user that the battery was low and needed recharging.

"Damn," Jake said to himself. "I must have left the damn thing on last night. I hope I didn't lose anything."

Reaching into his computer case, Jake quickly retrieved the recharger and brought the laptop safely back to life. The screen was open to the memorandum that Jake had written to Parker before coming to

Crosswind. Jake stared at the memorandum, then clicked on the windows menu to see which other files were open. He was surprised to find that all of his memoranda were open, although none had been changed.

As if hit by a small bolt of lightning, the hairs on the back of Jake's neck stiffened. He hadn't left his computer running. He had not used his computer since the prior evening when he had e-mailed a status report back to Parker, yet there was still power in the computer when he opened it fifteen hours later. He knew the battery in this computer would not last more than four hours even at rest. Someone other than he had retrieved his memoranda from his computer's memory and presumably had read all of his reports on the condition of his client and his thoughts about the case and the citizens of Crosswind. Whoever had been using his machine had done so recently, otherwise there would be no power remaining in the computer's limited battery.

Just as the subconscious mind sees things that the logical mind may discard as irrelevant, so the subconscious mind is capable of drawing inferences at speeds far beyond reason. There was no logical correlation between the muscular driver of the black Toyota and Jake's computer, but simultaneously with the recognition that someone had been using his computer, Jake's subconscious drew the further conclusion that it was this individual who had invaded his space and stolen his information.

The electricity that caused the hair on the back of his neck to rise quickly gave way to anger, then fear, then hypothesis as to why someone would want this information and how it might be used against Molly. Had he identified where she was and might be living after discharge from the hospital? Had he been too descriptive of her mental condition? Had he been too descriptive of his conjecture about the people of Crosswind? Had he identified Tom Mobley as a friend?

Jake clicked on to the electronic mail program in his program manager and was thankful that it required use of a password before anyone could gain access to the firm's files. He was relieved to find that most of his conclusions had been confined to his e-mails and that the memoranda were carefully written only to inform Mr. Parker of his progress and lacked many details that had been covered in telephone conversations. Tom Mobley was not mentioned by name in any of the memoranda.

After plugging the phone jack from his computer into the telephone console on the desk, Jake dialed in and quickly went through the series of procedures that put him directly into his computer in Detroit. There were four messages waiting for him. The first was a message from Mr. Parker. It read:

> Suggest you return to Detroit Thursday p.m. Understand your team has a championship game Saturday a.m. You shouldn't miss it. Plan to have dinner at my home Saturday p.m. to debrief. Martha understands and thinks I'm doing the right thing to help out. Bring Maggie. Parker.

The next message was from his secretary, Connie. It read:

> Concert was great. Stern was magnificent. Hurry back, I'm running out of things to do. Jackson case settled. Other side paid our legal fees in full. Your brief scared them. Connie.

The third message was from Carol Brooks. Her messages were usually short and to the point, and this was no exception. It said: "Not having much luck. Will keep trying."

The last e-mail also came from Carol Brooks. It read:

> Cancel last message. Just found out that a classmate at Michigan Law works for RT in DC. He agreed to check file on Red Rock. Will call tomorrow (Wed) and let me know if there is any info. If not confidential, will copy

> file for us. He owes me. We dated in law school. I kept his ego up among other things. He wants me to come to DC to discuss case. Says he needs another boost to his ego. I'm willing and have the time. CB.

Jake clicked on the "compose" icon and began drafting a response to Parker's message. He wrote:

> Concur. Ready for some R&R. Thanks for the invitation to dinner. Maggie will enjoy seeing Martha again and watching the freighters go by on Lake St. Clair. Hope it's not as hot there as it is here. Jake.

After pushing the send button, Jake composed another note to Carol Brooks.

> Go to DC. Find out as much as you can, especially about the founders of RRS&L, and an investment in White Sands. If any questions about trip, say it's for Parker. I assume the Resolution Trust has compiled a large file already. It had a team of investigators here several months ago. Reassigned to Arkansas to work on a politically sensitive investigation. President and first lady implicated. Much bigger loss. Good luck with your friend. Send me a memo with your findings ASAP. Thanks. Jake.

After confirming delivery of his message to Carol Brooks, Jake shut down his computer and headed for the registration desk of the motel to see if the man with the black Toyota was a guest at the motel or whether anyone had seen him. A young girl, probably in her late teens or early twenties, was the only person behind the registration desk.

She smiled as Jake approached the simulated marble counter and asked, pleasantly, "Can I help you?"

"My name is McCarthy. I'm in room 203. I noticed somebody in the parking lot that I think I may know. I wondered if you could tell me whether he's a guest here. He is kind of tall, has a very masculine face, and is muscular. I'd say maybe in his early thirties. Six foot two with dark hair."

"Oh, yes, Mr. McCarthy. Your brother arrived a few hours ago. He told me that you had promised to leave a key for him, but you must have forgotten. He was very nice, and I assumed you wouldn't mind, him being your brother and all."

"How long ago did you give him a key?" Jake asked in an unfriendly tone.

After a long hesitation and a sudden droop in the otherwise cheerful expression, the registration clerk said in a cautious voice, "About an hour ago. He said he had just come in from the east coast and that you were expecting him. Is there something wrong?"

A look of terror came across the registration clerk's face as she suddenly realized the potential impact of what she had done. "He wasn't your brother, was he? Did he steal anything? Are you okay? Was he there when you came in? Do you know who he is? Oh my gosh. I'm going to be fired. Oh my gosh. I'm so sorry. Why would he lie to me like that?"

"No, I don't think he stole anything. It is unfortunate but probably not catastrophic. These are electronic keys, so perhaps you could change the code on my room and give me a new key. And if the man ever comes back asking questions about me, please let me know and alert the other people that they should be on the lookout for him. He is not my brother and not a friend. I don't know who he is, but I intend to find out."

"Do you want to notify the police? I mean they would want to know about this wouldn't they? I mean is this guy some kind of a private investigator or something? I mean that's the kind of thing that Rockford would do. Oh my gosh. I'm going to be fired."

"No, I don't think it's necessary to alert the police right now. If you would just change the code on my room so that I can feel somewhat secure. I'll be checking out Thursday morning to go back to Michigan."

Returning to his room, Jake dialed the office number for Dr. Martinique Glasseur and was pleased to find that she was in her office and could speak with him.

"Hi Marty. Anything new with our patient?"

"Hi Jake," Martinique said in a mellow and inviting tone. "She is responding slowly to our work and is otherwise comfortable, secure and gaining weight. These things take time. We will probably need to discharge her in about a week although I may be able to talk the utilization management committee into letting me keep her a little longer. As a teaching hospital, we can extend some of our Medicare patients beyond the time authorized and charge off the time as an essential part of our teaching mission."

"I'll be driving into Oklahoma City Thursday morning, then taking an 11:00 a.m. flight to Michigan. Would you be available for about half an hour Thursday morning around 9:30 so that I can get enough information to take back to Mr. Parker? I'm meeting with him Saturday night for dinner, and he wants a full and frank discussion of Molly's condition."

"I'll be in a therapy clinic all morning, but I'll have copies of her medical records available for you to take back. I know you are not officially appointed her guardian, but I also know she has no one else to look out for her, and if I get in trouble for giving you these documents, I'm sure you will defend me. We have started her on a new program that includes a different approach to her condition. I want to discuss it with you. When will you return?"

"Can't say for sure, but I'm guessing next Tuesday or Wednesday. Monday is Memorial Day, and my kids are marching in the Rochester parade. Can't miss that. I'll let you know, and I'll want to see Molly on my return just to see if she remembers anything. It's been real hard to get any information around here."

"I'll be waiting," Martinique responded.

"One thing more, Marty," Jake said. "Someone broke into my room and may have gotten information about Molly from the memoranda that I had stored on my computer. Would you alert the hospital security staff to watch out for strangers?"

After hanging up the phone, Jake moved over to the picture window that overlooked the main parking lot of the motel just in case the black Toyota was parked where he could see it. He could see a large part of the parking lot from his room window, but there were no black Toyota sedans. Although nothing in his room appeared to have been changed or removed, the mere knowledge that someone had been scanning through his computer files without his permission instilled a very real sense that his privacy had been violated. Someone was snooping around Jake McCarthy's life, and he didn't like it.

Although there were no black Toyotas in the parking lot, what Jake did not notice was the tall, muscular man with a mean looking face sitting in the restaurant across the street from the motel in a position that allowed him to see Jake's car. He would know if and when Jake left the motel. He had just finished his fourth cup of coffee and a liver sausage sandwich with sliced Bermuda onion. His large, muscular hands wrapped around the porcelain coffee mug as he stared out the window waiting for something to happen.

CHAPTER 17

Jake did not emerge from his motel room until 7:00 p.m. Armed with detailed directions to the Casa Del Toro secured from the bellhop, Jake climbed into his Cadillac and started toward the center of town. He kept a sharp eye out for the black Toyota, but in doing so failed to notice that a white Chevrolet Lumina was following him at a discreet distance. He was too focused on following the directions that lead him way beyond any developed part of Crosswind and out into the plains north and west of the city.

The Casa Del Toro sat on a high bluff overlooking the Red River. It took Jake a full thirty minutes to get there, and there were no other homes or businesses within a half mile of the place. A single two-lane road had taken Jake from the extreme northwestern edge of Crosswind into the oil fields that had at one time made it a wealthy city. The wooden building had the appearance more of a nineteenth century saloon than a restaurant, and when Jake pushed aside the two swinging doors leading into the rustic bar area, he immediately thought of Clint Eastwood and scenes from any number of Class B Westerns. Judy Falsworth, clad in casual western attire, was sitting at the bar drinking a Dos Equis and chatting with the bartender.

"I'll have a Corona with a fresh lime, and fix my friend here another Dos Equis if she is ready," Jake said to the bartender as he sat down next to the bank manager. “This is a neat place out here in the middle of nowhere. Do you come here often?”

“Only when I have a good looking lawyer from Detroit to keep me company or when I have a big appetite for ribs and corn on the cob. It’s all you can eat, and the barbecue sauce is to die for, especially if you like it hot. Let’s go find a table before the place fills up.”

For the next half hour Jake and Judy Falsworth spoke generally about Crosswind and Detroit and Oklahoma City and the upcoming tornado season in southwest Oklahoma. She had lived in Crosswind all of her life and had worked at the First State Bank of Crosswind since graduation from high school. Her husband had died of liver cancer in 1993, and now she was alone but for her two adult children who lived in Oklahoma City.

Mr. Hathaway Senior, the founder of the bank, had hired her on the recommendation of a close friend because of her outstanding academic record in high school. She had proved worth the investment, and by the time of his death she had become a vice president of the bank responsible for the personal banking department.

“ Senior kind of took a special liking to me; I guess maybe because his offspring were less than he had hoped for or maybe because he never had a daughter. At any rate, when he died, he left me with an irrevocable option to buy 100,000 shares of bank stock at par value which is only a dollar per share and a lifetime employment contract that obligates the bank to buy my stock at $20 a share when I retire or end my employment at the Bank for any reason. In addition, the bank must pay me $100,000 cash if, for any reason, I am discharged prior to attaining age 65.

Tubby, oh, I’m sorry, our current Mr. Hathaway, resents the fact that I have this option and particularly resents the required $2 million payout if he ever tries to get rid of me. So he just kind of makes it tough for me. He took away my vice president title and put me back as the floor manager. But I don’t mind. I make enough money to live a very decent life, my kids are now through college and off making their own lives, and floor manager is actually a lot more fun."

At that point in the conversation, a hefty waitress in a red and white checkered cowboy shirt and too-tight blue jeans approached the table asking if they were ready to order.

"My friend here will have the all-you-can-eat country ribs special, easy on the hot sauce, and I'll have the baby backs. And you can bring us both another beer," Falsworth responded without even asking Jake what he might want. "Since this is your first visit to La Casa, you don't have a choice. You must have the ribs with all the trimmings. Next time I'll let you look at the menu, but I'll bet you come back for the same. Most people do."

"Did you really think that the office might have been bugged this afternoon?" Jake asked after the waitress had departed.

"I knew that Tubby was on his way in, and I thought he might have been listening at the door. I doubt that he is smart enough to try to snoop on his employees electronically. Anyway, I wanted an excuse to come back to Casa Del Toro, and I thought you might enjoy the ambiance. It's better than the Best Western Motel."

"Before those ribs get here, maybe we should try to finish our business so that we can each enjoy gorging ourselves," Falsworth continued, taking another long swig from her Dos Equis in preparation for what Jake assumed would be her third. "Until about eighteen months ago I was in charge of personal loans and sat as the Chairman of the Loan Committee for the bank. With one exception, every personal loan made by First State Bank had to be approved by the committee. That one exception was Richard Allen. When he first applied for a personal loan, Tubby Hathaway decided that he would process the loan personally, that he would authorize the loan personally, and that neither the Loan Committee nor I would be responsible for or have any knowledge of the loan. Since he was the boss, I really didn't have much to say about it, but bank policy strictly prohibits such practices. So, being a dummy, I reported the irregularity to our auditors, and guess what. Two days later I was made the floor manager and stripped of my title. I'd say there's something being hidden, but I don't know exactly what."

"When did Richard Allen first apply for a loan, do you know?" Jake asked.

"I think it was sometime back in 1992 or maybe early 1993. I seem to recall it was wintertime, and he had come to the bank looking for Tubby. He wasn't in at the time, so I asked if I could help, and Richard said he had some loan documents, which needed to be filed with the bank. I, of course, took the documents and assumed that they would be processed in the normal fashion. When I told Mr. Hathaway that Mr. Allen had been in to drop off the documents, Hathaway immediately took them from me, and I never saw them again."

"Were you surprised that Mr. Allen would be borrowing money from the bank since he owned a successful dealership?" Jake asked.

"Well, as a matter of fact, I was curious what it was for, but I guess I didn't give it much thought. Sometimes the people who seem to be the wealthiest end up having the most debt, and sometimes the people who seem to be living in poverty actually have substantial bank accounts but just don't like spending money. People are kind of funny that way.

"At any rate, that was the first and last loan document that I ever saw from Richard Allen until he died, and the bank filed Articles of Involuntary Bankruptcy against his estate. It turned out that between him personally and his dealership, we had loaned over $4 million of unscheduled debt. By unscheduled I mean not directly secured by the inventory of new and used cars that were covered under a separate floor plan. He had been making interest-only payments since way back in 1993. Even with his steady income from the dealership, it was highly unlikely that he could ever liquidate that $4 million debt. Granted, it was secured by everything he owned, including his house and the dealership, but out here real estate doesn't get you much. While he had a real nice house it only sold for $350,000. I can tell you for sure that the Loan

Committee never would have approved lending Allen more than about $1 million max, not with the big floor plan already held on the dealership's inventory. You know we were already factoring his receivables."

As Jake was trying to absorb this information, the hefty waitress returned to the table with a tray full of barbecued ribs, corn on the cob, coleslaw, baked beans and what appeared to be a whole loaf of bread sliced into inch-thick pieces and swimming in melted butter.

"Now you just let me know when you want some more of them ribs," the waitress exclaimed as she put the overflowing plate in front of Jake. "That there bottle in the middle of the table is Mexican hot sauce just in case you want a little more zip to them ribs. Band will be here at nine, so eat up so you got lots of energy to get out there and kick up your heels doing the West Texas line dance. Just holler if you need anything."

As Jake reached for a slab of the country ribs, he asked, "Are you able to get any of the details of those loans, or does Mr. Hathaway still keep them a secret from you?"

"I don't know. I found out how much he owed us because of the bankruptcy proceedings, but those proceedings were uncontested and the bank did not ever have to substantiate the amount of the loan. I'll see if I can dig out the loan records. I know that you have asked for them, so if I get caught doing something I shouldn't be doing I'll just tell Tubby Hathaway that I was trying to comply with your request and didn't realize they were meant to be kept secret. That should shut him up, especially if he thinks I might squeal on him to you or the court."

"That would be very helpful, and it will undoubtedly save me time on my next visit to Crosswind. For now, let's not push. I'll check over all the dealership records tomorrow. If he does not voluntarily produce all the loan documents, I will demand them on my next trip to Crosswind. I should be back in about a week. In particular I'd like to know why he borrowed the money. I don't think he was a gambler, and I don't think he led a separate life that would drain that kind of money. I know he invested in Red Rock Savings and Loan, but so did the other principal investors, and they don't seem to have suffered this economic loss."

"I'll see what I can do. Now let's eat."

Forty minutes and three beers later, Jake and Judy Falsworth polished off the last of their second helping of ribs and sat barely able to move in the wooden chairs that were just off the right side of the large dance floor. The small band had taken its position on a raised platform at one end of the restaurant, and Jake's last set of ribs had been interrupted on several occasions by the twang of an electric guitar being tuned against the tone of an electronic keyboard. As the waitress was clearing away the last of the dishes, the band started its series of western songs as twenty or so patrons stepped to the dance floor and formed several lines of dancers.

Jake watched as the lines went through a series of apparently rehearsed maneuvers that every so often ended with a great stomp on the floor, a form of do-si-do and two steps followed by a slight bow and another loud stomp. Some of the patrons were dressed in jeans and cowboy boots, and others were dressed in everything from a frilly Mexican dress to Bermuda shorts.

After ten minutes of watching this ritual of bending and twisting and stomping, Jake was ready for either another beer or a quick retreat. Before he could do either, Judy Falsworth preempted his plan by coaxing him to join her in the line dance, assuring him that it would be fun.

Half an hour later, protesting that he had to prepare for his next day's tedious work, Jake gracefully removed himself from the dance floor and stayed to finish one final beer while watching Judy Falsworth, the prim and proper floor manager of First State Bank of Crosswind, become fully engrossed in the rhythmic maneuvers of a West Texas line dance. She had done this before and appeared totally at ease doing a dance that rejected any concept of couples dancing together and emphasized group stomp and strutting to a steady western beat. When Jake left, Ms. Farnsworth was in high gear as she proceeded from one dance to the next without interruption. She waved as he left and shouted over the hammering of the music that she would do what she could.

CHAPTER 18

Wednesday morning in Crosswind was nothing short of perfect. The sun was bright, the air dry, and the heat had yet to reach its peak as Jake set off on a five-mile run. He had toyed with the idea of returning to Oklahoma City to see how his client was fairing under the care of Dr. Glasseur, but she had discouraged the trip by reporting no progress. Instead, Jake slept in, had a leisurely cup of coffee, then donned his running clothes and set off for his morning run. Although still unfamiliar with the streets around his motel, the giant rock was always in sight and made a perfect landmark.

After a quick breakfast, Jake called the Overlook Nursing Home to see whether Judge Stern was able to have visitors. He was pleased to find out that the Judge could have visitors for short periods of time, and there would be no problem with seeing him that morning. An hour later Jake was entering a beautiful, modern structure that looked more like a high-end condominium than a nursing home.

Overlook Nursing Home had been built on a prime piece of real estate overlooking the eastern expanse of Red Rock Park. Many of the wealthy families in Crosswind had coveted this location, but Horace and Mary Thompson had placed the land in trust in 1908 for the specific purpose of building an edifice in which the elderly residents of Crosswind could spend their waning years enjoying the beauty of their beloved Red Rock Park. At first the trustees had built a home for the aged that lacked nursing facilities but had a large veranda that accommodated all of the residents as they watched time pass by from wicker rocking chairs.

Through the good fortune of having a very conservative trust officer, the home survived the Great Depression, and then prospered from wise investment of the original endowment. As the value of the trust fund increased, the trustees were able to rebuild and refurbish the original home by adding needed indoor plumbing and giving the residents greater access through ramps and elevators. Ultimately it became necessary to construct a new, modern and fully accredited skilled nursing facility.

Mary Thompson had outlived her husband by nearly two decades, and through her efforts the trust that had originally been funded by her husband had grown impressively, and not entirely because of the prudent investments of its board of trustees. Horace Thompson had created the trust for the perpetual care of his parents, who were the first occupants of the home. They had not lived long after moving into the modest accommodations, and the trust was able to take in additional residents. Back in those days, there was no state or federal regulation of homes for the aged, and for the most part these facilities were modest but safe.

Horace handpicked the first board of trustees, but his interest in the home waned following the death of his parents, and Horace's cronies on the original board of trustees stopped coming to meetings when Horace retired as chairman and Mary took his place. Under Mary Thompson's guidance the board of trustees acquired members from the community, and soon local churches and wealthy families were contributing to the upkeep of the residence as a clean and safe home for their aging parents or, more commonly, as a place to send their domestic help once they became too old or infirm to keep up with their housekeeping chores.

Although the historical records credited Horace Thompson with having conceived of a home where the elderly residents of Crosswind could enjoy their last few years, it was his wife, Mary Thompson, who took charge of the project and turned it into a safe and comfortable place where the elderly could live out the remainder of their lives without being a burden on their family or former employer. While she was building an institution, Horace spent his time operating the only department store in Crosswind. Horace was considered a fair and honest businessman, but his extra-marital indiscretions with the widow of the Methodist Minister were fully ingrained in the folklore of Crosswind.

It was that affair that drove Horace to purchase a large cattle ranch for Mary in a remote area due south of the great rock and well away from Crosswind society.

Mary knew that Horace just wanted her out of the way, but the truth was that she loved the ranch more than she loved Horace, and was happy to see him spend his time in Crosswind with his mistress. After Horace's death, Mary resisted many offers to buy the cattle ranch even though the cattle business was hard and often unprofitable.

Most people thought her an old fool for staying on and trying to run the ranch after Horace's death and through the depression, but she stayed and ultimately died on her ranch at eighty-seven years of age. Mary had made the business marginally profitable despite the weak economy and beef surplus. When she died, Mary Thompson left the entire 10,000-acre ranch to the Mary Thompson Trust for the benefit of the Home for the Aged and construction of the Overlook Nursing Home. Before the trustees could figure out what to do with a cattle ranch in southwest Oklahoma, Standard Oil Company began its preliminary exploration of the Crosswind area in search of oil.

Mary Thompson's ranch sat on top of one of the largest oil reserves in the state, and within a year after her death the trustees of the Mary Thompson Trust presented the first of many royalty checks to the Overlook Nursing Home. Soon after the first well began producing high-grade crude oil, the trustees began planning construction of the new Overlook Nursing Home, which would lack nothing and continue to provide a safe and inexpensive place for the citizens of Crosswind to live out the last years of their lives, just as Horace had originally planned.

All of this information came from reading a copy of Overlook Nursing Home's annual report that lay conveniently on the coffee table in the nicely appointed waiting room. After reading of the Home's history, Jake glanced at the financial report and smiled as he reflected on the once-unimaginable value of Horace Thompson's rustic home for his elderly parents. The buildings and equipment were booked at a cost of $27 million, and the Mary Thompson Trust had over $100 million in assets administered by J.P. Morgan Bank. No wonder that a life-size portrait of Mary Thompson dressed in her ranching clothes was displayed prominently in the reception area of the nursing home. Just as Jake finished reading about this piece of Crosswind history, his concentration was interrupted by the singsong voice of a young assistant administrator.

"Judge Stern is able to see you now, Mr. McCarthy," the administrator said upon entering the waiting area. "We apologize for the delay, but he was feeling poorly this morning, and we were unsure whether he would be able to meet with you. Did you enjoy reading about our home in the annual report?"

"It was very informative. You have a lovely facility here, and with the endowment I am sure that it is possible for you to maintain a very high standard."

The tall, attractively dressed redhead led Jake down a wide corridor into a sitting room overlooking Red Rock Park. The entire wall was plate glass, giving an unobstructed view of the park and the famous rock. In a wheelchair by one of the overstuffed chairs sat a white haired gentleman with sharp features but an obviously frail and aging body. His head was held in a brace. A plaid blanket covered his hands and legs.

As Jake approached he saw that Judge Stern could follow him with his eyes, but the head and body were motionless.

"Judge Stern, this is attorney McCarthy. He is here to visit with you. Can you say hello to Mr. McCarthy?"

"Lo," was the only sound distinguishable from the former Federal District Court Judge. The sound was barely audible and resembled the broken speech of a stroke victim whose larynx is only half functioning.

"Hello, your honor," Jake responded. "I'm here on behalf of Molly Allen, who is my client." As Jake spoke the name of his client, he noticed a slight squint that led him to believe that the paraplegic judge recognized the name.

In a nearly inaudible bark the judge uttered the word, "trouble?" Then, after a few seconds of awkward attempts to say more, he called out in a whisper, "Rita!"

"Is she the lady that brought me in here?" Jake asked.

"No," came the slow, deliberate response. "Bell," the judge said, pointing with his eyes to a small silver bell sitting on an end table next to the overstuffed chair.

Jake rang it a few times, and from a door at the far end of the sitting room came a woman in her middle twenties, neatly dressed in a blue suit and carrying what looked like a Franklin planner. "Yes, your honor, what do you need?"

"Ask Rita," the judge whispered, and then became quiet as Jake began to ask questions about the judge's condition and whether Richard or Molly Allen had ever visited.

Rita McDougal introduced herself as Judge Stern's law clerk and sometimes nurse. In her third year of law school in Oklahoma City, she had applied for and received an internship with a Federal District Judge who turned out to be Judge Stern. "It's not exactly what I thought I wanted," she explained. "I sort of imagined sitting in courtrooms and hearing emotional closing arguments in major criminal cases. But after I had worked with the judge for a semester, I applied for a real clerkship after graduation and specifically requested Judge Stern. One of the great things about being a federal judge is that the appointment is for life. Because he is totally incapacitated, he receives disability pay that is very generous and the use of one law clerk.

"I am committed to establishing a reasonable method of communicating with the judge through whatever means are available. We have made progress. I am beginning to ask questions that he can comprehend and answer with his eyes. In a way this assignment has been good for me. After taking care of the judge and watching how the medical system works, I am now planning to specialize in health care law and focus on helping elder citizens who are unable to help themselves. Now, how can I help you?"

"I'm not sure," Jake responded truthfully. "I represent the widow of Richard Allen, who committed suicide late last year. I'm trying to figure out why and maybe recover some of his assets that were almost immediately taken in bankruptcy. Do you know whether Mr. Allen visited the judge late last year? They apparently had been friends for years, and I was just curious whether he came out here and whether he might have left something with the judge that would be helpful in my investigation."

"Well, sir, I remember seeing him, but it's hard to pinpoint exactly when. I know he didn't leave anything of value that might be of use to his widow. Let me check my planner to see when he last visited." Leafing through her Franklin planner, the attractive law clerk reported, "Richard Allen visited the judge on December 17th of last year for approximately twenty minutes. Nothing in my notes indicates that he left anything with the judge, but I was not present during the entire visit because we had exams coming up and I was studying in the back. My notes indicate the judge was upset after the visit. You can tell it in his eyes. The rest of his body may be cut off from the world, but his eyes are still bright and convey his emotions pretty accurately."

"That's only two days before he committed suicide," Jake responded. "Any idea what he got upset about?"

"I tried to find out without further stressing him. I'm not sure what he was trying to tell me. His eyes were angry, almost defiant, but I couldn't connect with whatever it was that had set him off. It's just not like the judge to be upset."

As Rita related this information to Jake, he turned to the crippled judge and watched as Stern's eyes flashed with excitement that contrasted mightily with his wholly immobile condition. His mouth opened as if to say something, but no words were forthcoming. Jake waited patiently and, without appearing to be condescending, moved closer to hear whatever words the judge was trying to expel from his badly damaged throat.

"No accident," the judge whispered.

"Did Richard have information about your accident?" Jake asked the judge.

Instead of an oral response, Judge Stern's eyes narrowed, and his otherwise pasty complexion became pinkish with signs of life.

Seeing this change, Rita immediately stepped in and stopped Jake from continuing. "He must not become agitated, or he may suffer a stroke. His neurologist is extremely worried about his high blood pressure," she said as she persuasively moved Jake away from the crippled body. "He was this way after Mr. Allen left, and it took weeks to get his blood pressure back into the safe range. You must stop now and let us get Judge Stern back to his routine."

Turning to Rita, Jake stated, "If you happen to hear or remember anything else about Judge Stern's accident or remember more of what Richard Allen may have said to him in December of last year, I am staying at the Best Western Suites Motel. I should be in town for three or four more days. Thanks for your time. It is very sad!"

It was early afternoon before Jake got back to his room at the motel, and after checking in with his secretary he asked to speak with Carol

Brooks to see whether she had been able to arrange her trip to Washington, D.C. As he listened to her voicemail message saying that she would be out of the office on Friday, Jake assumed, correctly, that she was on her way.

CHAPTER 19

Jake awoke early Thursday Morning, quickly packed his bags, and headed for Oklahoma City on the first leg of his trip home for the Memorial Day weekend. By eight AM he had checked out of the Best Western and was just leaving the City of Crosswind.

He was not the only early riser. The members of the Board of Directors of the now defunct Red Rock Savings and Loan were preparing for their long-anticipated trip to the Dozier Creek Ranch. Each, in his own way, sensed that this was most likely the last visit to the Ranch. Howard Stern had suggested the long weekend at the Ranch as a reward for successfully responding to the FSLIC and DOJ investigators, and, with the exception of Eric Beamer who rarely got excited about anything, the others had immediately embraced the idea.

The Dozier Creek Ranch is located on the eastern side of the Texas panhandle, just over the border between Texas and Oklahoma. Although ostensibly a dude ranch catering to would-be cowboys from Dallas or Oklahoma City, its clientele are select and carefully screened. It does not represent itself as a place for a family vacation. The cost for a long weekend at the ranch is fixed at $5,000 per person, in advance. This fixed charge covers all of the services available through the ranch's customer service department, and guests are asked to leave all of their valuables and their cash at the registration desk since there are no places on the ranch that will accept money or even a credit card.

Howard Stern had discovered Dozier Crook by accident on one of his inspection trips to the proposed resort and retirement community to be built on what their diviner had assured them was a mighty underground river capable of irrigating and servicing the White Sands area forever. The well diggers had been working for a month trying to tap into the underground river and were discouraged by the number of dry holes that had been drilled exactly where the diviner had specified. Stern had asked the foreman of the drilling team why his men were so discouraged since they were paid well even if they were unsuccessful. He had described to Stern the bonus that he had promised his crew if they struck water in the first two weeks of drilling–a weekend at the Dozier Creek Ranch. Once Stern head of the special attractions at the Ranch, he knew that he had to see for himself what it was all about.

The Dozier Creek Ranch offered the usual assortment of recreational activities found at a dude ranch. Horseback riding, fly fishing in Dozier Creek, hiking, and personal training at a large indoor gym complete with pool were always available, and guests had access to several hot tubs and saunas adjacent to the main lodge and at the remote sleeping quarters. Guests did not eat or sleep at the lodge. It was maintained primarily for its appearance as a working ranch with cattle and horses in abundance.

The ranch owned and staffed a number of remote facilities located throughout the ten square miles of wilderness encompassing the retreat. The Ranch staff referred to these buildings as "line shacks" because, to a large extent, they were located around the periphery of the ranch along the actual fence line. Before pickup trucks and helicopters replaced the quarter horse, large ranches constructed small cabins for the cowhands to live in while out for weeks on end repairing the fence and watching for rustlers. With the fierce weather endemic to southwest Oklahoma, the romantic concept of living out under the stars gave way to the more practical use of line shacks with watertight roofs and cots.

The line shacks at Dozier Creek Ranch were substantially more than their namesake. These "shacks" were fully equipped to feed, sleep and entertain up to ten guests at a time, and the support staff often outnumbered the guests by twice. Located from one to three miles away from the main lodge, none of the shacks was accessible by public or private road. A poorly maintained dirt track made it possible for four-wheel-drive vehicles to bring supplies and equipment to the shacks, but passage was intentionally kept difficult.

Although each line shack had all of the conveniences of modern living, great efforts were made to preserve the rustic atmosphere of a working ranch. Most of the guests would choose a horse from among the many maintained by the ranch, ride out to the designated shack, and be completely dependent on this mode of transportation for the entire stay. For visitors such as John Chambers, who refused to consider punishing any horse with his 350 pounds of flesh, the ranch would convey the guest in its modified Hummer to the desired location. But Chambers was the clear exception, and even Bill Hathaway agreed to subject his overweight body to the torment of an hour-long ride just to prove to the others that he had not yet succumbed to the morbid obesity that had sadly overcome his friend.

Although by day Dozier Creek Ranch appeared to be like any other dude ranch, by night it offered a different sort of adult entertainment that was its principal attraction. A significant part of the guest registration process involved a brief, private, one-on-one interview with the social coordinator, whose job included the assignment of guests to the appropriate line shack based on their individual tastes and desires. Each of the five directors of Red Rock Savings and Loan was assigned to a different line shack. For four of the five, assignment to a specific shack was a relatively simple task for the social coordinator. Each had already enjoyed the unique characteristics of a particular line shack, and none wished to change his personal taste. The only challenge was the accountant, Eric Beamer. He had tried several and had yet to find one to his liking. The social coordinator and her staff had anticipated this visit and thought they might have the right answer.

For John Chambers, whose wife had divorced him shortly after his father's death, the greatest pleasure in life came from two sources: food and liquor. His line shack, therefore, focused on making absolutely sure that its guests where satiated with the best whiskey, gin, vodka or other less traditional spirit, and food of the highest quality and quantity. The wait staff dressed casually, but their training was extensive. Each guest received individual attention throughout his stay. The purpose of a weekend retreat at this location was to treat gluttons to all of the food and drink that they craved without guilt or remorse. As with the other line shacks, this shack allowed its guests to indulge in their own vice of consumption without fear of criticism from the staff or rebuke from their peers. For most of the three-day retreat John Chambers and the three other men who had chosen this shack remained incoherently intoxicated and moribund.

For Bill Hathaway the selection was more complicated. Above all Hathaway was starved for affection. Although he had tried on his first visit to the Ranch to find affection through the Ranch's shack that was built as a replica of a French bordello, he was unable to satisfy his void through the carnal pleasures of a mistress or occasional dalliance with a prostitute. His visit to the bordello had been a disaster for him, but he was far too private with his personal life to have confessed his inadequacy to his friends. The social coordinator was notified immediately of Hathaway's inability to enjoy the myriad of sexual favors offered by the occupants of this line shack, and for his next visit she had suggested another venue whose staff consisted primarily of young men. Hathaway had immediately and adamantly rejected any such notions, so the coordinator started asking more questions in an effort to discover what would satisfy this rotund banker.

Hathaway had always been faithful to his wife, and it was his fear of the guilt that would follow him if he were to succumb to the Ranch's whores that prevented him from enjoying this release. Although his wife was similarly faithful and devoted to her husband, she lacked both the ability and the desire to satisfy her husband's needs for either physical or emotional love and respect. Intimacy had long since left their bedroom. She had no sympathy for and was personally repulsed by his chronic perspiration condition, and she had long since lost interest in his business or social proclivities. What kept her loyal was both his professed love for her and his income. Through him she could enjoy a standard of living that rewarded her tolerance of his ponderous weight and physical abnormalities.

After considerable analysis by the ranch staff, it was determined that what Hathaway missed most was his mother, who had divorced his father and moved to the east coast just as he was entering high school and experiencing the emotional dysfunction of a pubescent teenager. Mature women with large breasts and comforting hugs staffed his line shack. Rather than offering sexual favors, these women spent time with their guests. They all knew Bill Hathaway well enough to compliment him on everything from his manhood to his cleverness with numbers. They took care of him by laying out his clothes in the morning, making sure that he had fresh pajamas at night, and telling him as many times as he wanted to hear it that he was a good man, well respected by his peers, and truly loved by his surrogate mothers. Since his assignment to this line shack, Hathaway could sleep soundly, content in his fidelity to his wife and satisfied that he was a winner.

His shack consisted of a beautifully restored ranch house that exuded peace and welcomed relaxation. The instant perspiration that plagued Hathaway's life in Crosswind virtually disappeared in the warmth and kindness that personified his retreat. He relished the pleasure of sleeping late, enjoying a large breakfast masterfully prepared for him by one of his surrogate mothers, and walking casually around the ranch before preparing for an afternoon of fly fishing. At six o'clock he would appear in the small living room of the ranch house for cocktails with his mothers and the several other men who had selected this retreat. After a gourmet dinner and Cuban cigar, it was all that Bill Hathaway could do to stay awake long enough to reach his bedroom and restart the cycle.

Chapter 20

Although Howard Stern had the longest ride to his line shack, he enjoyed pushing himself and his horse. He craved the nighttime activities of the ranch, which could not be duplicated in Crosswind. The pounding of seat in saddle as he galloped toward his destiny effectively prevented him from enjoying the fantasies that consumed him in the days leading up to this weekend retreat. An old friend met Stern at the entrance to his shack.

"Welcome back, Chief Black Hawk. We have been waiting for your return all day. You are dirty from your long ride, and we must cleanse you in body and spirit. As soon as you change we will drink from the well of life, then begin the ritual. Here is your garment. I will be back in a few minutes."

"Thank you, Little Fawn. I, too, have been preparing for the cleansing that will bring our souls and our bodies closer," Stern responded.

As the slim, dark-haired girl left the room, Stern immediately removed all of his clothing, including his Rolex watch, which he carefully placed in his blue jeans pocket. Next he picked up the one item of clothing that Little Fawn had left for him. Through experience from prior visits, Stern skillfully slipped on his soft deerskin loincloth, which, he noticed with approval, had been carefully cleaned since his previous visit.

When Little Fawn returned she was colorfully dressed in authentic Apache clothes, which had been specially tailored to her slim, athletic body and long, graceful arms. "Come with me, Chief Black Hawk. The well of life awaits you." Little Fawn beckoned as Stern entered a room that had been decorated to resemble the inside of an Indian counsel house. "After you have had a drink from the well of life, you will be ready to begin the cleansing process to drive the impurities from your corrupt body. Then we will restore your spirit in the steam hut before retiring to our tent. Drink from this cup of water from the well of life while I prepare for the cleansing ceremony. Are you ready?"

"I have been ready since yesterday afternoon," Stern responded as he drank of the clear liquid, which he knew contained a distilled, powerful extract of peyote, the American Indian form of marijuana. He waited with anticipation for the mildly psychedelic effects of the stimulant to heighten his sensations before beginning the cleansing. "Are the squaws ready to begin?" he asked as he finished the cup of water.

"Yes, Chief Black Hawk, the squaws are ready for you. I will be waiting for you when you are clean and have expelled the unholy secretions from your body." With these words Little Fawn led Stern outside of the shack to a small pool whose waters were fed by Dozier Creek. Beside the pool were three women fully clothed in buckskins and wielding shammy cloths and scrub brushes made of hemp. Each squaw also had a small supply of willow saplings of about an inch in diameter with the tender bark peeled back to expose the bare wood.

Stern was first fully immersed in the cold water of the small pool, and then placed on a woven mat while the three women simultaneously began scrubbing his body with the hemp brushes using a cleansing cream made from cactus root. Stern did not remove his loincloth, nor did the women attempt to invade his privacy. Their focus was on his legs, arms and torso as they roughly scoured Stern's skin with the hemp brushes, rinsed with water from the pool and dried with the shammy cloths.

Satisfied that his skin was clean, the women each picked up two willow switches and began beating them against Stern's posterior from head to foot. With measured precision, they covered every exposed inch of his legs and back, then rolled him over and worked on his chest and abdomen. They did not strike hard enough to draw blood, but used sufficient force to cause Stern's skin to become inflamed. Using a systematic approach to this ritual, the women covered his body with small welts as Stern laid on the hemp mat without objection. The wet loincloth was insufficient to hide the massive erection that had overcome Stern as his body received this ritual lashing.

The pain inflicted by the willow switches brought with it intense sexual pleasure that Stern was unable to achieve through more conventional heterosexual or homosexual encounters. When he had met with the social coordinator he had complained about his inability to achieve true satisfaction from his normal or illicit sexual encounters. After an hour of questions into some of Stern's most private thoughts, the social coordinator began introducing pain into the sexual equation. It produced in Stern the most powerful climaxes that he had ever experienced. As each willow switch hit his back or chest, his mind rushed wildly with fantasies of hard-bodied Indian warriors covered with war paint and attacking white women and children. The fantasies grew in intensity as the stinging pain of the repeated beating of the willow saplings consumed his body.

The willow whipping lasted for half an hour, and by its conclusion Stern was exhausted. His sexual fantasies and the intensity of the physical stimulus had produced an overwhelming orgasm that completely drained his body and mind. He was ready for the steam tent.

For this part of the ritual, Stern removed his now-soiled loincloth, gently dried his angry skin with a soft cloth, and donned a clean, brightly colored Indian shirt and loose-fitting pants. Three other men were in the steam hut enjoying the cleansing power and relaxation of this part of the ritual. Although Stern had never witnessed another person undergoing the first part of the cleansing ritual, he had shared the steam hut with others. No one spoke. Each relished the glow of physical excitement and the introspection brought on by the hypnotic additives to water from the well of life. Whatever had been done to, for or with the other men, Stern was satisfied that for him the delicious pain delivered by the Indian squaws as they masterfully applied their willow saplings to his nearly naked body produced in him the highest level of sexual gratification.

An older woman tended to the fire, which heated four large stones located in the center of the steam hut. Every three or four minutes she would ladle water onto the rocks, which caused steam to billow out and around the now totally relaxed men. Smoke from the fire wafted up through an opening in the roof of the hut, but the steam-laden air in the hut was mixed with the smoke from the small fire. At regular intervals, one by one, each of the other men were led out of the steam hut by their Indian guide. After nearly an hour of smoke and steam, Little Fawn entered the hut to retrieve her chief. She was his for the rest of the night.

Throughout this process Stern had been silent, reveling in his fantasies, enjoying the pain and looking forward to the soft attraction of his concubine. "It was powerful this time, my Little Fawn. I have been drained of my evil fluids, my mind and body are clean, and you are my reward. We will enjoy the night together in peace."

Little Fawn smiled. Her customers always became sappy after the steam hut and possessive of her even though they knew that her talents were shared with other chiefs, each with their own sexual quirks. Some, like Stern, required pain to feel pleasure. Others had to witness pain inflicted on others. In most cases the ranch was able to accommodate its customers, and Little Fawn was well compensated for rewarding her johns with whatever they wanted. Rarely were they disappointed.

Finding an appropriate place for Jim O'Connor was simple because his tastes and desires were simple. He was a big person. He liked big horses, big cars and big-breasted women. He was not particular, and he did not view intimacy as something to waste on prostitutes. What Dozier Creek Ranch had to offer men like O'Connor was quantity. By the end of his weekends at the ranch, O'Connor was always exhausted, but confident in his manliness and physical ability to respond to the probing and caressing and kissing of multiple female partners.

O'Connor's shack was right out of the old west, complete with a cast of characters from the TV series *Gunsmoke*, including a marshal named Dillon, a head waitress named Miss Kitty, and a weathered sign on the front of the shack announcing that it was the Long Branch Saloon. The routine never varied, but was always fun for those who chose this venue. Although the bill of fare lacked gourmet foods, the kitchen at the Long Branch catered to big appetites for steaks, ribs and barbecue pork. The bar never closed, and the guests were treated to a variety of entertainment appropriate to the theme.

This was the most popular of the shacks, and O'Connor had enjoyed weekends when there were as many as fifteen men staying at the Long Branch. It was common to find boys in their late teens enjoying a gift from their father or older brother, and men in their seventies trying to see if they still had it in them. Throughout the evenings and nights, a steady supply of costumed bar maids would descend from the upstairs apartments seeking a willing male to return with her to her room for an hour or the night.

Booze and sex were not the only attractions, and the honky-tonk music from a player piano, gambling without money, and staged entertainment were only a diversion for those who chose to wait until the right woman enticed him to ascend into the upstairs apartments. The second most popular attraction of this line shack, and to some the even greater reason for returning to the Long Branch, were the carefully choreographed reenactments of many of the most famous gunfights from western movies. Guests could choose whether they wished to be a "good guy" or a "bad guy," and they were assigned black and white hats accordingly. Each person participating in these gunfights was required to wear clothing depicting a gunslinger or a sheriff, a frightened citizen or a hero. Authentic-looking replicas of the Colt .44 that were used in many of the western films were given to each combatant. Instead of bullets, these guns emitted a laser beam; and everyone had to wear a special transponder that, when excited by the laser beam, emitted a steady moan announcing to the other combatants that a gunman had been hit. Some of the participants also received similarly equipped Winchester rifles or sawed-off shotguns similar to the one used by Doc Holiday. Once hit, a combatant had to retreat into the Long Branch, where a staff member dressed in clothing suitable for an undertaker would solemnly silence the transponder. Unlike real life, once the sound had been silenced, the cowboy could resume the battle or turn his attention to the other attractions that were a constant source of distraction.

The last of the founders of Red Rock Savings and Loan was not a great supporter of the ranch, but agreed to join his cohorts as a final salute to the bankrupt company. In his first meeting with the social coordinator at the ranch, Eric Beamer had made it quite clear that he did not seek female companionship and was similarly not interested in men. He was a loner who liked skiing, hiking and mountain biking, but never in groups, and always as a test of his endurance. Although constantly looking for ways to test his endurance, Beamer had never tried the triathlon or participated in a marathon. He knew he would do well in these sports, but there were too many people.

Since catering to the individual vices and desires of its customers was the goal of Dozier Creek Ranch, finding a place for Beamer became a challenge unlike any the ranch had ever experienced. Each time Beamer had visited the ranch the social coordinator had tried a different event to test whether Beamer would find gratification or pleasure. None was entirely successful, although Beamer never complained or asked for a refund. For this visit the management of the ranch had devised a special program that focused on known traits of this difficult customer. Beamer was a loner who avoided crowds and rarely participated in any discourse other than that incident to his profession as a CPA. What the ranch hands discovered during prior visits was Beamer's natural ability to ride horses. On one of his visits he had been missing for over four hours, and the staff at his assigned line shack became worried that he had fallen off his horse or had a heart attack or stroke, events that had occurred with other guests. When Beamer finally returned to his shack just in time for supper, his only explanation was that he and the horse had gone for a walk into the wilderness.

It was that observation that led the social coordinator to suggest that Beamer be given a good horse, a map of the ranch, and enough food and provisions for the weekend. Tracking devices would be concealed on the horse and on Beamer's clothing so that the ranch helicopter could find him in case of an emergency, and he would have a cell phone to call for help. Otherwise, he would be on his own and could wander anywhere he chose over the ranch's four square miles of wilderness.

Beamer had jumped at the chance. He had the pick of any horse in the ranch's stable, and he chose two, one to ride and the other to carry his gear. The ranch outfitted Beamer from head to toe with the necessary clothing and equipment for his three-day ride. Included in his provisions were a matched set of long-barreled .45 Colt revolvers and a Winchester rifle. For the first time in his visits to the ranch Beamer was truly excited about his adventure. The weather was perfect. He could go and do as he pleased without answering to anyone, and his body would be challenged by the demand on his leg and shoulder muscles. His mind would be equally challenged not to get lost in the wilderness and to arrive back at the ranch house in time for his return to Crosswind.

CHAPTER 21

Before boarding the Boeing 757 at Will Rogers International, Jake had called into his office in Detroit to retrieve voicemail messages and see if Carol Brooks had gotten his e-mail of the previous evening. The voice-mail manager reported that he had seventeen messages, and he dutifully waded through all seventeen, making notes where necessary to remind him to return a call or provide assistance. The sixteenth message caught his attention. It was from Dr. Martinique Glasseur.

"Jake, it's Marty. Sorry I was unable to meet with you this morning. Hope you got the medical records OK. Haven't been back to my office to confirm. Molly is making progress, and we may even have overcome a small piece of the post-traumatic stress disorder. Call me when you have a chance, and when you return plan to spend some time in Oklahoma City before running off to Crosswind. What is your schedule?"

Jake pushed 3 and then the pound sign to delete the message, and then listened to the last message from Carol Brooks.

"Jake, it's Carol. Understand you're on your way back to Detroit. I won't be in the office Friday or Saturday. I'll be in DC and will work with Kevin Alexander, my contact at the Resolution Trust, on Friday and Saturday if necessary, then spend the rest of the long weekend sightseeing. Kevin has agreed to show me the sights. I'll be staying at his place in Georgetown. I'll overnight a package of materials on Red Rock and White Sands to the Hyatt Regency in Oklahoma City so it will be there on Tuesday. Let me know if I can do anything more for you. Parker OK'd everything. Thanks."

Jake gathered up his bags, laptop and boarding pass and boarded the stretch Boeing 757 for the long ride back to Detroit. There had been a fair amount of traffic on the drive up from Crosswind, and since the Memorial Day weekend was ahead of him, Jake left his briefcase and laptop in the overhead compartment and dug into a Clancy novel that he had picked up at the airport. Although the flights from west to east are generally faster because of the prevailing jet stream, it always seemed longer because of the time difference. The plane was in the air by 11:20 a.m., Oklahoma time, but the three-hour flight coupled with a two-hour time change put him into Detroit Metropolitan Airport at 4:30 p.m.

As Jake's plane was touching down in Detroit, Carol Brooks was preparing to land at Ronald Ragan National Airport in the nation's Capitol. The landing at Washington D.C.'s Reagan National Airport was fantastic. The cherry blossoms were in full glory, it having been a late spring on the east coast, and from the air the city sparkled. Even the Potomac River looked blue as it reflected the perfectly clear, deep blue sky. The Boeing 737 had come in low just to the south and east of the Pentagon, then turned north and west over the Potomac as it made its final approach to the airport serving the nation's capital. The Washington Monument and Lincoln and Jefferson Memorials glistened in the bright sunshine, masking the years of dirt that prior administrations had allowed to tarnish these national treasures. The Clinton administration was making an effort to clean and restore the Washington Monument to help preserve it for another hundred years, but work had not started. As far as Carol Brooks could tell, it looked great.

She had planned to scan through the stack of documents that she had downloaded off the Internet about Crosswind, Oklahoma during the hour-long flight from Detroit to Washington, D.C., but her ability to do any work was hampered by tantalizing memories of her yearlong relationship with Kevin Alexander, her now very important contact at the Resolution Trust. As relationships do, theirs had started slowly and entirely innocently. He and she were paired in a moot court trial against two teams of their classmates on an issue involving the right to privacy of minors. Their mock client was a sixteen-year-old female who was pregnant and seeking an abortion. The opposition consisted of the State of Michigan seeking to enforce the parental consent law and the National Association for the Preservation of Parental Rights or NAPPR appearing as an *amicus* or friend of the court.

At first it had been hard to work with Kevin. He was a corporate type, and Carol had focused all of her energy on being a trial lawyer. Moot court was a great opportunity to try out advocacy skills, and she relished the chance to demonstrate her ability to present cogent oral argument, while Kevin believed that success lay in the preparation of a bullet-proof trial brief and insightful cross examination of the key witnesses. After a week of trying to impress each other with their lawyering skills, Kevin finally conceded to Carol's strategy, which emphasized the fundamental rights of a person to determine what happens to their own body.

They had been working late at the world-class University of Michigan Law Library and were not quite finished as the library was about to close. Kevin lived in the law quadrangle adjacent to the library and suggested that they finish up in his room on the fifth floor of the central tower. All the way up the five flights of stairs, Carol Brooks had been restating and reinforcing her position that every person, no matter the age, has a God-given right to control what is done or not done to his or her body. Kevin had been parroting back all the laws that said otherwise with regard to the rights of parents to raise their children and the Michigan law requiring parental consent to an abortion by a minor.

By the time they reached Kevin's room, both were out of breath, but Carol was far from out of arguments. Kevin put up his right hand and stopped her in mid sentence. "Carol, I think you have it just about right. Let's build our case around your four points and try to distinguish the few bad cases that we know they will throw against us. Let's go through these last two cases, then I'll walk you back to your apartment."

An hour later, as Carol was completing her summary of the leading case defending the right of a parent to be notified of a child's intent to have an abortion, she asked, "Where is your roommate? He's out kind of late, isn't he?"

"He took off early for the weekend. He has no classes on Friday, so he runs home to Dearborn. Misses out on a lot that Ann Arbor has to offer on the weekends, but he has a girlfriend finishing up as an undergraduate at Wayne State, so he's out of here on almost every weekend. I pretty much have this place to myself. Want to stay here for the night?"

That night Carol Brooks had declined the invitation, but two weekends later Kevin had asked her out on a date, and after the concert at Hill Auditorium they had hit a couple of the bars on Liberty Street, and somehow ended up back at Kevin's apartment in the law quad. This time Carol did spend the night, and for the rest of that academic year she rarely stayed in her off-campus apartment on Friday or Saturday nights.

By the time the Boeing 737 began its descent, Carol had completely forgotten about Crosswind, had vividly recalled the nights when she and Kevin had explored each other's sexuality, and began to fantasize about what might happen this weekend. The combination of memories of long nights and late mornings in the quad and the expectation of seeing Kevin Alexander after four years was enough to trigger physiological responses in Carol Brooks that were only partially reflected in the crimson blush that had overtaken her normally pale complexion.

Kevin was waiting for her at the airport, and as their eyes met there was instant recognition of the anticipation that each had felt. Neither was married, neither was dating, and each had so deeply enmeshed themselves in their careers that they had almost forgotten the joy of sex.

Carol Brooks had taken the three o'clock flight into Washington rather than the early bird Friday morning flight so that she would have the entire day on Friday to review files, talk with investigators, and try to uncover information about Red Rock Savings and Loan. It was too late to call on any government offices, so the two of them decided to take in a few sights that would be open to the public until seven o'clock, then have dinner in Georgetown before heading to Kevin's apartment for the night. Carol was reasonably familiar with the city but had not seen the Roosevelt Monument, so they quickly decided to visit this impressive new testimonial to one of the great American presidents.

From the airport it took less than fifteen minutes to reach the monument, and soon the two young lawyers were wandering about the beautifully maintained gardens, gazing at the graceful waterfalls and rock formations that distinguished the national shrine from other more formal monuments. They took their time, reading of the remarkable achievements of the New Deal and the transformation of the country from deep depression to a growing economy, then the horrible onslaught of the Germans under Adolf Hitler, the invasion of Pearl Harbor and World War II. The tour ended with the incredibly impressive life-size statute of FDR, which artfully displays the tremendous strength of character that allowed this crippled president of the United States to command the respect of the entire world even as he sat in his wheelchair.

At first the distance between Kevin and Carol had been appropriate for two young professionals about to begin a research project into the legality of a defunct savings and loan. Gradually and perceptibly, however, they allowed their bodies to explore whether the closeness that they had enjoyed as second-year law students at the University of Michigan could be regained. It began while Carol was reading about the New Deal. Kevin moved in a bit closer than was necessary for him to read the same information. Carol did not protest.

As they were walking through the gardens surrounding the monument, Carol made a point of brushing up against Kevin. He did not object, and she did not apologize. By the end of the walk through the tribute to FDR, they were holding hands and each was anticipating an emotional evening together recalling their relationship while they were learning how to become attorneys.

From the Roosevelt Monument they walked past the memorial to the Korean War Veterans, the Vietnam Wall, and along the reflecting pond between the Capitol and the Washington Monument. The cherry blossoms were at their peak. The warm spring air, clear sky and overwhelming beauty of the most famous of national landmarks added to the tension that was building in each.

Kevin broke the spell. "I'm not really hungry yet; what if we head back to my place before going out to dinner? You can drop off your stuff, freshen up if you need to, and we can have a cocktail while we figure out which of my favorite restaurants to honor with your presence."

"Let's hurry," Carol responded without needing to say why.

Kevin lived alone in a Georgetown duplex four blocks from Dupont Circle. He enjoyed the luxury of an underground garage, but otherwise the apartment was a fairly typical two-bedroom townhouse with a small but adequate kitchen, living room and breakfast area.

After carrying her suitcase upstairs to the second bedroom, Kevin offered to show Carol around his modest home. Carol placed her briefcase and purse on the single bed, then turned toward Kevin and put her arms around him as they mutually gave in to the emotions that had been coursing through their bodies since they first saw each other at the airport.

"The only room I want to see right now, Kevin, is your bedroom, and I hope it has a bigger bed than this one." Their feet did not move as they continued their embrace and explored each other's lips and mouths. Carol reached for Kevin's belt as he helped her out of her navy blue blazer. Without hurrying but with a mutual sense of urgency, they migrated into Kevin's bedroom where a queen-size bed awaited their further activities.

As students their lovemaking had been hot and fast, but each understood the importance of establishing a basic harmony of purpose and directing their energies toward reasonable foreplay before bringing each other to climax. Four years of separation did nothing to change this understanding, and as they helped each other to remove their clothing they continued their gentle but focused touching of intimate body parts.

"I haven't had enough," Carol said ten minutes after they had consummated their reunion. "I have missed you, Kevin, and I think I'm going to miss you even more after this weekend is over. What ever happened to that girl you were dating senior year? I thought you and she were a done deal."

"Simple geography. I wanted to work in DC for a few years while I was young, and she wanted to go back home to her family in Cincinnati. When I turned down an offer from her father's law firm so that I could make half as much working for the government, she lost interest. Too bad that didn't happen at the beginning of the year rather than at the graduation dinner when her dad sprung his offer on me. What happened to you?"

"An opportunity came up over the summer to take a year off to study at Oxford in England, then I came back to finish up in Ann Arbor over the following summer. It was too good an offer to turn down; and then when I heard that you were dating Sally Fields with all of her blond hair and big boobs, I figured that I had lost out. I rationalized my loss with the experience that I gained in London, but it was a long summer during which my friends were all too eager to describe how perfect you and Sally looked as a couple. I guess they didn't know about your desire for government service. I'm so glad that we are back in the sack together. It's as if we never missed a beat."

Seconds later Kevin's lips were again exploring Carol's body, beginning with her lips, and relentlessly moving to other parts of her very female anatomy. Carol responded with particular attention to the very male parts of Kevin's now fully reawakened body. Dinner was all but forgotten as they more deliberately continued the erotic dance of two willing lovers.

CHAPTER 22

By the time Jake had retrieved his car from the Airlines Parking Authority located several miles from the airport and driven the fifty-five miles to Rochester Hills it was 6:30 p.m. By the clock it seemed like he had been en route for twelve hours, having left Crosswind at 6:30 in the morning, but he knew it had taken only ten hours or the equivalent of a normal workday. Nevertheless, he was exhausted.

The girls were doing their homework when Jake pulled into his three-car garage. When they heard the car door slam shut, they came running into his arms, and suddenly all of his fatigue seemed to evaporate. Their energy and excitement soon translated into an hour of show and tell as Kimberly and Ashley recounted all of their triumphs at school and on the soccer field. Maggie was quiet. Her turn would come later.

Saturday morning displayed a perfect Michigan spring day. The sky was a deep blue, the sun warm enough to dry the heavy spring dew and awaken the blossoms on every apple tree. The flowering crabapple trees that were planted throughout the subdivision were in full bloom, the sun was high and bright, and Jake was ready for the finals of the under-ten girls soccer league. He was early for this playoff final and was pleasantly surprised to find over half of his team already at the field passing the ball and chattering about the game. They seemed well prepared, and Cindy Smith, his assistant coach, was right there with them, encouraging, exciting and always friendly.

Jake had insisted that no parent or coach associated with his team would ever ridicule or belittle one of his players or the team. Cindy Smith was the epitome of positive reinforcement for the girls and, when needed, for Jake. At their first team meeting, which all parents were required to attend, Jake had expressed his philosophy of coaching.

"Proper coaching and instruction on the skills and strategy of soccer do not require put-downs. Coaches and parents criticize poor performance either because they lack understanding of why the performance is below standard or because they lack the communication skills to do anything but complain. It is much easier to find flaws in a normal person than to understand when that normal person has excelled. We laud and magnify the superstars because it is easy to know when they have made a great play or dominated a game. The media tell us. We see instant replays. Self-proclaimed experts comment over and over about the exceptional skill of our professional athletes. We know when to praise a Michael Jordan or Barry Sanders.

"Observing amateur and recreation-league athletes is much more difficult. Finding and praising exceptional achievement requires a lot more work and a profound understanding of the capabilities of each individual. We must watch all the time for success in our children and in our lives. There are no instant replays in recreation-league sports or in life.

"Our children are born with certain talents," Jake continued, "and it is up to us as parents and coaches to do what we can to develop those talents. We need to teach through instruction, by encouraging good behavior on and off the field, and most of all by letting our kids know how proud we are of them no matter what they do or how well they do it. We know when we have done less than our best, and our kids are no different. We don't need to tell a ten-year-old girl when she has done something wrong. We need to show her how to do it right and then praise her when she tries, whether or not she eventually succeeds. I need parents who are willing to encourage us to excel and who do not let us become discouraged by small setbacks."

His parent pep talk had ended with a pledge from each parent that so long as their child was on Jake's team they would never be negative about their child's individual performance, about the team, and especially about any other child on the field, whether on the Royals or on the opposing team. The result of this continuously positive reinforcement had been an undefeated season and a wonderfully cohesive team. What had been a surprise even to Jake was the report from a number of parents that their girl had started getting better grades in school, watched less and less TV, and in many non-soccer related activities had adopted a "can-do" attitude. Positive reinforcement of every child's innate abilities had worked.

Several times during the first few games of the season one or two of the parents had openly criticized their daughter for not running hard enough or missing a tackle or toying with her pigtails. When that happened Jake immediately left his place along the sidelines and asked the parent to join him out of earshot of the other parents.

The game continued under the watchful eye of his capable assistant while Jake carefully and clearly reminded the parent that such negative encouragement would not be tolerated. After a few of these sessions with parents unable to contain their derogatory comments, the team suddenly coalesced and the parents not only became best of friends with each other, but also were the best source of positive encouragement for their daughters and the other girls on the team. As required by FIFA rules and enforced by Jake, no parent ever criticized the call of a referee or linesman. The same could not be said for the other teams in the league.

"Cindy!" Jake called to his assistant coach as he jogged onto the practice field. "I have never seen the team so pumped up for a game. You are fantastic. The girls look ready for a great finals."

"Thanks, Jake, and welcome back. I knew you wouldn't miss this game," Cindy Smith responded. "Here's the line up. Everyone's coming, and the Andersons are responsible for oranges at half time. Right after the game we're all going out for DQs, so we can go over the details of the Memorial Day parade while we're getting our ice cream cones. Let's not bother the girls with that now."

The game was close in score, but the Rochester Racers were no match for his Royals, who seemed to control the game from the opening whistle. The three-nil score would have been more one-sided had not the Racers' goalie made five spectacular saves. Jake made a special point of congratulating the goalie for her outstanding game despite the three goals that she had no chance of stopping. Her coach, on the other hand, could only focus on the loss and was busy berating his team for not playing up to their potential. All the Racer players were interested in was getting their runner-up trophies and enjoying the rest of the long weekend.

That evening Jake and Maggie drove the thirty-seven miles south and east to "The Pointes," where Reginald Parker lived in a large home overlooking Lake St. Clair. The house, located on St. Clair Shores' Nautical Mile, was a quarter mile north of the Grosse Point Yacht Club and sat on one of the few pieces of land that did not have Lake Shore Drive or Jefferson Avenue between it and the lake. Another quarter of a mile north was the historic Edsel and Eleanor Ford Home, which had been preserved in its art deco style and converted into a meeting place for charitable events and non-profit organizations.

The chairman was in rare good form as he and his wife hosted Jake and Maggie and three other couples. During cocktails Jake was able to fill Mr. Parker in on most of the details of his investigation and outline his plans for the coming week.

"The key is still Molly. If her mind does not respond to treatment, we may end up with nothing more than a charity case. Her doctor provided me with a copy of her medical record, which I will leave here with you. Perhaps you can have one of your Detroit Medical Center colleagues look it over. My review showed nothing of any help. I have confidence in Dr. Glasseur," Jake continued, "and my last message from her indicated that Molly was showing signs of progress. I am anxious to get back to Oklahoma City and see whether we can pry a little more information from her."

"You're in charge," Parker responded after Jake had finished his brief report and was in the process of pouring another gin and tonic. "I concur with your logic that Richard should not have been the only one of the investors to feel the pain of personal bankruptcy. From what you have said, none of the other investors had independent wealth sufficient to sustain them through the loss of millions of dollars. Richard had a thriving dealership with steady cash. Why was he so far in debt?"

At dinner Jake realized that the other guests were in fact potential new clients of the firm. Jake sat next to the president of a mid-sized company whose former president and CEO had just sued for wrongful termination, claiming that he had been forced to retire without cause. At issue was whether the board's discovery of major irregularities in the books of the company constituted sufficient cause for discharge. The other two were contemplating suing suppliers who had failed to deliver on time and had caused major losses in revenue and reputation. Jake was all ears and ready to take up their causes, and by the end of the evening they were just as eager to retain him and the firm.

CHAPTER 23

Jake was booked on an 11:30 Tuesday morning flight from Detroit Metro to Oklahoma City, and he had already decided not to make a stop at the office on the way to the airport. After the Memorial Day parade in downtown Rochester, Jake had reluctantly driven into the city and spent four hours wading through piles of correspondence–mostly solicitations to sell everything from office supplies to multi-volume treatises on ERISA–that had piled up in his absence. After sorting through the important correspondence, Jake dictated a half dozen letters, a motion for summary disposition and a week's worth of time (spent almost entirely on the Molly Allen case). He left the tapes for his secretary, and then dove into the stack of deposition summaries prepared by the two litigation law clerks under the supervision of Carol Brooks. He could have used another day or two, but Parker had insisted that he concentrate on Molly and let the firm pick up his caseload.

Knowing that his flight didn't leave until 11:30, Jake uncharacteristically stayed in bed after Maggie got up to fix breakfast for the girls and get them off to school. It was a warm, spring morning, and the sun came streaming through the large windows in the master bedroom. Jake awoke out of a light sleep to see Maggie standing in the doorway of the bedroom with a large coffee mug in each hand and an even larger smile on her face.

"It's been a while since you've slept in on a business day, Jake McCarthy!" she said. "How about a cup of coffee?"

Jake sat up in bed, smiled and reached out for the steaming cup of Starbuck's breakfast blend. Maggie was wearing her light blue chiffon bathrobe that Jake had given her for Christmas the year before. As Jake took his first sip of coffee, Maggie moved to her side of the bed, placed her coffee cup on the bedside table, quickly unbuttoned her bathrobe and dropped it to the floor. Her naked body glistened with expectation as she slid between the sheets of the king-size bed. Jake quickly put his coffee on the night table next to his side of the bed.

"I like having you home in the morning, Jake," she purred.

"Keep this up and it may become a habit," Jake said as he responded to his wife's advances. "I'm still turned on from last night. Are you trying to spoil me?"

"Mmm," Maggie purred as she began chewing gently on Jake's right earlobe and running her hand along his abdomen as it traveled to its intended destination.

The flight to Oklahoma City was uneventful, and after picking up a rental car at the Hertz lot, Jake made his way to the Hyatt Regency to check in and see if the overnight package promised by Carol Brooks was waiting for him at the hotel. He was not disappointed. Carol had assembled fourteen different news articles on Red Rock Savings and Loan that she had found through the Internet from financial publications, local newspapers and several trade publications on the savings and loan industry.

She had also assembled a substantial number of documents and reports from the insolvency proceedings before the Resolution Trust; a list of assets held by Red Rock Savings and Loan at the time of its bankruptcy; a complete list of its shareholders from inception showing their various interests; and copies of the articles of incorporation, bylaws and other corporate documents filed with the state of Oklahoma and with the federal regulatory agencies. Red Rock had not been publicly traded, so there were none of the SEC filings that would have provided further information about this now-defunct organization.

It was nearly 4:00 p.m. by the time Jake checked into the hotel, settled into his room and scanned the stack of documents awaiting his review. Before reading any of them, Jake placed a call to Dr. Glasseur at her office.

"Dr. Glasseur's office, Jan speaking. Can I help you?" came the cheerful voice of Dr. Glasseur's attractive, young receptionist.

"Hi, this is Jake McCarthy. Is Dr. Glasseur in?"

"I'm sorry, Mr. McCarthy, she has left for the day. She did ask me to tell you, if you called in, that she would like you to come to the hospital tomorrow morning at 8:00 a.m. She wants to discuss with you the therapy that your client is receiving. Will you be able to make it?"

"I'll be there."

After hanging up the phone and removing his suit jacket, Jake unscrewed the cap on one of the complimentary mini-bottles of Jack Daniels, poured the entire contents over a glass full of ice, and took a sip of the straight bourbon whisky before wading into the documents on Red Rock Savings and Loan.

When he had finished scanning the title pages of the many documents assembled by Carol Brooks, Jake turned to the fourteen-page memorandum that she had prepared as a summary of the documents. As usual, her report was well composed, well formatted and capable of submission directly to a client or, with a proper caption, to a court. She was good, and Jake knew that within a year or two he would have the pleasure of co-sponsoring his industrious associate for junior partnership in the firm. Jake hoped at the same time to achieve senior partner status even ahead of his peers, based primarily on the $3,000,000 judgment that he had secured while defending Tecumseh Products against a breach of contract claim by Takawara Iron Works, a Japanese conglomerate. After a week of poring over documents and drawing many diagrams of the deal that had apparently been struck, Jake decided that his client was not only innocent of any breach of contract but had also suffered substantial losses as a result of Takawara's dumping of inferior metals with a Tecumseh competitor. Jake promptly filed a substantial counterclaim against Takawara for wrongful dumping of its metal products, interference with a beneficial contractual relationship, libel and slander of the Chairman and CEO of Tecumseh Products, and assorted other counts.

Typically these counterclaims become a bargaining chip in the settlement of complex commercial litigation. In this case Takawara refused to settle, and a jury in the United States District Court for the Eastern District of Michigan, sitting in Ann Arbor, awarded Tecumseh Products and its Chairman and CEO a combined judgment in excess of three million dollars.

"The Japanese may know about efficient manufacturing techniques and how to develop a loyal workforce through a promise of lifetime employment," Jake recalled telling his client after the jury verdict, "but they never fully understand the American judicial system and the power of individuals and corporations to defend against manipulative people using their power and financial leverage to damage legitimate business. Use of power and influence is endemic to the Japanese business culture and one of the main causes for the decay in its economy."

The chairman of Tecumseh Products had personally thanked Jake for his defense and rewarded the firm with a $50,000 bonus for the unexpected recovery on the dumping claim.

These thoughts raced through Jake's mind as he forced himself into the far less exciting task of digging through piles of information from which he hoped to glean a small kernel of insight into this worthless company that had cost Richard his life and Molly her life's savings. Jake worked his way through the lengthy memorandum and randomly looked through the pile of documents and news clippings assembled by his associate.

Four hours and three Jack Daniels later, Jake finished the last of the documents, carefully ripped out his seven legal pages of notes from the almost empty pad, clipped the notes together with an oversized paper clip and put all of the papers and notes in his briefcase. Within minutes he was in bed and sound asleep.

CHAPTER 24

Jake arrived at the University of Oklahoma Medical Center in time for a weak cup of coffee in the hospital cafeteria and a bagel with cream cheese. Since recovering the voice message from Dr. Glasseur while waiting to get on the plane to Detroit, Jake had mentally prepared himself for everything from a remarkable breakthrough where Molly Allen was completely recovered and full of vital information, to mere improvement where she could at least recognize who and where she was. By a quarter of eight, Jake was sitting in the physicians lounge on the psychiatric ward waiting for Dr. Glasseur.

As he reached over to the oak veneer end table to retrieve one of the dog-eared magazines, a short, thin, dark-skinned woman dressed in a carefully tailored, dark-blue suit entered the room and crossed over to where he was sitting. "Are you Mr. McCarthy?" she asked with a distinct British accent that was in contrast to her noticeably Far Eastern physical characteristics. "I am Suba Reddy, the chief therapist on this floor. I have been taking care of Mrs. Allen for the last several weeks. Dr. Glasseur asked me to invite you to come watch our therapy session so that you might understand how we have been able to achieve our successes with Mrs. Allen."

Jake rose to his feet and followed the slightly built therapist down a long corridor and into an observation room. One wall of the room had a one-way mirror through which observers could watch without interfering with the therapy sessions. Dr. Glasseur was waiting for Jake in the observation room. The therapy room was empty.

"Hi Jake," Dr. Glasseur said immediately upon Jake's entering the room. "I'm so glad you could make this session. Molly Allen has made such wonderful progress, and we owe so much to Dr. Reddy. We have used a series of conventional and unconventional therapy in our efforts to break through to Molly Allen. None of us is willing to say for sure which of our treatments has met with success. Perhaps they all contributed, but my guess is that one or both of the modalities that you will see this morning was the triggering event that caused her reversal. Are you interested in what we have done so far?"

"Of course," Jake responded. "How is she doing, and when can I see her?"

"You will see her in a few minutes. Let me explain what we have done so far.

"We have applied four different programs to help relieve the post-traumatic stress that has interfered with Molly's ability to recall the recent past. First, we have worked to improve her physical health through careful regulation of her diet, frequent and varied exercise, and a strong dose of high potency multi-vitamins and minerals. Although far from chronically undernourished, Mrs. Allen was pretty bad when she entered the hospital. She had lost weight. We could tell because her clothes were so loose on her, and her electrolytes were grossly out of balance. We have restored her to good physical health for a woman her age, and she seems to have enjoyed our exercise routine that involved step aerobics in the morning, working on the treadmill in the afternoon and swimming in the evening just before dinner."

"I will let Dr. Reddy explain her part of the therapy," Dr. Glasseur continued. "She is in charge of our alternative therapies department and has applied many of the skills that she acquired from her training in Bombay, India. Suba?"

"Thank you, Dr. Glasseur. I will not be lengthy since my therapy session will begin in fifteen minutes, and I must prepare. We have applied two separate modalities in an effort to restore the balance of electrostatic forces surrounding and protecting Molly Allen from physical and emotional injury. Dr. Gupta on our staff has written his Ph.D. thesis on the teachings of Dr. Mikao Usui and the healing powers of Reiki. Dr. Usui discovered the existence of an aura surrounding every human body that protects us from external forces through a powerful electromagnetic force that is energized by the body's heat. When that force is interrupted or torn through physical trauma or intense emotional stress such as the loss of a loved one, or through other forces beyond our rational cognizance, the whole body suffers. As therapists trained in the healing powers of Reiki, we try to restore that invisible force and bring the individual's aura back into balance so it may continue to protect the unity of the body, mind and soul of the person."

Jake said nothing and carefully repressed the desire to laugh at this bizarre recitation of an obviously weird therapy cult. His opinion of Dr. Glasseur dropped a few notches.

"Dr. Gupta spent three days with Molly Allen attempting to locate and quantify the break in her aura," Dr. Glasseur interjected, as Dr. Reddy was about to continue her explanation of Reiki. "On the third day he was successful in finding what he believes is a giant tear extending from her right temple to her waist. He has been using superficial massage therapy to work this area back into its continuous field around her body. He, of course, is claiming credit for having found this serious fracture in her aura, but it is yet to be seen whether he can heal it or if it really exists. We have seen some progress."

Dr. Glasseur then asked Dr. Reddy to continue. "For the last two years, we have been working with another very new and even more controversial program developed at one of the leading medical facilities in Africa. It uses the rhythmic cadence of special drums as a means for healing the body through harmonization of the living force around the body with the mental and physiological essence of the body. Because the two disciplines seemed to compliment each other, we decided to combine them into a single therapy. It is difficult to explain how music reacts with the body and soul of a person, but it has been recognized for centuries that it does have healing qualities. In the late 1980s, a group of African therapists, lead by a physician trained at Johns Hopkins, achieved a breakthrough in music therapy as a physiological phenomenon. They discovered that people suffering from severe trauma could be rendered pain-free through repeated exposure to percussion instruments played continuously for periods of up to eight hours."

Dr. Glasseur again interjected. "Working with traditional physical therapists and several highly skilled musicians from Kenya, a team of researchers was able to document with scientific verifiability that curative effects were achievable from the application of certain kinds of music. Scott Parker, a young musician interested in the para profession of music therapy, received a $200,000 fellowship to develop a program of music therapy in our alternative therapy department here at the University of Oklahoma Medical School. Fortunately, his fellowship was approved just before Molly entered the hospital, and she became his first subject. He, of course, claims that Molly's improvements are a reflection of his therapy. No matter who is responsible, we are satisfied that she is improving daily and seems to like and respond well to these sessions."

Trying not to be sarcastic, Jake finally spoke. "This is incredible. I had no idea that a hospital of this size and reputation would experiment with procedures that have no scientific support and almost no recognition in the medical field. It seems mighty strange to me, but I will watch. What else has Molly been exposed to?"

Dr. Glasseur had a sparkle in her eye as she responded to Jake's question. "Me," she said, adding emphasis by pointing to herself. "We are fortunate that we can experiment with these programs, and yes it is very unusual that an institution of this size and reputation would permit such experimentation. Not everybody knows what we're doing, and we would just as soon not advertise it until we have some better statistics. The hospital's Chief of Staff knows that we are trying out these remedies, especially on people for whom there is no apparent cure. We have been able to show several successes or partial successes, so he has been lenient with me and has been willing not to tell Hospital Administration and the Board of Trustees that we are experimenting with alternative procedures. Of course all of this is totally harmless, unlike the experiments of the early sixties that used electric shock therapy.

"We do not desert traditional psychiatric treatment, so on top of these other therapies, Molly spends a lot of time with me. If she is cured, I guess we can all claim a bit of the credit. Suba, perhaps you and Dr. Gupta should be getting ready for your therapy session. Will Scott be performing today?"

"Yes ma'am," Dr. Reddy responded. "Scott will be bringing his African goat-skin drums into the therapy room momentarily. It is interesting to watch the expression on Mrs. Allen's face as these various alternative procedures are applied. I will be in the room documenting physical and apparent emotional changes as she is exposed to these two different therapies."

After Dr. Reddy had left the room, Dr. Glasseur walked over to Jake and flashed her sparkling smile at him as she said, "I'm so glad you're back in town. Are you free for dinner tonight, and would you like to use my spare bedroom rather than the hotel?"

"Yes and no," Jake responded. "Yes, I'm free for dinner tonight and would be delighted to have dinner with you, and no, I won't accept your offer of the spare bedroom."

Several minutes later, as Jake and Martinique watched through the one-way mirror, Molly Allen entered the treatment room. In addition to the set of drums now occupying one corner of the room, there was a single, padded, treatment table with fresh sheets but no blankets or other coverings. Moving more briskly than Jake had recalled from his earlier meetings with her, Molly walked directly to the table and easily lay down upon it, face up. The young attendant then pressed a button on the side of the padded table and raised it to a higher elevation.

As it was elevating, a young man with long, blondish hair and a small earring in his left earlobe entered the room and went directly to the set of African drums. Dr. Gupta was right behind him and went immediately to Molly Allen's side. Suba Reddy sat in one corner with a notepad to document the session for inclusion in the report to the grant committee.

"How are you this morning, Mrs. Allen?" Jake heard Dr. Gupta ask as he began to run his large hands over and around Molly's slim body, softly touching parts of her skin but not rubbing or applying any pressure.

Jake could not hear Molly's reply, but Dr. Gupta appeared to be satisfied with the response and continued. "We are pleased that Mr. Parker is here to play his drums for us, and we will proceed with our efforts to restore your kinesis. I can feel that you are stronger today, but here, in the area around your right shoulder and connecting on up over your head, there is still a gap in the field that we must work on. Now just relax while Mr. Parker and I go to work." All the while Dr. Gupta was gently massaging Molly Allen's shoulder and back until he was satisfied that she was fully relaxed and ready to respond to the therapy.

Molly said nothing, but Jake had the sense that she had been listening and was not asleep. Dr. Gupta nodded to Scott Parker as he concluded his gentle touching and soothing comments, and on that signal, Parker began to construct a rhythmic sequence of drum beats that were neither loud nor staccato but consisted of a combination of rhythms and tones that were pleasing even to Jake's skeptical mind. The tempo was soothing yet had a compelling rhythm that drew attention to the sound of the drums and away from other thoughts.

While Parker applied his music therapy, Gupta continued to run his hands over and around Molly Allen's body, occasionally stopping to softly massage a small area, but always delicately and on the surface. Occasionally Gupta would rest his hand over an area of her body, especially around her right shoulder, neck and hand, and would leave the hand there for several minutes as if trying to heal a wound through simple touching, without the application of pressure or friction.

"We have read much literature on the healing quality of physicians who touch their patients, either through efforts at diagnosis or in reassuring the patient that a wound will heal," Dr. Glasseur said, interrupting Jake's fascination with the unusual form of treatment. "The old concept of a 'hands-on physician' has been overlooked by many modern medical schools in deference to surgical intervention and wonder drugs. We believe many illnesses and disorders are generated through the complex interaction between the brain and its extension out into the nerve system of the body. The laying on of hands and touching in those areas that are troubled can provoke a cure that is equally effective without the surgical intervention or chemical treatments promoted by most medical schools. We have made good progress with Molly Allen."

"Marty, I am fascinated with this. Does it really work? What about those drums?"

"Music therapy is in its infancy in this country; however, it has been used for years in Africa and Asia. There are groups around this country who are only now beginning to explore some of the healing characteristics of sound. What we try to accomplish through music therapy is the resurrection of the natural harmony in the body fibers that serves as a protection to the person. These remedies have been practiced in other cultures for centuries, but Western civilization was raised on the Greco-Roman reliance on the five senses. If you can't see, feel, smell, hear or taste it, then it doesn't exist. The theory of Kinesis, or a force around the body that we can't see or feel, is the underlying concept for the Reiki movement. I know it's hard to figure out logically, and for lawyers that can be a problem, but think of it in terms of the people you know who are the so-called 'fast healers' who seem never to get sick and when they do they only stay sick for a short time. Then there are the people you know who are always ill. The fast healers are in harmony with themselves and use their own healing powers to cure whatever is wrong with them. The chronically ill individual is out of harmony with his body, and his natural force offers no protection from injury and illness.

"Enough of this lecturing," Dr. Glasseur said as she turned toward the observation window. "Let's see how the therapy is going. As you can see, Scott keeps a basic cadence and volume. Over the last week we have tried a number of different tonal programs from loud and fast to very slow, calming and quiet. As we try different tones we alter the cadence and intensity of the drum sound. Dr. Gupta is able through his training to sense Molly's autonomic or spontaneous reaction to the music. Two days ago he sensed a real change while listening to a particular combination of tone and cadence generated by the drums. Notice that we do not use music in its ordinary sense, either classical or modern, because it is too complex. The mind focuses on the song or harmony instead of allowing the whole body to absorb the sound. We want the body to feel the drum beat without thinking or relying on sight or the normal sensory perception of sound. If the music is too complex, the mind takes over and there is no benefit. We keep the drums to three or four different tones and a consistent although slightly irregular cadence."

The therapy session continued for another thirty minutes, during which time the drums and Dr. Gupta continued uninterrupted by outside sound and without speaking to the patient. Jake had no idea whether or not Molly Allen was awake through this session. She did not move throughout the procedure. At the end of the session, the drums stopped and Dr. Gupta invited Molly to sit up on the bed with her legs hanging over the side.

"How do you feel, Molly?" Gupta asked in a quiet and friendly voice. "I could feel the healing that was going on in your body. Could you feel the healing?"

"I feel much better. My mind is not so confused, and I can remember so much more than yesterday. It's as if someone turned on the lights in the room, and I can see what's there. I don't understand what you're doing, but I want to keep going until all of the lights in the house are on, and I can see and remember everything." As she said this, a wistful smile crossed Molly Allen's face, and Jake could see a faint twinkle in her beautiful deep blue eyes that he hoped was an indication of greater cognition than he had ever seen in her before.

"We will continue for as long as it takes, Molly. Scott and I are here to restore your whole body to its former equilibrium. We are making progress, and you should be proud of yourself," Dr. Gupta reassured her.

Molly Allen smiled back at Dr. Gupta, waited as he pressed the button to lower the treatment table, then stepped off and left the examining room with the assistance of the attractive young attendant who had originally brought her in.

"I really don't understand," Jake said as he turned away from the one-way mirror and looked at Dr. Glasseur.

She responded with a simple explanation. "We in this country are only just beginning to understand some of the healing remedies that have been used in other countries for years. You have a right to be skeptical since you, like so many others in this country, are accustomed to traditional treatments supported by the AMA and drug manufacturers. There is nothing physically wrong with Molly Allen. We have established that through blood tests and physical examination. Through our nutrition program here at the hospital and a regular course of non-stressful exercise, Molly Allen is physiologically healthy and physically fit. But we all know that something very serious is troubling her mind.

"Just as we have no way of actually knowing what an animal sees, we have no way of actually sensing what a mentally confused person sees or smells or hears. We take for granted that red is red, but sometimes to them red is black or green or yellow. We assume that people can hear what we hear, but sometimes the translation is all wrong and, to the mentally impaired, it's like hearing Chinese or the shrill tones of a facsimile machine. Part of our therapy rests on finding out whether the patient is experiencing any of these aberrations in what we take for granted as our basic senses. Until we know more about what she sees, feels, smells and hears while she is in her transcendent state, we don't want to attack the problem chemically. We could only do it on a hit or miss basis. Long therapy sessions might break through the wall of silence, but it could take a long, long time and each session might add to the basic problem. So, we are trying something different and non-threatening.

"Think of it this way," Dr. Glasseur continued almost as a schoolteacher might instruct a precocious child. "Molly Allen's mind is like a puzzle with many pieces all scattered about waiting to be reassembled. Sometimes we can reassemble those pieces through consultations and group therapies where individuals basically try to sort themselves out with a little help from us. In Molly's case, consultation was inappropriate. Even the gentlest probing resulted in her lapsing into the unconscious world of her fears. Since that method of therapy would have only limited chances of success, we tried something else, which, I will admit, is somewhat experimental."

Raising his hand, Jake interjected. "Enough. I don't understand how it works, but she looks better to me. When can I see her and ask her a few questions?"

"Based on our observations so far," Dr. Glasseur continued, "we believe the best time for you to ask her questions will be immediately after her morning therapy. Will you be here tomorrow?"

"You bet," Jake quickly responded.

"I have a full schedule of patients this afternoon, but I should be done by six," Dr. Glasseur explained. "I'm glad you are free for dinner tonight. I want to hear about your trip to Crosswind. How about I pick you up at your hotel around 7:30? Dress casual."

"It's a deal," Jake responded. "I'm at the Hyatt."

CHAPTER 25

Jake waited outside the front entrance of the Hyatt Regency, enjoying the warm evening breeze that helped to clear his mind from the tangle of information combed out of the stack of documents assembled for him by Carol Brooks. After his morning meeting with Dr. Glasseur and observation of Molly's alternative therapy session, he had returned to the hotel and spent the rest of the day reading and trying to understand the relevant information. His mind was exhausted, and his fingers were tired from taking notes that would allow him to go back to certain documents and study them more carefully. As so often happens in complex cases, Jake had the sense that there was an unexplained inconsistency. It was his task to bring his mind to focus on pieces of the facts; to analyze them, check their basic logic and consistency, categorize them, and then store these facts and inferences in the legal part of his mind. As he analyzed each piece of the puzzle, he would bounce new facts against old and hope to find a clue. The legal mind works twenty-four hours a day, and in Jake's experience the answer to nagging questions, the clue that ultimately points to the solution, often presented itself in the morning during a hot shower, at lunch with colleagues discussing a completely unrelated matter, or sometimes during those rare moments in the office when the phone did not ring.

As these thoughts were crashing through Jake's mind, a black Peugeot convertible with its top down pulled into the circle drive in front of the Hyatt entrance, and Martinique Glasseur flashed one of her beaming smiles at Jake as he strolled toward the car. She looked more striking than ever. Her black hair lay softly on a white silk blouse unbuttoned just low enough for Jake to see the start of her cleavage. A single strand of small, white pearls graced her neck. She wore no other jewelry. As Jake climbed into the spotlessly clean convertible, he quickly noticed and approved of the stonewashed jeans that fit her trim body like a glove.

"I thought we'd hit one of the Tex-Mex restaurants over on the south side of town. Are you up for a little burrito with hot chili sauce, or maybe a barbecued pork fajita?"

"Sounds great," Jake yelled over the throaty roar of the Peugeot as it accelerated away from the Hyatt Regency Hotel.

One hundred and twenty miles away another dinner was already in progress. The food around the solid oak table in the private dining room of the Crosswind Country Club was, to a large extent, a reflection of the people who had ordered their meal. Hathaway, the corpulent banker, had ordered the club's special 22-ounce T-bone steak with a side order of scalloped potatoes and fresh asparagus. Beamer, the accountant, had ordered a grilled chicken salad with dressing on the side. Stern had ordered surf 'n' turf—two African lobster tails, a six-ounce filet mignon and julienne of vegetables. It was the most expensive meal on the menu. Chambers, owner and editor of the weekly newspaper, had ordered prime rib of beef, which came floating in beef gravy with a side order of garlic mashed potatoes and Yorkshire pudding. Rounding out the cast of Crosswind elite was the newest member, Jim O'Connor, owner of the Ford dealership. His plate contained a large porterhouse steak and huge Idaho baked potato smothered in sour cream, butter and cheddar cheese.

As usual, Hathaway took the lead and raised his half-full glass of merlot in toast to his comrades. "Gentlemen, we have reached a milestone. I understand that probate of the estate of Paul Chambers has, as of this week, finally been settled and that John is now truly the owner of the Crosswind Gazette." Hathaway raised his wine glass several inches higher to salute his friends around the table, nodded at John Chambers, who appeared to be uncomfortable about anyone toasting the death of his father almost six years ago, then drained his glass of merlot before returning the empty glass to the table.

Dinner was swift with each man aggressively stuffing the oversized portions of food into a willing mouth. After the meal, as several men sucked on expensive cigars and others played with their after-dinner drinks, Eric Beamer interrupted the indulgence.

"I hate to mix business with pleasure, but yesterday I received a statement from our associate, Mr. Kruger, for his most recent services on our behalf. He attached to his statement a log of the activities of Mr. McCarthy while in our fair town including several trips to Red Rock Park and a rather lengthy dinner meeting with old man Mobley here at the Country Club. He even went out to dinner with your floor manager, Bill. Kruger didn't report what they said. Too noisy out in that Del Toro dump. Kruger charged $200 per hour, which is twice his normal rate. His cover letter attempts to explain the high rate by the urgency with which we requested his services and the excuse that he had to set aside other business in order to service us. While the hourly rate seems unreasonably high, I don't see that we have any choice other than paying his fee. He knows far too much about us and our master plan, and he participated in too many of its parts for us to risk his leaking information to the authorities. What say you?"

"What's it total up to, Eric?" O'Connor asked.

"$27,573.22 including costs," Beamer responded in a monotone voice.

An assortment of groans, whistles and sounds of disbelief emanated from around the table. Finally, Hathaway spoke. "That's more than Kruger charged us for any of his other services which were far more difficult than simply tracking someone around town. Did you check with him to see if maybe he made a mistake?"

Beamer again spoke in a near monotone voice, "I called but he was unavailable. I then checked his time records and realized he was on a 24-hour clock for the entire time, beginning with our call to him in Little Rock and his return to Little Rock. He charged us for every hour at $200 per hour. The math is correct."

"Do you think he's trying to blackmail us?" Stern asked. "I mean, does he think he can charge us any amount of money, and we'll pay just to keep him from telling people what he did? I mean, he's as guilty as we are."

"Yeah, we paid him to do it, but he did it. Do you think he'd really tell the police?" Chambers asked. "I know I just got dad's estate, but it cost me a lot of money, and I don't have a lot of money. I own the damn paper, but it's so far in debt that I doubt it will ever be worth anything. It's running me dry."

Hathaway spoke up in his officious voice and said, "That comes to about $5,500 a person. Surely you have that much money from your old man's estate, John. Quit crying poverty. My old man made it so I have to live off the money I make out of the bank and the small amount that his trust pays me. I suggest that we not use Mr. Kruger again. You're right, he knows too much about our business and is personally responsible for too many of the skeletons in our closets, if you know what I mean."

"That's not even funny, Bill," Stern said angrily. "I still get nightmares thinking about what we have done, and it doesn't help for you to make light of it. Does the log or any of Kruger's report tell us much about what happened while McCarthy was in town?"

"Not really," Beamer responded. "He did manage to get into McCarthy's computer, and some of the memoranda back to his office are revealing. I guess poor Molly Allen is a fruitcake. According to one of the memoranda, she doesn't remember anything. I don't think she's a threat to us unless somehow they are able to restore her memory. Even then, I don't think Richard told her very much about his business or Red Rock."

"Eric, you and Howard have told us all along that legally and financially all of the tracks have been covered. Have you checked again?" O'Connor asked.

"I am confident that there is nothing in the legal documents that could possibly implicate any one of us," Stern responded. "We were careful then, we are careful now, and we need to be careful in the future."

"Richard's books are clean as a whistle," Beamer chimed in. "They weren't bad before, but just to be sure, I went back and redid the entire journal entry and reconciliation program before the Feds came into town. If he was stupid enough to put his entire dealership and his home up as collateral for the development, then he was stupid enough to lose it all. I hate dealing with stupid people. It's too bad that Richard happened to be a nice, stupid person."

"Then we are ready to begin the next phase of our efforts?"

"I still need some cash to pay this bill," Beamer retorted. It comes to $5,514.64 each, and if you would prefer not to write checks at this time, I must have the money in our investment company account by the close of business tomorrow. Any method of transfer is fine. I don't think Mr. Kruger is going to take any discount in this fee, and I agree with Bill that we should probably not use him again although he has been very valuable to our cause. With the exception of Howard's father, he was very efficient."

Several checkbooks came out on the table, and checks made payable to Crosswind New Generation Investment Company, LLC, were handed over to Eric Beamer for deposit into the company account.

"Are we agreed that the next phase of our endeavor will be to get Howard appointed to the federal bench to replace Judge Swain when he retires this summer?" Hathaway asked.

Muffled responses in the affirmative accompanied by the nodding of heads came unanimously from around the table. "Good, because I have already set wheels in motion. I am having coffee with President Clinton at the White House Thursday after next, and I have been assured that I will have time to speak privately with him about Crosswind and Howard's appointment to succeed his father. After I received the invitation two weeks ago, I had to convince my board that it was in the bank's best interest for me to attend this coffee with the president. It cost the bank a lot of money, but this is an election year, and the president's campaign advisers have hinted that the President is considering 'modernization' of the banking industry by focusing new regulations on small, local banks with the possible intent of forcing mergers with the regional or national banks. That is what I told my board, and I now have specific instructions to speak directly with the President to try to stop this new pan. I'll put in a good word for my bank, but I primarily want to bring up Howard's name. It is critical that we have influence on the federal bench in Crosswind."

CHAPTER 26

Jake rolled over in his king-size bed on the top floor of the Hyatt Regency and opened his left eye just enough to see the digital readout on the clock radio. He groaned, rolled off the side of the bed and slowly made his way to the bathroom for his morning ablutions. As the hot shower cascaded down on his pounding head, Jake began to sort through the information and feelings that had occupied so much of the night before.

Dr. Glasseur had taken him to a small Tex-Mex restaurant well out of the downtown Oklahoma City area on the southwest side. Although Jake doubted whether the restaurant could ever have passed a health inspection, he had to admit that the food was good, very spicy, and plentiful. Of more serious concern at the moment, however, were the quality, size and ingredients of the margaritas, a pitcher of which had appeared on the table even before he or Martinique had ordered drinks. The pitcher never went dry, and the spicy food encouraged consumption.

Dinner at El Sids was an event rather than just a meal. Unlike many Mexican restaurants where menus are standardized and profits are made through volume of meals sold rather than quality or presentation, El Sids expected its customers to come for the evening, stay for the entertainment, and drink. Food was secondary, presentation non-existent. El Sids was, above all else, a watering hole for those who love tequila and spicy food cooked in Mexican olive oil. Its mark of distinction was its total lack of pretense. Its patrons liked El Sids for what it was and what it wasn't.

The food service was intentionally slow while the barmaids seemed to anticipate a need for refill of whatever particular brand alcoholic beverage may have been desired. Half an hour after their arrival, a swarthy Mexican, probably in his fifties and wearing a large sombrero, entered the main dining room through a small door in the back of the building. He walked directly to a platform that had been placed approximately in the middle of the dining room area. On the platform were a stool and a guitar stand into which the Mexican placed a highly polished Gibson guitar without apparent electrical amplification.

The Mexican ceremoniously removed his massive sombrero, retrieved the guitar from the guitar stand, and placed his colorful hat on the guitar stand. Perched on the stool with his guitar strapped over his shoulder, he began playing and singing a continuous series of Mexican ballads. Three and a half hours later, when Jake and Martinique finally stood to leave El Sids, the Mexican was still sitting on the stool and still playing and singing Mexican tunes. Neither his voice nor the dexterity of his fingers seemed to falter even after Jake and a number of the other patrons had conveyed their appreciation through free drinks and $20 tips.

Jake had never found it difficult to talk with Martinique, and dinner at El Sids was no exception. The music was a wonderful backdrop for their chatter, and business did not interfere with the relaxed euphoria that resulted from an overdose of spicy pork and refried beans and more margaritas than Jake could count.

Through the haze of his hangover and the driving relief of the hot shower, Jake remembered asking about Molly's condition and marveling at the clarity of Martinique's explanation of her treatment even as Jake was having trouble absorbing the information. Either Dr. Glasseur had a very high tolerance to alcohol, or she was a consummate actor. As Jake leaned forward in the shower to try to stretch out a few kinks in his back, he recalled her description of Molly's condition as physically strong with no apparent brain damage. He wondered whether the same were true of his mental and physical state following a night out with Dr. Glasseur. As he lathered up his body with the Hyatt's hand-blocked body soap, Jake's mind focused on the broad smile that crossed Martinique's face showcasing her perfect teeth and supple lips as she dispensed with the business part of their dinner meeting before convincing Jake to relax and forget about Molly Allen until the following morning.

"You are still planning to come and observe tomorrow's session?" Martinique had asked.

Jake had responded in the affirmative, and Martinique quickly set the tone for the rest of the evening. "In that case, let's not talk business any more. You can ask me all the questions you want tomorrow morning while we're waiting for the therapy session to finish. Then you can ask Molly a few questions."

Jake smiled as he reached for his can of shaving cream, taking special care not to lose his balance. His head and body were still suffering from tequila, limejuice, refried beans and hot chili peppers. Jake was not sure what El Sids put in its margaritas, but he remembers how good it tasted at the time and how bad it felt this morning. After lathering his face, he carefully reached for his disposable razor and proceeded with the morning routine of scraping yesterday's growth of hair from his angular face.

His recollection of the rest of the evening was less precise. As he pulled the razor across his face, a rapid succession of vivid flashbacks of the drive back from the restaurant with the top down and the warm Oklahoma night air bathing them in the sweet smell of spring. He remembered Martinique pulling her car off the main road and into a small park that overlooked Oklahoma City. Off in the distance the city lights dwindled to insignificance against the vast western sky that was ablaze with stars. Only a sliver of a crescent moon diminished the near absolute black of the sky as it contrasted with the sparkle of a billion lights. The immenseness of the universe was breathtaking as Jake and Martinique tried to comprehend the sanctity of a perfect display of Mother Nature's brilliance.

Thirty minutes later and ten minutes late for the start of the therapy session, Jake entered the observation room on the fifth floor of the hospital where, the day before, he had first seen the application of music and touch therapy on his client. Dr. Glasseur was talking to a group of young residents and Ph.D. psychology candidates about the benefits of multiple kinds of psychiatric intervention and the importance of exploring different modalities looking for the key that would unlock a disturbed mind.

"What makes this program different from other unconventional therapies is the conjunction of music therapy with massage or touch therapy," she concluded. "See how Dr. Gupta communicates with Scott Parker. This is good. I have not seen Dr. Gupta quite as excited. I think he's making significant headway."

Although Jake had arrived too late to hear Dr. Glasseur's full explanation of Molly's treatment to her entourage of residents and therapists, he was able to watch Dr. Gupta through the observation window as he went through his routine of gentle massage of the invisible force around Molly Allen.

He looked on Dr. Glasseur with a new appreciation. He had wondered how she would look this morning after their indulgences of the night before. Until then she had been entirely professional in her relationship with Jake and Molly Allen, but her consumption of spicy food and tequila during their dinner and as they enjoyed the warm night under the endless Oklahoma sky were far from the usual persona of the chairwoman of the department of psychiatry. He greeted her with an enthusiastic "Good morning" and a slightly sheepish grin as the words sent a sharp pain through his head. His body was still trying to overcome the natural consequences of his over-consumption of the food and drink at El Sids.

"And a very good morning it is," responded Dr. Glasseur with a twinkle in her eye and a broad smile which Jake took as a sign that she had powers of recovery way better than his. She introduced Jake to the residents who appeared to be skeptical of the program, but they were respectful of the department chair and listened intently.

"Those drums are really unique. I don't suppose they were purchased out of any medical supply catalogue?" Jake asked lightheartedly after the students had left.

"West African. Parker is just getting started in this business, and there isn't much money in it. We got a grant from the O.U. Foundation for Alternative Medicine to further our research into holistic medicine. We were able to purchase those drums for Parker on condition that he help train one of our interns who has expressed an interest in learning more about the philosophy of music therapy. Those drums are Scott's most precious possession. See how he has developed a constant rhythm. He and Gupta have found a synchronous tone and cadence that seem to be working." The excitement in Glasseur's voice was evident.

Twenty minutes later she and Jake waited in one of the small conference rooms for Molly Allen to be brought in by Dr. Reddy. Jake was not prepared for what happened.

When Molly entered the room in the company of Dr. Reddy, Jake immediately noticed a far more relaxed composure, complete with a broad smile on her face and twinkle in her blue eyes that had been totally lacking in his prior encounters. The demons that had controlled her mind for the past several months were at bay, and at least for the time being she appeared normal and responsive. Jake hoped that the transformation was permanent; however, Dr. Glasseur had warned him that post-traumatic stress disorders often are recurrent and impossible to eliminate completely.

"How are you, Molly?" Jake asked as she entered the room.

"I feel like a great weight has been lifted off of my head and shoulders, and suddenly for the first time in a long time I can remember things without struggling. I feel well. Dr. Reddy is taking me over to the big swimming pool at the university this afternoon, and I hope to do at least a hundred laps. How are you, Mr. McCarthy?"

"I'm fine," Jake responded, and after complimenting her on how well she looked, asked, "and how is your memory of what happened back in Crosswind?"

"Jake, I found Richard's body. They say he committed suicide, but I know my Richard, and he could never have committed suicide. He lacked the courage. He was a good and a loving husband. I know he was terribly upset over our financial situation, but we had worked out a plan. The night before his death we had enjoyed an evening full of hope and promise. We were prepared to sell the dealership and our home. We had even picked out a more modest house on the east side of town out toward cattle country.

"Richard told me that he had recently found information concerning his partners in Red Rock Savings and Loan that cast a whole new picture on the venture. He wouldn't discuss it with me, but he as much as told me that White Sands, where we were going to retire, was a sham."

"Did he tell you how he got so far in debt?" Jake asked, trying not to act overly excited or to put undue pressure on his client.

"Not really. We talked about possibly losing the dealership because of the Red Rock losses, and he talked about not being able to rely on his friends. The funny thing about it was that those fellows have been doing things together all their lives, and for the first time that I can ever remember Richard finally figured out what the rest of us had known pretty much all along. He was calling them nasty names and vowed that he would not let them get away with it, whatever 'it' might have been. It seemed to me like Richard had a mission that he was undertaking, and that would just not fit with his going out and committing suicide. Mr. McCarthy, I lived with Richard for forty-eight years, and he just wasn't that kind of person. I hate to say it, but he really did lack the courage to do it."

"Molly, did Richard have any other office or place where he might keep documents that could explain why he was so far in debt?"

"No. He used his dealership office for all of his business. We had a small office in our house, but Howard said I didn't need to keep any of his personal papers since he had copies. They were destroyed when the liquidators sold off our furniture. That happened so fast, but Howard kept assuring me that it was the only way to protect what value there was left in our assets. We did have a safe deposit box at First State Bank, and there might be some papers there."

"I'll check," Jake said, "Do you have a key?"

"I have a key in my purse. Richard gave it to me the night before he…died. I don't know what it is to, but he told me to take good care of it."

"Great!" Jake exclaimed, showing a sense of relief at possibly finding a clue. "Did Richard have any relatives or friends with whom he might have confided about his newfound information?"

"No," Molly responded. "Richard was an only son, and Richard's father had no siblings. Richard's mother had an older sister who lived in Illinois, but she died several years ago. We were the last of the Allens. I think Richard was always upset that we didn't have an heir to carry on his family name, but he refused to consent to any extraordinary means for us to conceive, and for him adoption was out of the question."

"How are you feeling, Molly?" Dr. Glasseur asked, interrupting the flow of questions.

"I feel fine," she quickly responded, then resumed her conversation with Jake. I don't know what happened to me after Richard's death. It's like a void in my life that I hope someone will fill in, but I feel like I am on the other side of that wall of confusion."

"Did you and Richard ever own a cottage or cabin or someplace where he might have put information on whatever he had discovered about Red Rock?" Jake asked.

"We had a cabin up on the lake about an hour northeast of Crosswind, but we had to sell it in 1993 to cover some of our debts. Of course, we were thinking of buying a place in White Sands once the resort community was about halfway done, but that didn't work, and we had no other places. We loved our house, and Richard loved his country club. I'd like to think that his papers are boxed up somewhere in storage, and maybe they are, but I seem to recall watching all of our possessions being auctioned off and taking a cab to the motel with only a suitcase full of my personal clothing. It was terrible. I had no one to protect me. I think if anything pushed me over the edge, it was seeing my life disappear and not being able to do anything to prevent it."

"Jake," Dr. Glasseur interjected. "Go easy, and Molly, don't let these questions upset you. We have plenty of time to sort this all out."

"I want to get to the bottom of this, and I won't rest until we do," Molly responded with a defiance that contrasted with her demure passiveness of a few weeks earlier. "What else can I tell you, Jake?"

"Didn't you have any legal help?" Jake asked.

"Of course, Howard Stern and his law firm represented me in the bankruptcy proceedings and in the probate of Richard's will. They did it for free, but it seemed like they pushed the process along pretty fast. Howard tried to console me, but he kind of made me mad because he kept putting all the blame on Richard, who was unable to defend himself."

Molly paused, her mind working on some thought as yet unformed. Doctors Glasseur and Reddy stood ready to intercede, but before they could stop her, Molly continued. "Richard was quite a car nut even when we were first dating. His father always provided him with a nice car, and he maintained them perfectly. I don't think I ever rode in a dirty car, and Richard changed oil more often than he changed filters on our furnace."

Jake was momentarily stunned by the rapid change of topics and Molly's ability to reflect on the good times when she and Richard were first married. He said nothing as she continued.

"Richard had some old cars that he kept out in the work shed at the back of the dealership property. His dad kind of gave him that shed as a place where he could go and be by himself. Richard would spend hours working on his cars, making sure they ran just right, polishing the chrome and cleaning the upholstery. His cars always looked perfect. I can remember visiting him out there one day when he was working with steel wool on the wood panels of his old '48 Ford wagon. That's the one he always took in the parade. Each year he'd strip it down and put a really fine coat of varnish on the wood, just in time for the next parade. My but we loved that wagon." A wistful smile came over Molly's face as she again paused to gather her thoughts. This time the two doctors sat tight waiting for the next bit of information.

"That old shed wasn't much to look at, and after he sold off his cars in the spring of 1994, he didn't go back there much. I kind of recall his having a small office out there to keep his repair manuals and documents on the authenticity of his cars. If there were a place that he might keep important pieces of paper and stuff other than his office in our house or his office at the dealership, it just might be out there in that shed. He used to call it his hideaway and safe house, but it isn't much more than an old run-down repair shop that has long outlived its usefulness. I think Richard's father would have torn it down but for the pleasure that Richard got from just puttering around in that old place." As Molly spoke these words her voice trailed off to a whisper and her eyes began to focus on nothing. She spoke no more.

"Molly, I am about to go back out to Crosswind," Jake said softly, trying to divert Molly's mind away from the tragedy that pushed her into her stress disorder. "I want to continue my investigation into the circumstances of Richard's death and the disposition of his assets. Mr. Parker has secured a very comfortable apartment for you to use not far from here, and Dr. Glasseur has assured me that she and her staff will continue to work with you to minimize the impact of those horrible memories. You are scheduled to be discharged Friday morning."

Molly made no response.

"Is that okay?" Jake asked after a short pause waiting for some sign of recognition.

Finally, Dr. Reddy gently took Molly by her hand and led her back to her room.

"I have undone all of your good work," Jake said, turning to Dr. Glasseur in alarm. "She seemed so normal and spoke so freely of Richard, then…."

"This is to be expected, Jake," Dr. Glasseur responded quickly. "Her mental condition is still very fragile, but she must realize that she soon will be required to cope with society and living by herself. We can only keep her here in her acute phase, and she is now almost through that phase and well on the road to recovery. Remember, it is a long process, and there will be stumbling blocks along the way. You have done no permanent damage. That damage was done by the trauma of Richard's death. She is still having trouble coping with the vision of Richard's mangled body. It must have been horrible."

CHAPTER 27

The digital temperature gauge on his rental car read 104 degrees as Jake pulled into the parking lot of the Best Western Suites Motel in Crosswind. When he stepped out of the comfortably air conditioned car, Jake was met with a blast of hot, humid air made only slightly more bearable by the breeze that cascaded over the western plains, driving sand and tumbleweed into Crosswind. After leaving Molly at the hospital on the day previous, Jake had spent the entire afternoon and well into the night restudying the pile of documents that Carol Brooks had assembled on Red Rock Savings and Loan. The venture was doomed from its inception. It was both undercapitalized and staffed with inexperienced and often underpaid management.

Although the members of the executive committee of the board of directors were each paid $200,000 a year for their services, the chief operating officer of the savings and loan received only $75,000 in salary and the next highest paid employee dropped to the level of a retail clerk. Predictably, Howard Stern was the attorney for the Savings and Loan, and Eric Beamer its accountant. William Hathaway was elected president of the board of directors and acted as its CEO. Richard Allen was a member of the board of directors, but was not an officer or on the executive committee. He received no compensation. O'Connor's name appeared nowhere.

Carol Brooks had run all of the corporate documents and financial statements through the mergers and acquisition department of the law firm and the tax department for comments. Each had prepared a memorandum of their findings and observations. Each concluded that there was little or no substance to the S&L, that it was improperly formed, undercapitalized and poorly managed. Despite that fact, both departments reported that the documents were well drafted and in good order for purposes of filing with the Federal Savings and Loan Insurance Corporation, state and federal bank regulators and the Internal Revenue Service. The form was proper. The content, had anybody taken the time to read it, was full of holes.

After changing into his lawyer's uniform of blue pinstriped suit and red tie, Jake drove to the First State Bank of Crosswind to meet, once again, with William Hathaway. When he arrived at the bank, Judy Falsworth was waiting for him in the parking lot and beckoned Jake to follow her into a coffee shop through a rear entrance that backed up to the side of the parking lot. Jake followed without saying a word.

Once seated, Ms. Falsworth began speaking softly but with a rapid cadence. "You've got him scared. He's like a frightened walrus. He and Mr. Beamer have been talking to each other all morning about the questions you asked yesterday afternoon when you called to make the appointment to continue your review of the financial records. I wasn't able to hear what they were saying, but I know Beamer did most of the talking."

"Do they have something to hide?" Jake asked. "I figured that I might stir them up a bit, but I must confess that I was kind of shooting in the dark. All I really planned to do was look at the loan documents and review the bank records on Allen Ford. I did check with Ford Motor Company, and there just doesn't seem to be any good reason related to car sales for Richard to have been in such bad financial condition. Of course, if Mr. Hathaway is a little anxious, I wouldn't want to let his anxiety dissipate by not being there on time."

"No, Mr. Beamer is gone, and Tubby…Mr. Hathaway has calmed down. You can always tell with him. He starts sweating like a pig, and then pulls out that pillowcase that he calls a handkerchief and just starts mopping up the water. Out of respect for Allen senior, and just maybe for Mr. Hathaway senior, I thought I would suggest some things that you might look for among Richard's papers. After you left last week I managed to find and read some of the loan documents.

"As you know he was deeply in debt to the bank. From 1991 through the summer of 1994, Richard Allen borrowed in his own name or for the dealership over four million dollars, pledging as collateral not only all of his stock in the dealership, but also his house and literally everything he owned. He even borrowed against his pension. The bank, and I fault Tubby for this, allowed him to get in way over his head. Poor Mrs. Allen signed every one of the loan documents. She trusted Richard, and he trusted his banker, who, after all is said and done, allowed him to go so far in debt that he…well, he killed himself."

After a few seconds to regain her composure Falsworth continued. "What seemed a bit strange to me was that all of the loans carried a relatively high rate of interest, sometimes over 14%, but mostly in the range of 12.2 to 13%. Other customers of the bank were borrowing at 8.5 or 9 percent, but his loans were always double digit. I had assumed that these loans were taken to provide working capital for the dealership, but after you were here last time I began to think about the revenue generated from that dealership and wondered why Richard would require all this cash. As I told you, I am normally on the loan committee, but for these loans Mr. Hathaway acted alone. We never saw the documents or the terms of the loans. I think Stern drafted them for the bank.

"I checked, and during that period Mr. Allen didn't build a new house, didn't buy any expensive toys, drove dealership cars, and didn't live beyond his means, yet he borrowed all that money. I don't know why. After Richard committed suicide, it was the bank that moved immediately to put the probate estate into bankruptcy. I always thought that was ruthless of Hathaway to go after his ex-friend's estate like that, but I never said anything."

"Anything else?" Jake asked after a long pause.

"That's all I know, so maybe you better get on to your meeting," Falsworth responded, noticeably more relaxed after imparting this information.

"Thank you very much for your information, Judy, I'll be sure not to mention it to Mr. Hathaway or Mr. Beamer. Perhaps you should stay here and finish your coffee while I walk over to the bank."

Leaving a few dollars on the table to pay for the coffee that he had barely touched, Jake departed for his meeting, and in a few minutes entered the bank and was pleased to be greeted with a hearty welcome from its president.

"Well, Mr. McCarthy!" Hathaway bellowed as Jake entered through the massive front door. "Have you been successful in unearthing any new assets for the Allen estate? How is dear Molly? For that matter, where is she? I would like to write her a note of sympathy about the death of Richard and offer my services to help her reestablish her life here in Crosswind, if she has a mind to return."

"That is very generous of you, Mr. Hathaway, but Molly is in good hands right now and recovering nicely from her ordeal. When she is ready, I will tell her that you would like to help get her back on her feet, and I'm sure she will contact you." By this time they had reached Hathaway's large office, and Jake was invited in.

"I would like to ask you some questions about Red Rock Savings and Loan," Jake continued, as he sat down in one of Hathaway's green leather chairs opposite his massive mahogany desk. "I believe you were its president and CEO? Is that right?"

"Yes," Hathaway responded hesitantly.

"How was it capitalized?"

"Well," Hathaway paused, "I guess I'm not at liberty to say, it being a corporation and all. I'll need to talk with the board and get approval to discuss it with you."

"Perhaps you can tell me who promoted the idea of the White Sands Land Development?" Jake continued as if in a deposition. No response. "Do you maintain the books and records of Red Rock Savings and Loan here at this bank, or are they located somewhere else? I would like to go over those books and records so that I can get a better understanding of the losses incurred by my client's deceased husband." The last questions were intentionally pointed and strung together so that Hathaway had no chance to think of an answer to one question before the next was asked. Jake had used this technique on cross examination when he knew the witness had the answers but was refusing to talk. Sometimes if he shot enough penetrating questions the witness would try to stop him by answering one seemingly innocent question which would lead to more until the witness would either clam up completely or come clean with the information. About half the time it worked.

The sweat on Hathaway's red face was popping like the moisture on a cold pitcher of cherry Kool-Aid on a humid midwestern summer afternoon. Jake noticed a slight tremor in his hands as he reached for his oversized handkerchief and began wiping away the streams of sweat before it hit his shirt collar. The bellowing voice that had greeted Jake upon entering the bank was replaced with a slow, deliberate and forced response.

"The books and records are kept by Eric Beamer, the accountant and CPA for Red Rock. I have none." Hathaway said no more in response to the string of questions.

"I understand from looking at the court records that Richard Allen had borrowed a substantial amount of money from this bank. Do you recall making those loans to him?" Jake asked, trying to keep pressure on the fat banker.

"No, I don't recall, but this bank makes thousands of loans every month and it would be unlikely that I would recall any specific loans to Richard or anyone else. Do you know when or how many?"

"I think the records indicated loans were made between 1991 and August of 1994. Since the bank was Allen's and Allen Ford's major creditor and was the first creditor to petition the Circuit Court to place the dealership and the Allens in involuntary bankruptcy immediately following Richard's death, I would think that you would have remembered loaning money to your longtime friend. Now do you recall?"

"I vaguely remember reluctantly approving the filing of bankruptcy papers on poor Richard's estate after his death. It was a terrible thing to do to a dear friend, but business is business and I needed to protect the bank. We had probably over-extended our loans, and Richard crumbled under the strain."

"You do recall making loans, then?" Jake asked.

"Yes, now that you mention the filing for bankruptcy, I do recall some loans."

Jake waited a few moments before responding, and then carefully choosing his words asked Hathaway, "I understand that Richard personally borrowed over four million dollars from the bank between 1991 and 1994. Can you tell me exactly why he borrowed this money?"

"That is confidential information between a banker and his customer, and I am not at liberty to tell you what was told to me in confidence by Richard Allen. I'm sorry, but if I told you, then the state banking regulators would be all over me, threatening to take my license for divulging a secret." Hathaway reached into the rear pocket of his suspendered pants and retrieved another large white handkerchief with which he mopped his face and neck. The perspiration had trickled into the corners of his left eye and down one of his cheeks as he worked at drying the ever-present wetness.

"The air conditioner in here seems not to be working properly. Would you like to take off your suit coat?" Hathaway asked as he feebly attempted to change the subject.

"No thanks," Jake responded. "The temperature in here seems to be just about right. Now, Mr. Hathaway, you and I both know that there is no banker-client privilege recognized in the laws of this state, and furthermore that whatever privilege there may have been died with Mr. Allen. You also know that I represent Molly Allen and that I have her power of attorney to review any bank documents and gather any information relating to her or her husband. You have two choices. Either you disclose those loan documents to me in their entirety with all backup materials, all credit checks and all supporting memoranda, or I go ask the court for a subpoena forcing you to disclose those documents to me. Which one do you want?"

"I will need to call Mr. Stern. Would you mind waiting in the office across the hall? I will have an answer for you shortly," Hathaway responded, apparently pleased that he had found a solution to his current predicament.

Jake rose from the green leather chair and walked across the hall to the small office that he had occupied a week before. His blood was at the boiling point, yet externally he maintained his composure and allowed his temper to subside as he waited for Hathaway to check with his lawyer. Apparently the information Judy Falsworth had provided struck a sensitive nerve. It was now time to ask the question that he hoped would unlock the mystery of what happened to Richard and why. "I would also like to have access to Mrs. Allen's safe deposit box. I have her key," Jake said to Hathaway as they were about to enter the small office set up for Jake.

Half an hour later Hathaway came to the door of the office. Judy Falsworth was carrying a carton full of legal documents, which Jake assumed were the loan documents he had demanded. From the doorway Hathaway almost triumphantly reported to Jake that the Allen's safe deposit box had been opened by the Probate Court and the contents had been surrendered to that Court for disposition. Jake accepted the information without visible sign of regret, but his one possible lead had just dried up.

"Stern said to let you see the files, so here they are. Hard to believe that Richard could go so far in debt. I really had no idea. I'll be in my office if you need me." Howard Stern had successfully defused the cross examination, but Jake knew Hathaway's weakness. Jake could resume the interrogation at any time. Hathaway was smart enough to be stupid in his responses to direct questions.

Jake immediately began studying the documents and drawing a small schematic of the loan transactions that had commenced in 1991 and seemed to continue on a regular basis until just prior to Richard's death. The documents did not disclose the purpose for the loans, so Jake looked carefully through all of the documents and attachments to see if there were any reasonable explanation for the substantial indebtedness. From his prior look at the bank records Jake knew that the dealership was throwing off pretty decent monthly payments to Richard, so why did he personally borrow four million dollars over four years? And why was there nothing to show for it? From all accounts Richard was not a gambler, and his vintage car collection could not have cost that kind of money.

As Jake came to the bottom of the box he found in one of the last of the loan files an unsealed envelope addressed to Richard Allen with the bank's name and trademark on the face of the envelope. Jake opened the envelope and removed the single-page letter. He was surprised to see that it was a letter from Allen to Hathaway.

> Mr. Wm. Hathaway, President,
> First State Bank of Crosswind
> Crosswind, Oklahoma 73926
>
> December 10, 1994
>
> Dear Bill,
>
> White Sands has nearly bankrupt me. I have been forced to borrow well beyond my means from your bank

in order to meet the capital calls required of the shareholders. The most recent letter from Eric requiring another $50,000 has done me in. I neither have the cash nor the inclination to borrow another $50,000 from your bank. I will not make this call. I want out of this venture and demand a full accounting for my contributions and a return of my capital. What should I do? I wish the rest of you well on this project and hope that none of you has had as much difficulty keeping up with all of these capital calls as I have had. When may I expect an accounting?

Molly sends her regards to you and to Jane.

Best regards for the holidays,

Richard

Appearing on the bottom of the letter was a handwritten note, neatly penned in near-perfect script. Apparently, it was a response from Hathaway to Allen. It read:

Eric tells me that this will be the last capital call! Hooray! We did it! We have all been suffering from this financial drain. With this $50,000 contribution from the partners, we should be able to save White Sands, and Eric forecasts a modest profit in 1995. I spoke with Howard and Eric, and they have agreed that your $50,000 will be applied towards your down payment on the beautiful retirement home that you have planned for Molly at White Sands. Come by the bank and we'll make out the necessary papers. We know your credit is good, and the economic forecast is bright both for the car business and for land development.

Bill

Although Richard Allen's name appeared on the face of the envelope, there was no address and the envelope was unstamped. Jake assumed the response from Hathaway never made it back to Allen, perhaps because of his suicide. Jake confirmed that Allen had not borrowed another $50,000 from the bank in late 1994. Was it this call for more capital that pushed him over the brink? Jake wondered.

Jake refolded the letter, and instead of placing it back in the pile of documents that had been brought to him by Ms. Falsworth, he carefully tucked the letter in the inside pocket of his suit coat. Next, he placed a call to the offices of Eric Beamer.

In response to the cheerful hello from the receptionist at Beamer's office, Jake asked, "Will Mr. Beamer be in this afternoon?"

"I will put you in to his secretary," the receptionist responded. "She can schedule an appointment for you."

Two hours later Jake was sitting in the modest waiting room of Beamer and Associates, PLLC, waiting for his appointment with Eric Beamer. "Mr. McCarthy," came the almost too cheerful salutation from Eric Beamer. "Bill Hathaway and Howard Stern have both told me about you and your mission to help out Molly. She and Richard were close friends, and it was such a tragedy when Richard ended his life so violently. How is Molly?"

"Molly is doing well. She is recovering slowly from her trauma, but it may be some time before she is completely restored to her former self. Thank you for asking."

"What can I do for you?" Beamer asked as he ushered McCarthy through the door adjacent to the reception desk. "My secretary tells me that you are looking for not only the Allen financial records, but also the documentation relating to Red Rock. Did you also want to see documents on Allen Ford? When Richard took over the dealership after his father's death, he transferred the corporate accounting to me, and we were responsible for that account as well."

Beamer was short, dark-haired and deeply tanned. Jake couldn't decide whether the tan was from time spent in the Oklahoma desert, a normal pigmentation of his skin, or regular sessions in a tanning salon. Jake sensed that Beamer was intelligent, focused and very high strung.

As he ushered Jake into a small conference room, Beamer said, "I had my staff pull the Richard and Molly Allen personal files from 1990 forward and the dealership files from as far back as we had responsibility. We also pulled the corporate documents relating to Red Rock Savings and Loan. There are many, many more documents stored in our file room in the basement of this building, but we keep this working file on hand for review by persons such as yourself or the representatives of the FSLIC or Resolution Trust, which just finished its investigation and gave us the all-clear. We have nothing to hide. We just got caught up in the interest rate fluctuations of the early nineties and had the misfortune of lending money at low interest rates and then having to borrow money at higher interest rates. Like so many other savings and loans, we just couldn't weather through until the value of our underlying properties increased sufficiently to cover the value of our loans."

"How was Red Rock capitalized?" Jake asked.

"A bunch of us got together and put $200,000 each into the corporation. The Red Rock stock was $2.00 par, and we each owned 100,000 shares. We intended to go public with Red Rock as soon as we had enough loans under our belts and could demonstrate a positive bottom line. Unfortunately that never happened, so we each ended up losing all of our capital investment."

"Was everyone's capital paid up in full?" Jake asked.

"Yes," Beamer responded, sensing a shift from friendly chat to professional inquiry. He offered no further information.

"Tell me about White Sands. How was that investment made and when did it occur in the course of the life of Red Rock Savings and Loan?" Jake asked.

Beamer hesitated, and then responded deliberately, carefully choosing each of his words. "White Sands was a joint venture between Howard Stern, myself and three or four outside investors including Richard Allen. He had the largest investment in the venture. It was kind of his pet project. You will see in some of the documents that we have laid aside for you in this conference room that we put together a very strong pro forma of the potential revenue to be derived from development of White Sands. I don't know if you have ever gone out to that part of the desert, but we still believe that White Sands sits on top of a major underground river that could provide unlimited water to create an oasis in the middle of the desert. If you have ever been to Palm Springs in Southern California, you will understand the importance of being able to irrigate and cultivate parts of the desert. We envisioned creation of another Palm Springs. We were about to break ground when the FSLIC forced us into bankruptcy, and the Resolution Trust took over the property."

Questions and half-answers continued for another forty-five minutes, then Jake stood and extended his hand to Beamer, saying, "Thanks for your information. I don't have time this afternoon to study the books and records of Red Rock and Allen Ford, but I would like to come back and spend a day going through them."

"Just call to let us know when you are coming, and I will make them available," Beamer responded as he began to walk toward the door. "We are here usually between nine and five every day."

Jake left the accountant's office with an uneasy feeling, but he could not decide whether it was the same uneasy feeling that he always got after talking to a CPA, or something related to the case. At any rate it would have to wait until after his dinner at the Bar M Ranch with the Mobley family.

CHAPTER 28

"Bill, this is Howard. We need to talk. Not by phone. I'll pick you up in twenty minutes."

"Will you be gone long, Mr. Stern?" the attractive receptionist asked as Howard Stern left his office on the way to pick up his friend, Bill Hathaway. "Remember it's Thursday, and you have a five o'clock appointment with the Kayhills to do an estate plan that has already been postponed twice."

"I'll be back. Just going out to do some errands," Stern replied as he left the office.

Ten minutes later Howard Stern stopped in front of the First State Bank of Crosswind to pick up Hathaway, then stopped four blocks later to pick up Eric Beamer, who was standing in front of the office of one of his clients. Chambers and O'Connor were next.

"What's this all about, Howard?" Beamer asked. "I'm up to my ass in alligators right now, and I don't have time to be fussing around with you and Bill over this Red Rock problem. Let's make it quick!"

"I went out to visit my dad at the nursing home at lunch today. Couldn't get out there after the Memorial Day weekend since I took the family up to Lake Powell to our cabin. His nurse law clerk told me that the attorney from Detroit had been out there talking to him."

"I didn't think the judge could talk," Hathaway responded.

"Well he can't talk much, but he can talk, sort of. I have never seen my father so agitated. He kept growling at me between the little grunts that serve as his only communication. When he made his grunts he looked straight through me as if he somehow thought that I had caused his injury. He was so visibly upset that his nurse asked me to leave until he had recovered his composure. Do you think McCarthy suspects something and told my old man? What could he have told him that would make him so mad at me?"

A cold sweat had already broken out on Hathaway's forehead prompted by the fear that their plan was unraveling. He reached for his oversized handkerchief and swiped at his brow but said nothing. Beamer, who consistently assured his partners that everything was completely in order, was typically analytical in his response to Stern's question.

"We paid good money for a pro, and now is when that money will pay off. I don't know what McCarthy suspects, and I don't care. Now that Richard is out of the way there are no loose ends. McCarthy was at my place this afternoon, but didn't stay and didn't seem too concerned about all those documents that we have worked so hard to perfect."

"He was in again to look at bank records, and asked a whole lot of questions about Richard's loans," Hathaway interjected before Beamer could comment further on Jake's visit. "He told me when he left that he would be back to see all of the documents for the dealership and any records the bank has on Red Rock and White Sands. When he returns I'm going to stall, of course, just to make it hard on him, but eventually I'll be forced to give the records to him, assuming that Molly's power of attorney is still good. Howard?"

"Why don't you destroy the bank records?" Stern responded. "You have no obligation to maintain records once your client is dead."

"Howard, you never were much of an attorney," Beamer interrupted. "Of course Bill must keep those records, and of course he can't destroy them now that they may be under scrutiny. It would as much as admit liability where none exists. Just keep your cool, both of you," Beamer responded.

"I knew it, I knew it, I knew it. We are in deep, deep shit," Chambers whined from the back seat of Stern's Lincoln Town Car. "Just when I finally settle my dad's estate, the roof caves in on us, and all because of some city lawyer that doesn't know shit about Crosswind and what we all have done for this city."

"We've got to get rid of McCarthy," O'Connor responded to this outbreak from the rotund editor of the Crosswind Gazette. "It's the only thing to do, and we have to find Molly, and get rid of her too."

The car was suddenly silent as it cruised around Crosswind, stopping occasionally at a stoplight and staying generally in the small downtown business district. Each of the men thought in his own way of the ease with which one of their members was talking of killing another two humans, including one who had never done any of them any harm. Finally, Beamer spoke up.

"Before we run off half-cocked, let's see what the possible downsides are. First, even if McCarthy suspects that the accidents weren't accidental, how can he prove anything? The coroner's reports on all four clearly established the cause of death as accidental. Howard, can McCarthy change that?"

Stern hesitated, then responded, "He might be able to have the bodies exhumed, have the coroner perform a more complete autopsy, etc., etc. Hard to figure how the coroner could conclude anything but accidental. I guess it's theoretically possible."

Once again O'Connor spoke, this time with more conviction. "Look, Molly Allen has no kin. With no family and no property, it is unlikely that anyone will miss her. If we eliminate her and McCarthy and make it look accidental, there's no one else who will come snooping around. The Feds are through with us and spending all their time down in Little Rock. I doubt whether McCarthy's law firm up in Detroit will send down another attorney, gratis, if their client is dead. I move we take care of them both, and soon."

"But I can't afford any more of our consultant's time," Chambers said. "I've already spent most of dad's money on computers. Is there some way we can do this ourselves?"

"Leave McCarthy to me," O'Connor said. "My manager and I have experience in this kind of thing, and I'm confident that we can accomplish the task without our friend Kruger. Do I have your approval?"

Each of the men nodded their assent and simultaneously thought how fortunate it was that one of them was willing to step forward, and how scared they were that their grand scheme, having failed so miserably to convert their family's modest assets into a billion-dollar land development, might ultimately be discovered.

Jake was looking forward to his visit to the Mobley ranch, although he had no clear concept of what a large, modern cattle ranch might be like. From his frame of reference of 1960's westerns, he envisioned a comfortable but modest wood-frame house with a large covered porch overlooking the barn and a bunkhouse for the hired hands.

Following directions given to him by Tom Mobley, Jake drove fifty miles due east of Crosswind and had no trouble finding the entrance gate to the Bar M Ranch. It was the only driveway for nearly a mile after the small town of Korbett that served this ranching community.

The gravel driveway was just over a quarter-mile long and passed through occasional thickets of wood, open prairie and little else.

Unlike Crosswind, which was basically flat but for the large rock jutting out of the plains, the land east of Crosswind became gently rolling hills leading to a small range of foothills, not tall enough to be called mountains but substantial nevertheless. As Jake came over a small rise he saw before him the Mobley ranch. The main house was a large stone and log structure that sat alongside a stream that eventually led into a small man-made pond about the size of two football fields. At the southern end of the pond, which abutted the driveway, was a small concrete weir that caused the formation of the pond.

In addition to the farmhouse there were five other buildings within a compound circled by a white board fence similar to those found in Kentucky horse country. It was difficult for Jake to determine from the exterior just how large the ranch house was, but clearly it was not small. There was, as he had envisioned, a large covered porch facing west and overlooking the stream and the pond.

As Jake drove into the parking area on the north side of the house, Tom Mobley emerged from the front door and briskly walked over to Jake's car. "Welcome to the Bar M Ranch. Just leave your car here, and no need to lock it. We never lock anything around here, and nothing ever gets stolen because any thief would know better. I see you found yourself some comfortable clothes, so how about we go out back and check on the horses in the corral before we go in for dinner. I have a small icebox out in the barn and keep a few cold beers on hand so I don't get in Dolores' way when she's cooking. Me and the boys like to come out here before dinner and just kind of take in all of this wonderful world that we live in."

Several minutes later Jake and Mobley were standing by the corral looking at several quarter horses that Mobley's foreman was in the process of training. One had already been broken and the other was being broken by one of the younger ranch hands. Each of the observers had a cold bottle of Budweiser, and they were enjoying both the performance of the bucking quarter horse and the cool taste of the beer.

"You knew Richard Allen pretty well," Jake said, disrupting Mobley's enjoyment of the exhibition of horsemanship displayed by his foreman. "Do you think he was capable of committing suicide?"

Mobley did not answer the question immediately but stared across the corral at the surrounding foothills searching for an answer. "Richard was not terribly bright, nor was he a good businessman. But that never seemed to bother him, and he was always very decent, very polite and a friend to those who knew him. I cannot recall his ever being depressed, but for that matter I can't recall his ever being excited about anything except his antique cars. He was just kind of a mellow person who went along with life, good or bad. So I guess if you are looking for the profile of a person given to committing suicide, Richard did not fit. But that does not alter the fact that he put a bullet through his head."

"What if it was made to look like a suicide?"

"You've lived in Detroit too long, Jake. Things like that don't happen out here in the great western plains. Besides, why would anyone want to murder Richard Allen? He had no enemies. He never did much with his life to create enemies, and he certainly was not a threat to anyone. No, I think the news reports had it just about right. He had lost his money, lost his dealership, had no kids and had nothing to live for, so he took the coward's way out and left poor Molly to her own devices."

"I think it goes much deeper than that," Jake continued. "I think Richard's friends were ripping him off, and I think he may have found out about it and confronted them with the facts. Would they have been capable of eliminating Richard Allen and making it look like a suicide?"

"I've thought some bad things about those boys, but I never would accuse them of going that far. You better have solid evidence before you go public with those kinds of accusations," Mobley responded in a stern but fatherly tone.

By this time the sun had set over the flat plains to the west of the Bar M Ranch, and a chill had come into the air that prompted Mobley to suggest that they return to the house for dinner. "I wouldn't mention these matters around the dinner table. After dinner, I want to continue this discussion and include the two older boys. They know Stern and Hathaway better than I do, and perhaps they can shed some light on this theory of yours. I'll suggest that we go for a drive around the property. That way we can talk in private, and I know the two boys will be very discreet with any thoughts that you may have."

"Sounds great, and I really am getting hungry. Must be this fresh air."

An hour later Jake was the first to say, "Dolores, dinner was marvelous." He had just finished a sizable piece of homemade apple pie, and his stomach was protesting against his belt. "Those steaks were as tender and tasty as any I have had, and your muffins fresh from the oven were a treat, not to mention this apple pie that has set my diet back a month."

"Well, Jake, you're welcome anytime. It's not often we get an attorney from Detroit to come all the way out here for dinner. But for the funny way you talk, you're really not so much different than we are."

Jake had to smile at her comment about his way of speaking, as he was working hard simply to decipher the words being spoken by this Oklahoma native. The Okies had a language unto themselves, and for those who were not exposed to the leveling influence of TV and national talk shows, the accent was nearly indecipherable.

"Jake, why don't you, me and the boys go for a short driving tour of the ranch? Perhaps we could see some deer out on the prairie or maybe even scare up a mountain lion. Jim, Frank, do you want to come along?" The boys knew better than to decline.

Ten minutes later Jake, Tom and his two older sons were driving slowly along a perimeter road that followed the fence line that extended around the entire property owned by Mobley and his four sons and grandchildren.

"We strung our fences in such a way that we could drive the entire perimeter, then took a dozer and leveled a road along the fence line. It took a bit of work, but the boys love to use the dozer, and it sure makes a difference when we have to check to see whether a fence is broken or we've got some intruders coming in after our cattle. Although each of us owns a piece of the entire ranch, we treat it as if it's one big spread, and we all help each other take care of the place."

"These two boys of mine knew Richard Allen pretty well. He was quite a bit older, but both boys bought several trucks from him when he was running the dealership. Ask them the question you asked me earlier today, Jake."

"I asked your dad whether he thought Richard Allen was the kind of person that was capable of committing suicide. What do you guys think?"

"Well, I guess he did, so I guess he was," Jim, the younger of the two boys, responded after a few moments of thought. "Hadn't given it much thought, though. You think it might have been something else?"

"You know the report of that suicide never did sit square on my plate," Frank, the older son, reflected. "Richard wasn't the kind of guy that would blow his brains out. He was kind of a neatnik. Always polishing up his cars and making everything shine, and I just don't think that he'd make that kind of a mess, at least not consciously. If he was to commit suicide, I figured he would take some pills or maybe gas himself in the garage. He loved cars, so why not die in something you love? I guess from reading the newspapers that he had reason to be upset, but you know I never thought he was that kind of person. So I think I'd have to say that he was probably not the type that would commit suicide; and I'd go one step further and say that if he were, he wouldn't do it with a pistol to his head. But there you are and there you are. He did it, and there's no use worrying about whether he would or wouldn't."

"Your dad tells me that you know Howard Stern, William Hathaway and Eric Beamer pretty well. What are they like?"

"I call them spooners," the younger son immediately piped up. "Born with a silver spoon in their mouth and not smart enough to know how to use it. Rather than using the spoon to feed themselves, they left the spoon in their mouth and just grabbed with their hands trying to put as much more in their mouths as they could."

"Why James, that's about as poetic as I've heard you get. Where did you come up with that observation?" his father asked.

Jim had a sheepish look on his face and confessed, "Well, I guess it really wasn't my way of putting it. Sammy Franklin used to say that about the three of them when they were back in high school. It kind of stuck in my mind as a pretty good description."

"I know the three of them well enough that we do not use Howard Stern or his law firm for any of our business, we do not bank at the First State Bank of Crosswind and we certainly don't use Eric Beamer as our accountant. I don't trust any of them, especially after the Red Rock fiasco that cost a few of our citizens a lot of money and, fortunately, didn't cost us anything because we didn't invest in that turkey. Of the three of them, Stern scares me the most because I think he's basically dishonest. But Beamer comes in a very close second only because he's a lot smarter than Stern. Bill Hathaway is just a buffoon. Are they somehow mixed up with Richard Allen? He was older than they. I am surprised that they would have anything to do with him."

During their discussion, the Chevy Suburban had worked its way up to a plateau overlooking the ranch. "This is the high point of our property," Tom Mobley explained as he parked the truck and turned off the headlights. "In the dark you can really feel close to the heavens with all of those stars up there holding untold mysteries. There's the ranch house way off in the distance. That's Jim's house over there, and Frank's is over there. I love this spot because it shows how vast the universe and how small our little 110,000-acre spread. Right boys?"

The younger son chimed in, "Right, dad. We know the lecture."

"You know these individuals," Jake continued. "Are they capable of violence? Just how hungry are they to satisfy their need for more? Jim, you said they were spooners, but you also described them as grabbing at everything they could to satisfy their need for more. How greedy are they?"

The four men were silent as they stared off into space, each thinking his own thoughts and rapidly tying together questions concerning the possibility that Richard did not commit suicide and the potential for violence by the other investors. This time, the older son spoke first.

"I have never told you this, dad, but when we were in eighth grade, Howard and I used to go down to the old sand pit for target practice. He wasn't much of a shot, and I guess it was mostly my suggestion that we go down there in the first place. But he got the idea that it would be fun to use live targets. I wouldn't do it, but one time he caught a prairie dog and tied one leg to a string and hung him from a branch. Now that was bad enough, but his idea of target practice was to zero in on a leg and shoot three of the four legs out before aiming for other parts of the body. I did not join in, and after that we never went back together. So, Jake, you asked me if they were capable of violence. I would have to say yes, at least as to Howard Stern. If he could do that to a prairie dog, I think he could be equally sick and do violence to people. Now mind you, I've shot a few rats down at the dump, but that's different. They're not tied up, swinging in the breeze."

"Jim, do you know anything else about these guys?" Jake asked.

"I'm five or six years younger than they, so I didn't pal around with them very much. But I used to date Sally Ann Jacobs in high school. She was the queen of the homecoming game our senior year, and I was proud as punch that she was my date. Little did I know that she and Eric Beamer had been corresponding. He was away at college and kind of a big man on campus, and she up and decided to invite him to the prom and left me high and dry. Well, things took their course and eventually they got married. I didn't see much of Sally Ann after that until about four years after their marriage, and one day she drove all the way out here to the ranch to see me. She was a mess. I mean she was one gorgeous lady in high school, but four years with Beamer had brought her down to puffy eyes, a sallow complexion and, as she graphically demonstrated to me, some major bruises and scarring from a series of beatings to which Eric had subjected her. I put her in contact with our lawyer, and within three months they were divorced. She moved out of the state, but we still exchange Christmas cards. If you're asking me whether Beamer is capable of violence, ain't no question."

They had been parked for nearly an hour marveling at the spectacular display of billions of stars shining down on the Mobley Ranch. The discussion about the Allens had come to a close, and for several minutes there was silence in the Suburban as each of the occupants enjoyed the quiet simplicity of nature and reflected on the quality and potential of their existence. The silence was broken by Tom Mobley turning to Jake who was seated next to him in the front of the car.

"You have formed some theories about this case and some suspicions, Jake, can you share them with us? You can trust us not to discuss any of these matters with anyone, am I right boys?"

As if one, the Mobley sons responded in the affirmative.

"Well, in September of 1989, Red Rock Savings and Loan was formed by the heirs of four of Crosswind's prominent families. Each agreed to invest $200,000. We don't know anything about O'Connor, but he shows up as another major investor in July of 1992.

"I haven't been able to make the connection between Richard Allen, who at his death was sixty-eight years old, and the other four investors who, one would guess, are in their mid-fifties. There seems to have been a bond of friendship and trust to the extent that Richard Allen was willing to place all of his personal and financial business with them. They knew all there was to know about Richard Allen's finances, and he knew virtually nothing about theirs.

"Because Judge Stern survived, Howard has not inherited his estate, which I assume is substantial, and apparently Hathaway Senior left his estate in trust so that his son earns only what he makes at the bank plus a little income from the inheritance, which ultimately will go to charity. Neither Beamer nor Chambers had wealthy parents, so their assets are limited, and our research indicates that the Gazette is nearly bankrupt. So how come these other major investors are still doing business while poor old Richard Allen winds up a pauper?"

"Holy cow," the younger Mobley son exclaimed. "Do you think that Richard Allen was bankrolling the savings and loan and his so-called friends and partners were using that money to pay themselves?"

"So what do you think happened to Richard Allen?" Tom Mobley asked Jake.

"I don't know for sure, but everything I have been able to find out about Richard Allen leads me to think that he was not the kind of person who would commit suicide, and like Frank said, not with a gun to his head. There is no question that he was in financial trouble. Hathaway had allowed him to mortgage everything he owned, including his house, well beyond its appraised value. Dealership revenues were factored to the hilt, at a very high interest rate, and there really was no way out for Richard. Still, you knew him, and Molly knew him better. She says it was impossible for him to commit suicide, and from what I've been able to gather, he just wasn't the kind that would kill himself."

"What then?" Mobley asked again.

"I think he may somehow have figured out what happened, maybe even found some evidence of what his friends and partners had been doing. But I have absolutely no proof."

"Why not go tell the police?" the younger Mobley asked.

"I have thought about that, but we're dealing with some pretty prominent people in Crosswind. You can't just make accusations based on speculation without getting burned in the process. I trust you guys because I know your father, and you have all convinced me that you are not part of that crowd. Obviously if they knew I suspected this kind of behavior, either they would have me in court for slander or they would add me to their trophy collection. I don't wish either consequence. Until I have firm evidence, I just need to keep on poking into their business and asking questions. Tomorrow I go pull the autopsy report. Maybe that will give me something to work on."

"Well, Jake, it's getting late and it looks like you have a full day's work ahead of you tomorrow. Me and my boys here will help any way we can.

We know a few folks in town, and I think they can be relied on to keep this thing under wraps. Of course, we won't say a word about your theory, but I am a personal friend of the State Police Commander in town. When the time comes, I can certainly make an introduction. I agree with you, however, that until you have both barrels loaded and aimed in the right direction, you should not pull the trigger. You can't afford to show your hand until you have hard proof."

CHAPTER 29

Jake's eyes were barely open before he detected the smell of fresh-brewed coffee and cinnamon rolls that Dolores Mobley had fixed for breakfast. Rather than drive back to Crosswind after his tour of the ranch, Jake had accepted her offer to stay the night even though he had no fresh set of clothes or shaving gear.

"Ah don't you mind," Dolores Mobley had said cheerfully. "My boys sometimes go three or four days without shaving or changing their clothes, and I'm right used to it. Come on and stay the night, and I'll fix you some home-cooked cinnamon rolls to go along with a good country breakfast. Then you can drive on back to town and get citified."

Jake splashed some cold water on his face and ran his fingers through his dark, wavy hair that, he again was forced to notice, was beginning to show signs of thinning. He retrieved his clothes from a wooden high-backed chair that had served as his closet for the night, and proceeded downstairs to the source of the wonderful aroma. Only Dolores Mobley was present in the kitchen.

"Tom and the boys were up early this morning. Weather changed last night. Looks like a cold front will be moving through sometime this afternoon, and you know this is the beginning of tornado season in this part of the world. They got out early this morning to go round up some of the cattle and move them up into the higher ground where they won't be bothered by the high winds."

Jake glanced out the window and saw no change from the clear sky and constant sun that seemed to prevail in this part of Oklahoma. Dolores Mobley must have seen him glance out the window and look perplexed.

"Don't look no different, but stick your head out the door and you'll probably feel the humidity. That's a dead giveaway that severe weather's on the way. I figure it'll start raining here round about six or seven tonight, and if the cold front comes down from the north like they're predicting, it could whip us up a real good storm. We've been through some dandies out here in the past, but this house is built real solid and our barns and outhouses are all built to withstand pretty much anything but a direct hit. Our biggest fear is the cattle, 'cause they just kind of stand there and take it, and if they're in the way of the tornado, they'll just wait for it to take them away. They're dumb animals, but we love them and they provide us with a pretty good living out here. How about a cup of coffee?"

Forty-five minutes later Jake thanked Dolores Mobley both for the fine dinner the night before and the sumptuous breakfast. "Tell Tom and your sons that I was sorry to miss them this morning but understand that they had work to do. He sure was quiet getting out of here this morning. I didn't hear a sound."

It was nearly noon before Jake had returned to his motel, showered, shaved, put on fresh clothes and checked in with the office in Detroit. By then there were clouds rolling in from the west, but no rain. The local weather channel had a fifteen-minute discussion of tornado-like conditions, but concluded that this storm probably would not result in really severe weather. Jake decided the coroner's office could wait and that it was time to check out the shed behind the Ford dealership.

"Can I help you look for a new automobile?" a young salesman asked as Jake entered the dealership. "I see you're driving a Caddie. Maybe you would like to look at one of the new Town Cars. Much better ride than a Deville, and better legroom in the back seat. How do you like driving them big cars? Me, I like a sports car like that Mustang over there or a pick-up truck with a half cab."

"No thanks, I'm looking for Mr. Tyson, who helped me out several weeks ago. Is he in this afternoon?"

"No sir, he left here the end of last week, kind of sudden like. I guess he and the new owner had a kind of fight, and Mr. O'Connor just up and fired him on the spot. Too bad, he was a real good salesman and had a lot of customers who came back every three years or so for a new car. Reckon he'll find a job with the Chrysler dealer over on the other side of town. Most of the good salespeople left here after Mr. Allen's death and have already gone over to Chrysler or the new Saturn dealership. Must have happened just after you saw him. He'd been here a long time. Nice guy. Really knew his cars. Taught me a lot. He was making good money, too. People liked to buy cars from him. How about a Crown Victoria? Great car, great price, and we can make a deal. Factory is offering a rebate of $2,000."

"I'm really not interested. Is the owner around today?" Jake asked.

"Nope. O'Connor owns the place, but he's not here much. He kind of leaves management of the place up to Vince over there. You're not going to complain about me are you?"

"Oh no, you're fine. I just need to speak with whomever is in charge."

"Well, if you ever need a new car, here's my card. Don't forget me. I'll take care of you. I can even get you a new Expedition, and you know they're hard to come by."

Smiling, Jake walked over to the office manager and introduced himself. The dark-haired man in his mid-thirties wore a finely tailored black suit that appeared out of place in a west Oklahoma town like Crosswind, and perhaps out of place in any automobile dealership. Jake bought most of his suits from Carl Sterr's, a small boutique men's clothing store located in Birmingham, an upscale town southwest of

Rochester. He was accustomed to finely tailored suits and could see the office manager's was expensive and looked new.

"Can I help you?" the manager asked in what Jake immediately recognized as a South Boston accent. "Was Ronnie unable to show you what you wanted?"

While Jake was courting his wife, Maggie, he had spent at least half a dozen long weekends with her parents in Boston. They were not from the south side of town, but Jake had explored more than a few of the many Irish bars in Boston and could distinguish between the blue-blooded aristocrats such as the O'Tools and the blue-collared democrats that had propelled the Kennedys to power. As soon as the manager spoke Jake knew that he came from the blue-collar side of Boston. His nametag identified him as Vincent McBride.

Jake introduced himself and explained why he was there without disclosing his interest in finding clues that might explain Richard's unexpected suicide.

"Mr. O'Connor is attending an important meeting this afternoon, and I don't have the authority to permit you to go into that shed."

"Perhaps you could call or page Mr. O'Connor if you feel you need his approval to proceed. Of course, I don't want to interrupt him, but I am on a fairly tight time schedule and had really hoped to get through this process this afternoon. If I find anything of value, I am duty bound to disclose it to the Probate Court. All we are looking for are some familiar parts of Richard Allen's life, you know, pictures and mementos to help Molly overcome her emotional trauma. She doesn't remember anything," he lied.

"It's been a while since I've been back there, and I can't promise you there won't be some critters in there that you might not want to deal with. We got us a few rattlesnakes around here that are big enough to bite your leg off. I can try to reach Mr. O'Connor, but it may take a while. He's not one to hurry in returning pages. Wait here just a second while I try to find him."

Jake waited while McBride walked into his small office. As with many dealerships the office walls were mostly glass so that the salesmen could see potential customers and the manager could tell if his people were doing their jobs. Inside, the dapperly dressed manager moved quickly to the telephone console on his desk and pushed a speed dial button that automatically dialed the cellular phone that O'Connor always carried. Within seconds the manager and O'Connor were discussing Jake's request to search the old shed behind the dealership that had once been Richard Allen's retreat from the world.

"Did he say what he was looking for?" O'Connor asked.

"Just some personal belongings that his old lady client thought Richard might have left out there. Nothing specific. He says because he's a lawyer, he would have to report anything of value to the Probate Court, and the estate's creditors would scarf it up. Ain't nothing of value out there no how. I poked around in there a couple of months ago out of curiosity, and it's just an old shed with a bunch of old rusted-out parts for old cars. I don't see how it could do no harm."

After a lengthy pause, O'Connor finally said, "Okay, take him back there. But take your time. Make him think you are having trouble reaching me. I want to talk things over with the rest of the group, then decide how we want to deal with this opportunity."

The manager sat down in his high-backed leather swivel chair, re-lit one of the fine Cuban cigars that he had recently acquired through one of his Canadian friends, and waited nearly thirty minutes. Finally he reached over to the telephone as if to answer a call, appeared to speak to someone, then emerged from his office saying, "Sorry to keep you waiting, Mr. McCarthy, couldn't find the boss right away. He finally called in, and when I explained why you wanted to look, he said it was OK.

"I've only been out to that old shed once or twice since I've been here. It's pretty run down, and we don't use it for anything since it's not completely weatherproof. Auto parts are too expensive to use it as a storage shed. If you leave things out there they just rust up. I'll get my truck, and we'll drive back."

Although there were a few more clouds in the sky, only a light breeze was blowing, which had not cooled the still-sultry air that had descended upon the area the previous night. The two men moved quickly to the manager's Ford F-150 truck, then drove the several thousand yards to the back of the dealership property. The shed was a wood-frame building about the size of a five-car garage. The roof was sagging at one end, and the wooden siding looked like it had been painted many years before, but most of the paint was gone, probably ground off the side by the relentless wind and blowing sand driven off the western plain. There were several small windows facing toward the dealership, but only one had its full compliment of glass. At one end of the building was a large overhead garage-type door, but the manager drove to the other end of the shed where there was a smaller door, which the manager quickly unlocked.

Once inside the shed, the manager said, "How long do you think you'll need out here? I must get back to the dealership since O'Connor isn't there. We have several sales pending, and our salespeople will need my signature. Tell me how long you'll need, and I'll come back and pick you up."

Jake looked around the old shed, and then said, "Forty-five minutes, maybe an hour at the most. It looks like most of this is junk, and I doubt that I will find anything worth looking at. But my boss asked me to go through everything looking for things that might be of use to her."

"Okay, I'll be back in about an hour. You can always walk up to the office if you get through sooner." After reminding Jake to keep an eye out for snakes, McBride left, closing the door behind him.

As the truck pulled away from the shed, Jake began the process of looking for any potential hiding place where Richard Allen might have kept important documents concerning his investment in Red Rock Savings and Loan. Although several windowpanes were missing, the shed was basically dry and relatively clean but for the dust that had accumulated through non-use. There were many signs of animal life that went with the noticeable smell of rodent droppings.

Jake flipped on the light switch and was pleased to find that power to the shed had not been disconnected. Before going too far into the building, Jake made a quick check for snakes, remembering McBride's warning. Fortunately there were none.

The walls of the shed were unfinished, showing the two-by-four studding and the underside of the exterior, wooden, tongue and groove boards. The electrical wiring, such that it was, was visible and appeared to have been installed well after the shed was built.

The front two-thirds of the building had a poured concrete floor while the back third had a slightly raised wooden floor that appeared significantly newer than the rest of the shed. Scattered around the front part of the shed were old car parts now badly rusted, several 55-gallon drums that held what appeared to be old motor oil or other petroleum products, several pieces of metal furniture that Jake guessed may have been discarded from the dealership waiting room, and not much else. The walls were empty. There were no cupboards or cabinets, just a room full of old car parts and trash. Jake guessed that Richard's vintage cars had been stored in this part of the shed, and once they were sold there wasn't much use for the space except as a catchall for old junk.

Jake moved deliberately, taking his time checking in, around and under everything in this part of the building, but there were no good places to store or conceal anything. The half-dozen boxes that might have contained documents were filled with used auto parts and old *Car and Driver* magazines.

Stepping the half step up onto the wooden flooring covering the back third of the shed, Jake moved immediately to a small wooden desk placed neatly against one wall just below the one small window that still had all of its glass. The top of the desk had a thick layer of dust on it, and otherwise was bare but for a small picture of Molly Allen taken when she was probably in her early fifties.

Moving the old-fashioned wooden swivel chair aside, Jake gently pulled open the large center drawer only to find an assortment of pencils and erasers, a few paper clips and a magazine, which Jake assumed from its cover had to do with the restoration of antique cars. From the grease stains and dog-eared pages, Jake also guessed that this was one of Richard's favorites. On the cover it had a picture of an old Ford station wagon with wood paneling.

Retrieving the swivel chair, Jake began looking into each of the other five drawers. The three drawers on the left side of the desk were filled with new auto parts, many still in their boxes. The smaller drawer on the right side of the desk contained several repair manuals, one for a 1933 Ford roadster and the other for a 1948 Ford wagon. Jake had saved the large filing drawer on the right side of the desk for the last, hoping that it would contain some meaningful records. It was completely empty.

Controlling his disappointment, Jake resisted the temptation to slam the large filing drawer shut. A quick look around the room confirmed Jake's fear that Richard had cleaned the place out of anything significant. Most of the floor was covered by a large area rug, possibly twelve feet square. On the walls were several pictures, one of which Jake recognized as the giant red rock giving rise to the name of the now-defunct savings and loan. Like a private eye in some grade B movie, Jake peeked behind each of the pictures on the off chance that Richard might have hidden a key or some other bit of helpful information. He found nothing.

On one side of the room there was a small bookcase that contained repair manuals, two complete shelves' worth of magazines on antique cars, and what appeared to be a complete set of Tom Clancy novels. Jake began a random check of the manuals and magazines to see if there were any loose papers. There weren't.

Jake was now thoroughly discouraged. There simply were no other places to keep records or store documents. The office area was neat but lacked any filing cabinets or obvious storage places other than the shelves of old magazines and books. He walked back across the room and sat down in the wooden swivel chair. Molly had been so hopeful that Richard may have kept some of his personal records out in this building that Jake had convinced himself that this old shed would provide the solution to the riddle of how a decent, conservative, normal man could go so far in debt without anyone knowing it. He glanced at his watch and saw that he had at least another twenty-five minutes before Vincent would return. He thought about walking back, but decided to stay put. Maybe he had missed something in the front part of the shed. He would go over it all one more time.

Turning away from the desk, he stared across the office area and into the larger part of the building where the old parts had been randomly tossed on the floor. The contrast between the cold cement floor littered with old parts and the neatly kept though rustic office with its wooden floor and large carpet were dramatic. As his subconscious mind compared the two areas of the building, Jake's conscious mind focused on a small crease in the carpet approximately four feet from one of its edges. Jake realized that he had looked over and under almost everything in the room, except for the carpeting.

"This is really stupid," Jake said out loud to himself as he stood up from the wooden chair. "But I guess if I'm going to do this right, I might as well look under the carpeting to see whether something is hidden there. It isn't any more stupid than looking for something taped to the back of a picture." Moving to one corner of the carpeting, Jake pulled back the edge just far enough to see the area that had shown the slight crease. There were no documents. He pulled further until approximately half of the area under the carpeting had been revealed.

In the middle of the floor Jake saw a three-foot square panel cut through the plywood floor. The fit was near perfect but for one side that left about a half-inch gap, just enough to cause the small crease in the thin Oriental carpet. There were no handles or hinges, and except for the easily missed wrinkle in the carpet, no one would have suspected anything but a solid floor under the carpet. Two holes just large enough to insert a finger in each had been cut in the middle of the wooden panel.

Jake carefully lifted the panel as his heart began beating a little faster. He again glanced at his watch: at least twenty more minutes. He got down on his hands and knees to see what was underneath the wood flooring of this part of the shed. The first thing he saw was what appeared to be the rungs of a ladder leading down into the area below the wooden floor. Without a flashlight, he could see nothing else.

Looking around for anything that would provide light and finding nothing, Jake decided to at least take a few steps down the ladder to see what lay beneath the floorboards of this part of the old shed. "If there are snakes to be had," he said out loud, "this is where they'll be!"

Carefully stepping through the opening in the wooden floor, Jake lowered himself slowly into the dark until he had gained solid ground approximately six feet below the level of the flooring. It was cold and dank, and Jake imagined scurrying rats and snakes and other unpleasant creatures, but so far he neither heard nor felt anything.

Slowly his eyes became adjusted to the dark. The small amount of light coming through the trap doorway was just barely enough to enable him to make out the shapes of a few objects in the small compartment. The first object that he noticed was a metal four-drawer filing cabinet that sat approximately three feet away from the ladder. As his eyes continued to adjust to the dark, he saw on top of the filing cabinet a small desk lamp. Jake carefully moved to the cabinet and was relieved when the light sprang to life and quickly showed the rest of the contents of this sunken pit. The area was only three to four feet wide, and its walls were made of cinder block. Jake guessed that the area had been a grease pit used to service cars before the days of hydraulic lifts.

There was little else in the area save a small wooden chair sitting at the far end of the pit and a neatly folded blanket that appeared old and tattered but once of good quality. It sat on a rectangular piece of sheet metal that served as a makeshift shelf. Above the shelf was another, smaller shelf just wide enough to hold a variety of memorabilia, including ribbons and trophies from classic auto shows, and a picture of Richard and his father looking at a 1987 Ford Thunderbird Turbo Coupe and holding a replica of the Car of the Year Award. At the far end was a small picture of Molly taken years earlier and even in the uneven light of this underground hideout her bright blue eyes and creamy white skin were immediately noticeable. The shelf contained nothing of apparent value, yet Jake guessed that on this small platform in a subterranean pit was a montage of Richard's life.

As Jake moved down the narrow passageway past the file cabinet and toward the end where the chair was located, he noticed propped in the corner by the file cabinet a tripod with a video camera attached. Hanging from an old nail hammered into the side of the cinder block was a satiny red mechanic's jacket with "Allen Ford" emblazoned across the back in large white letters.

The metal file cabinet was old and locked. Although the Key which Molly had entrusted to his care seemed far too big for a file cabinet, Jake noticed that the lock was large and might take the key that Molly and Jake had assumed was for the safe deposit box. Before Jake could retrieve the key from his briefcase, which he had left on top of the oak desk, the light in the small grease pit suddenly went out. Jake was again in pitch-black darkness. He stood motionless waiting for his eyes, which had become dilated with the bright light, to readjust to the sudden darkness.

Before his eyes could react, however, his sense of smell, followed almost immediately by his sense of hearing, detected another change in conditions. The smell was smoke and the sound was the unmistakable roar of a very hot fire. Jake looked up and saw white smoke dancing across the three-foot square opening in the floorboards of the shed. He moved quickly to the opening and began climbing the ladder, only to realize that the entire shed was engulfed in flames. Quickly surveying the possible avenues of escape, all Jake could see were flames on all sides. The only window and the wall adjacent to it were an inferno.

Ducking his head back into the grease pit, Jake smelled the unmistakable odor of singed hair, and a quick touch confirmed that the intense heat had licked at his unprotected head. Smoke was slowly infiltrating the underground compartment through the opening that was Jake's only escape. Jake's mind tried to analyze the situation and devise a plan, but the heat was becoming oppressive as flames leaped from the wooden sides of the building. Jake instinctively threw his left arm across his mouth in an effort to filter out the deadly fumes as they tried to consume his lungs.

The only door out of the shed was at the extreme other end, and Jake knew from his first look that the far end of the shed was fully engulfed in flames. The window was ablaze. There was no escape. Panic suddenly seized Jake as he looked for a way out of Richard's shed that had suddenly become his crematorium.

Black clouds of smoke were now circling into the sky as the flames quickly ripped into and through the ceiling of the shed. From somewhere in the front end of the shed came a double explosion as the drums of old motor oil and solvents added fuel to the fire. Pieces of roofing material began falling around Jake as he stood dumbfounded half in and half out of the grease pit searching for an escape.

Finding none and reverting to instincts he did not know he had, Jake overcame the panic that had nearly paralyzed him, realized that it was impossible to avoid the intense heat and smoke that now filled the old shed, and decided in a matter of seconds that his only hope lay in staying in the pit underneath the fire and hoping that nothing would come crashing through the wooden ceiling.

Quickly Jake felt around in the blinding smoke for the trap door that he had carefully lifted and set aside as he descended into the pit. Finding it still untouched by the fire, Jake slid it over his head and immediately immersed himself in the pitch darkness of the grease pit that would become either his coffin or his cave.

The smell of burning wood, asphalt shingle and insulation seeped into the pit even after closing the trap door, but the carpeting that lay over most of the pit area helped slow the flames that had by now completely engulfed the old wooden shed. With every breath Jake choked with the stench of acrid smoke, but closing the small door had momentarily slowed the infusion.

Moving back toward the chair, Jake banged into the filing case, and then brushed against the red parka hanging on its nail-hook. Although intended as a shield against the cold dampness of the sunken pit, Jake stripped off his now filthy suit coat and donned the parka as an insulator against the heat of the fire. He then grabbed for the wool blanket that sat neatly folded on the sheet metal shelf.

As he struggled in the darkness to protect himself from the fire, Jake knocked the video camera that had been propped against the metal filing cabinet, and it came crashing to the floor of the pit. Ignoring the damage that such a crash would have done to the camera, Jake proceeded to roll himself in the wool blanket covering his hair and his face, then lay down on the floor of the pit as far away from the small trap door as possible.

He lay still, trying not to breathe deeply, and thus avoid the choking smoke that was infiltrating his space. Using his suit coat as a further shield between his face and the heat of the fire, Jake listened as pieces of the shed began falling on the floor above him.

Suddenly, the darkness of the grease pit was shattered. A piece of the wooden flooring came crashing down on Jake as he lay rolled up in the woolen blanket. Although burning wildly when it dropped to the floor of the pit, Jake was able to extinguish this first invasion into his space by rolling over the burning embers and kicking at them with his feet. The wool blanket produced an awful smell as it smoldered in the heat of the plywood flooring that had fallen through, but it did not ignite. The stench of the burning wool and smoke from the hole left by the fallen piece of flooring made Jake choke uncontrollably. Coughing repeatedly, he was unable to clear his lungs. Pulling the wool blanket up over his mouth and nose in a last, desperate effort to avoid the smoke, Jake fought to keep his consciousness even as the subterranean pit filled with more of the black, caustic smoke now coming from the underside of burning plywood floorboards that had once hidden this secret place.

As Jake gasped for air, he became only distantly conscious of the crashing and banging above him caused by pieces of the shed falling in on the wooden flooring only to be consumed by the very flames that would soon consume him. The roar of the flames became deafening, then suddenly there was silence as Jake slid into a smoke-induced coma.

CHAPTER 30

"Are you absolutely sure he was in the shed?" O'Connor asked of his manager as they stood watching the flames consume the old shed that had once housed Richard Allen's prize collection of antique and classic cars. "I would have thought that he would have tried to get out or at least made some noise calling for help. I didn't hear or see anything."

"Yes sir," Vince responded. "There's only that one door that works, and when I left him out here I put the padlock back on the door just as you said so I know he didn't come out that way. That old overhead door is busted, so he couldn't use it, and from here we can see the only windows in the place. Unfortunate accident. Must have been overcome by smoke before he had a chance to get to the windows. Or maybe he wasted precious time trying to open the door. Who knows, and who cares. He won't be asking no more questions."

O'Connor chuckled, "Yeah. Only the good die young. He never should have come around snooping in the first place. Remember, he was never here and never asked to see the shed. We didn't even know he was in there. Might have tried to save him if we'd known he was in there. Must have climbed in through a window because the door is still locked, right? Real sad, but he was trespassing. If we had known we would have tried to save him. Right?"

"Yes sir. Real sad, but bad things happen to people who stick their educated butts into other people's business."

At this last remark an electrifying bolt of lightning followed almost immediately by a tremendous crash of thunder announced the start of a torrential downpour. "Hurry, let's get back to the dealership and call the fire department. That old shed just got hit by lightning. Lucky no one was working there. You take care of the Caddie?"

"Yes sir," the manager again responded promptly. "I was able to hot-wire it, then drove it back and left it at the motel where the late Mr. McCarthy was a guest. I wore gloves so there won't be no prints, and I was careful not to let anyone see me. Tom picked me up at the cafe across the street. I told him you were supposed to pick me up but got called away on business."

As the two men ran back toward the dealership, the rain and thunder and lightning attested to the awesome power of an Oklahoma spring storm. Within seconds the two men were drenched. The wind began to drive the rain in great sheets of water later reported by the local news station to have been over four inches in less than an hour.

As they reached the door of the dealership and stepped into its protective cover, O'Connor exclaimed to his manager who was two steps behind him, "That lightning must have hit that old shed dead on for it to go up so fast." Then he whispered, "What did you do with the gas cans?"

Shaking the water out of his hair and brushing it off the black wool suit that Jake had found so out of place earlier in the day, the manager responded, "They're back in the repair shop where they should be. We didn't leave no evidence out there, and this rain will wash away our tracks and every other sign that anybody was there. I told you, we don't need to bring in no professionals like that Kruger fellow. It didn't take much to handle this attorney fellow from Detroit. Next we need to think about Mrs. Allen."

"Were there any tornado warnings out this afternoon, Vince?" O'Connor asked, acting relaxed but concerned about the weather as they walked back towards his office.

"Yeah, I think there was a tornado warning, but I don't know if any were sighted. It's that time of year. That rain sure is driving down hard though."

O'Connor picked up the telephone on his desk, dialed 911, and soon was speaking with the dispatcher for the Crosswind Volunteer Fire Department. "Yes ma'am, we have this old shed out behind the dealership that must have been struck by lightning. It's burning pretty good out there. I figure by the time you get here, it will be nothing more than ashes. I've been meaning to tear the old thing down, anyway. Guess Mother Nature helped me out on this one. Hate to get your boys out in the middle of this storm."

Twenty minutes later the Chief of the Crosswind Volunteer Fire Department was standing just outside the foundation of the old shed, which had been reduced to a smoldering pile of rubble. The intensity of the storm had not abated, and even before the Fire Department showed up, the driving rain had all but extinguished the fire, leaving nothing but puddles of gray and black ash.

"Well, I guess we can leave this until the morning, Jim," the Fire Chief said as he turned away from the shed and walked back toward his truck, water cascading off of his Fire Chief's red hard hat. "It's too dark, too wet and too late. We'll come around tomorrow morning to make sure that there are no fire pockets left. Lucky the lightning didn't hit your dealership."

"Thanks, Eddie," O'Connor said as he closed the door to the Fire Chief's Dodge pickup truck. "These storms are nasty. Leveled that old shed in less than ten minutes. We've got lightning rods on the main building. See you tomorrow."

Jake awoke from his smoke-induced coma to the sound of rain splattering on the charred remains of plywood and roofing shingles that covered his body. The abandoned maintenance well that was Richard's secret hiding place had become Jake's refuge from the fire that

O'Connor and his manager had set in an unsuccessful attempt to eliminate him. The carbon from the charred remains of the shed had blackened Jake's face and clothing, which were soaked. Already several inches of rain had puddled on the floor of the pit, and the badly singed wool blanket that had protected Jake from the heat of the fire was now saturated and stinking of wet, burnt wool coupled with the unmistakable smell of singed hair. Jake had no idea how long he had been unconscious, but damp cold had replaced any heat that remained from the fire. He had a splitting headache.

Coughing to clear his lungs of the acrid smoke that had nearly taken his life, and trying to refocus on where he was and what he should do next, Jake unwrapped himself from the tattered remains of the wool blanket and in the process sat on the video camera that had gone crashing to the floor of the pit as Jake struggled to protect himself from the heat and flames of the fire. The camera had broken open in the fall, and as Jake lifted the camera out of the way, a videotape fell out of the camera and onto the wet blanket that was now lying in a heap on the floor of the pit. Jake's first instinct was to protect the tape from the rain and the standing water in the pit. It was about the only salvageable item, so Jake decided to take it with him in case it had family pictures or scenes of Crosswind that might help Molly regain her memory.

Jake unzipped the Allen Ford jacket that he had used as another layer between him and the fire, unbuttoned his shirt, which was the only semi-dry clothing he had, and placed the videotape inside his shirt. Slowly and deliberately, Jake pushed aside the remains of the plywood floor that had fallen into the pit, poked his head above the level of the floor and looked around for any signs of life. He was astonished to see that the entire shed had burned to the ground and lay smoldering even as the rain doused the last remaining embers. A bolt of lightning raced across the sky as Jake carefully pulled himself out of the maintenance pit. Nothing but charred pieces remained of the oak furniture that had once comprised Richard Allen's office. His briefcase with Molly's key was destroyed, and although the key may not have melted whatever remained was sitting in a pile of smoldering ash.

As another bolt of lightning flashed down to earth several miles away, Jake was able to gather his bearings and began to walk back toward the automobile showroom. His head was aching from the lack of oxygen, and he had trouble focusing on the terrain as he worked his way toward the road and the haven of his car.

The pitch-black night and pouring rain made it difficult, but Jake was in no hurry and he was already as wet as he could get from the wind-whipped rain that had saved his life. The Allen Ford parka that had protected him from the deadly heat of the fire now shielded him from the cold rain that signaled the passing of the cold front that had caused the torrential rainfall. Several yards away from the charred remains of the shed, Jake thought he smelled the faint odor of gasoline. At first his mind dismissed the smell as one likely to come from an old maintenance shed, but as his mind began to clear from the smoke, Jake thought again. As he had done on many occasions in the past when presented with a problem, Jake instinctively began the process of lining up the facts and reaching a logical conclusion. It was not raining when he entered the shed, and it was not raining when he had thought about walking back to the dealership just before he found the sunken grease pit. He had heard no thunder and seen no lightning prior to smelling the burning shed. By that time the building was half consumed. Assuming that he would have both heard and felt a bolt of lightning if it had actually hit the building, Jake quickly dismissed the easy explanation for the fire. The building was half destroyed before the storm started. Another whiff of gasoline hit Jake's nostrils as his mind reached the next most obvious conclusion. The fire was intentional and meant for him. A cold chill raced up Jake's back just ahead of a rising anger that kicked his adrenaline into high gear and drove him forward.

Becoming more accustomed to the dark and aided partially by the street lights that were several thousand yards away, Jake chose an indirect route to the front of the dealership property. He headed for the western edge of the property, and then using the rows of parked cars as a screen, he worked his way toward the front of the dealership. Although late, the lights were still on, and Jake did not want another encounter with O'Connor or his manager.

It took Jake over twenty minutes to get back to the front of the dealership where his car was parked. It was not there. At first he thought he had forgotten where he had parked it, but there were no cars out in front of the dealership, not his or anyone else's, and he knew that he had left his large Cadillac right in front of the Allen Ford showroom. Being careful not to stand up in a clear area in case someone were watching, Jake began to survey the entire dealership parking area for his car. Several bolts of lightning aided him in his search, but there were no Cadillacs among the rows of Fords. His car was gone.

Maintaining his crouched position, he quietly left the dealership property and began walking back toward the center of Crosswind, avoiding streetlights and maintaining a low profile even in the dark. The rain had slowed to a steady cold shower. Jake's head was pounding from the effects of oxygen starvation, and he knew that he should feel the cold, but his adrenaline was pumping hard in his system. He was emotionally somewhere between furious and frightened. He stepped up the pace as he drew further away from the dealership. Only then did he start to regain his equilibrium.

After walking for half an hour Jake came to the Cavalier Motel, a small and seedy place that looked to be less than half full, although cars were pulling in and out of the parking lot. Jake saw a public telephone near the door marked "office" and decided to seek help. Quickly crossing the half empty parking lot, Jake made his way to the telephone booth and welcomed the opportunity of stepping out of the rain and into a dry but uncomfortably close environment. The smell of burnt hair, wet clothing and charred wood were overwhelming as Jake placed a call to his only friend in town, Thomas Mobley.

"Hello," came the energetic voice of Dolores Mobley, whose comfortable house Jake had left barely eight hours earlier.

"Hi, Dolores, this is Jake McCarthy. Is Tom there?" Jake responded, trying not to sound either angry or scared.

Jake heard Dolores call, "Thomas, Jake's on the phone, and he's in trouble. Come quickly."

"Hello, Jake, what has happened?" Mobley asked.

Quickly Jake relayed the events of the last hour, including his suspicions following the smell of gasoline and his inability to find his rented car.

"Go into the motel, try to get warm and dry off, and I'll be there as soon as I can. It should take me about an hour," Mobley ordered. "Rent a room if you need to, they are cheap there if you don't order their brand of room service. The ladies come in all sizes and shapes and will do almost anything you ask as long as you pay them. The police have been trying to shut the place down for years, but it goes on serving its clientele. Don't hang out in the bar. I'll see you in an hour."

Fifty-five minutes later, Jake sat in the front seat of Thomas Mobley's Suburban wearing a dry set of clothes provided by Mobley and beginning to tell the story of how he ended up in the maintenance pit underneath the false floor in Richard Allen's shed.

"That pit saved your life, and you were smart to hunker down in it rather than try to find a way out through the blazing fire. Since heat rises, the smoke goes up with the flames rather than seeping down below the fire. In some cases there might have been a fear of consuming all the oxygen, but with an old shed out in the middle of a parking lot, there was plenty of air to fuel the fire."

"Before the fire started, I found an old metal file cabinet, but it was locked and I didn't have time to find a key. I was hoping that Richard might have hidden one down there," Jake related, "but before I could finish my search the place was falling down around me. I don't know whether the file cabinet survived the fire, but I'm sure going to try to find out. The only thing I could salvage other than that wonderful Allen Ford parka was this videotape. "

"We'll crank up the VCR tonight to see if it has anything on it," Mobley responded. "I suspect Richard used it to show off his cars, but maybe there are some family shots that Molly would enjoy."

Mobley then pulled his cell phone from his jacket pocket and punched in a series of numbers. "Hello, Wilma. This is Tom Mobley. Is Mark there?" Jake listened as Mobley spoke.

"Mark, this is Tom. Hey, one of my friends was caught in a fire set by one of the lightning bolts. He suffered what appears to be smoke inhalation and a few cuts and bruises. Think you could come over to the ranch in about ten minutes and take a look at him? Doesn't look too serious, but he's coughing pretty badly and maybe needs something to help him with the smoke problem. Thanks, Mark. See you in about ten minutes."

Mobley explained, "Mark Davis is a physician friend of mine that lives several ranches over. He works out of an urgent care center down in Crosswind and helps out on the Indian reservation, but mostly he likes to take care of all of us ranchers out on the east side of town. Former Navy, but got tired of the ocean and came way inland. Good man, but I don't think we need to fill him in on all the details. We need to know more about what happened and why it happened, and until we do we probably ought to keep this pretty close."

Jake was happy that someone else was making decisions for him, and he simply nodded as the Suburban made its turn down the long driveway into the Mobley ranch. The rain had returned with a vengeance, and a cold wind was driving it almost horizontal as Mobley's SUV came to a stop at the back door to the ranch house.

As Jake and Mobley ran from the Suburban to the front door of the ranch house, a Toyota Four Runner pulled into the circle in front of the house, and Mark Davis, M.D., quickly exited his vehicle, grabbed a small black bag and a tank of oxygen, and entered right behind Jake and Mobley.

"Hello Mark," Dolores called as he entered the house. "I've fixed some hot soup for Tom and Jake to take the chill out of them from this nasty storm. Care to join them for a bowl?"

"Sure, but first I want to take a quick look at my patient to see if his medical condition is sufficiently serious to justify postponing that invitation."

Half an hour later, Jake was clean, reclad in yet another set of Tom Mobley's blue jeans and a flannel shirt, and sporting several fresh bandages. "Thanks, Dr. Davis," Jake said as they emerged from the guest bedroom, where Mark Davis had given Jake a complete physical after Jake had taken a hot shower to wash away the grime and soot and fear from his now extremely tired body. "That shot of oxygen sure cleared up my head in a hurry. I really feel much better."

"You were lucky, Jake. Smoke inhalation is not something that most people survive. I'm not sure that I fully understand where or what happened, but it doesn't look like you suffered any permanent damage, and those cuts and scratches should heal quickly."

"That bruise on your left leg will probably change colors several times over the next month. If it is superficial, then you have no particular fears unless you were planning to enter into a beauty contest. On the other hand, if that leg begins to ache, don't ignore it. The biggest fear we have on these lower extremity bruises is a deep vein thrombosis that could become dislodged and end up with a pulmonary embolism or cardiac arrest. Check out your leg periodically, and if it hurts or seems hot to the touch, get back to me immediately so that we can start you on some blood thinners and antibiotics. Now let's go have some of Dolores' soup. And if you're a friend of Tom's, then you better start calling me Mark. Out here we set aside formalities."

An hour later Jake and Tom Mobley were sitting in front of the television in Mobley's living room as Richard's videotape began to play. At first there was nothing save wavy lines and a low hiss. Then a bright blue screen appeared with the time and date of the video, 1:15 p.m.,

Wednesday, December 19, 1994. Finally an empty chair appeared on the screen.

"That picture was taken in the shed. That's Richard Allen's desk chair. I sat in that chair three hours ago looking through the drawers of his desk," Jake reported. "It's nothing but a charred pile of wood now."

After several seconds of empty chair, Richard Allen entered from the right hand side of the screen and sat down in the chair. He began speaking, at first in an unsteady voice, but gradually becoming more direct in his presentation.

"To my beloved Molly and to those who have been hurt by me and by the people with whom I have mistakenly shared friendship for the last thirty years, I want to say that I am deeply sorry."

Richard Allen appeared nervous and unsure of himself as he sat looking into the impersonal lens of the video camera. From the minute Richard spoke, Jake knew that this was his suicide note to Molly and the world.

For several minutes Jake and Mobley listened as Allen rambled on about his family and his life in Crosswind. As he spoke, his arms and facial expressions, which had been nearly emotionless during the first several minutes, became more animated. His voice took on a stronger and more confident tone.

"If you are viewing this videotape without me, Molly, it probably means that I am in jail or worse. I want you to know from the bottom of my heart that our investment in Red Rock Savings and Loan and the White Sands community was undertaken in a sincere belief that it would bring us financial security and a beautiful and lasting retirement home. All I longed for was to create something of my own that we could enjoy during the waning years of our life together. You are the best thing that ever happened to me, Molly, and I always felt that I failed you by not giving you children, by not building my own business and living off what my dear father built. All I ever wanted was to please you and build for us a beautiful place of our own to retire and spend the rest of our lives together.

"Now all of that is gone, and most likely I, too, am gone." Allen shifted uncomfortably in his wooden desk chair, and then resumed his monologue. "Several days ago I went to see Howard Stern and pointedly asked him how I could get out of White Sands Development. After all, I had invested over four million dollars in the project and had mortgaged my home and my dealership to support a project in which I believed but which seemed to be going too slow. I was now living month to month and having real trouble keeping up with the bills, especially the growing interest payments to Bill's bank. Although the bank's factoring of the dealership's accounts receivable kept us technically solvent, the interest and handling charges were strangling us. We had no money to put back into the dealership, and our facility was beginning to look shabby. I needed out of White Sands and wanted my investment back. Eric had just notified me of another capital call for $50,000, and I was determined not to borrow any more for this project. I wanted out. It was time to call it quits.

"I looked around at Howard's fancy office, and the thought crossed my mind that none of the other partners seemed to be having the same financial problems that I was having. For years the dealership had done much better than either the legal or banking business. I know that John Chambers doesn't have millions to throw around, and I heard that Bill's inheritance was placed in trust. When I asked Howard about White Sands and how I could get out, he answered with almost the identical words that Bill had used earlier when he tried to talk me into another $50,000 loan. It was as if they had rehearsed their response. I got suspicious.

"Next I went to John Chambers to see if he had seen the light and wanted out, but he knew less about the project than I. So I went to Eric's office to look at the books of Red Rock and White Sands. Oh, I had asked to see them on several occasions before, but for one reason or another had never actually got around to it. There was always a reason why they were not available, and I never gave it much thought. After all, they were my best friends. I trusted them completely.

"As partners in White Sands we all were supposed to contribute equally, or at least that is what I was told. When I checked out the actual books it turned out that I was the only one putting money into White Sands, and my friends were using my money to pay themselves large salaries for doing nothing. I would have blown up at Eric if he had been there, but he was off on another one of his trips. I'm convinced that the only reason I got to see the books this time was because Jenny, his young receptionist, figured I had a right to see them.

"When Eric returned I questioned him, but he refused to explain anything. Instead they convened a meeting of the partners at the Country Club. Molly, it was awful. I guess they had met earlier without me. It was apparent from the way they were talking that they had been drinking pretty heavily. When I entered the room they kind of shut up, but after a few minutes of pleasantries, Bill Hathaway started talking about their master plan for Crosswind. He dwelled on all that they had done to create Red Rock Savings and Loan just to help Crosswind develop more industry. I listened for a minute or two, but was not interested. I wanted my investment back, and I told them so in so many words. It stopped Bill in his tracks.

"Howard told me that the money was all gone. When I confronted them with what I had found at Eric's office, they all started talking at the same time about the lack of water, shifting sands not suitable for good foundations and a lot of other excuses. None was willing to tell me where my $4 million went, so I told them. It went right into each of their pockets. I covered the large salaries that they were paying themselves, and I picked up the tab for their trips out to White Sands, which I now know usually ended up at Dozier Creek Ranch. I told them point blank that I would sue to get it back, and that they had better start looking for the money right now. There were four of us. I put in $4 million;

they put in nothing beyond the initial capitalization of $50,000. The math was simple. They each owed me a million dollars.

"This must have scared them. All of a sudden they became quiet as they all looked to Howard to say something. What followed was despicable, vile, and horrible. I am still in disbelief about what I heard. It is impossible to think that rational men would be so greedy. Either it was one great big lie made to scare me into submission, or these former friends are outright criminals capable of doing the most heinous acts. I don't trust any of them to tell me the truth, especially Howard. I hope what he said was an ugly joke. I don't think I should go to the police until I know for sure. They had all been drinking, and I just can't bring myself to believe what they said was true. Instead, I am recording this for you, Molly, because I know you will do what is right if I am gone.

"Howard and Bill are coming out to the house this afternoon to try to convince me to stay with the project. I suspect that they will offer a solution, hopefully a recapitalization and payback that will get us back on our feet. We need the money. If they do not assure me that what Howard said last night was false and done only to scare me into backing off of my demand for refund of my investment, then I will put this tape in the only safe place I know of and hope that you find it before it is too late. Then I will go to the police. You always were smarter and stronger than I. If I am unable to defend myself, maybe this tape will add credence to what I report.

"Here in a condensed form is what Howard told me last night, followed by his overly pious legal opinion that I am as guilty as they are since I was part of the conspiracy and enjoyed the fruits of their crimes. I don't know what the law says, and I assume they would all lie about my involvement anyway. I swear on the grave of my dear father that I had nothing to do with this, and I will report them even if I end up in jail. Please forgive me for being so naive and trusting. It hurts me even to think about what Howard said last night, but I also need to record it."

What followed on the tape was an anguished recitation of how the others had hired Herman Kruger, a professional hit man, to methodically murder Paul Chambers, Bill Hathaway Jr. and Judge Stern so that they could inherit their father's wealth without having to wait for them to die a natural death. "Perhaps his drinking brought out the darker side of Howard, or maybe he is just mean, but he did not even act remorseful when he described how their man had staged accidents that resulted in the deaths of two and the total disability of Judge Stern. He kept saying it was for the good of Crosswind, which needed the younger generation to step up to the plate. I think it was just greed. They all lusted for the success that their fathers had achieved, and they thought that all it would take was a little seed money.

"Howard then went on to tell me that because his father did not die and Bill's left all of his money in trust, their plan to secure substantial capital failed. Poor John Chambers always thought his father had millions stashed away. He used to get so mad at old Paul Chambers because he never invested in the Gazette. We all knew Paul had no money, but his overweight son thought he knew better. When the hoped-for inheritances didn't pan out, they renewed their friendship with me. Howard knew through his former law clerk who now works at the Farley firm that I would inherit my father's entire estate, including the profitable Ford dealership, without any restrictions. Dad's trust in me may have sealed his tragic death. Once Howard and his cronies had me believing that I was part of their inner circle, they called in Kruger to stage my father's accidental death."

By this point in the recitation Richard's eyes were red, tears were trickling down his cheek, and he was nearly unable to speak. After wiping his eyes and blowing his nose, he continued, and his remorse gradually changed to anger and a desire to avenge the murder of his father.

"I tried to convince myself that this was a joke and that Howard was fabricating an explanation for the accidents that had taken these fine men, but Howard proceeded to provide details on how the accidents were orchestrated. He relished in relating the planning that had preceded each event and the efforts that they and Kruger had made to convince the police and the coroner that the deaths were accidental. With the exception of John Chambers, who had fallen asleep probably from too much bourbon and beef, they all seemed pleased with their ability to maim and murder old men without being caught.

"Howard warned me that I was just as guilty as they were as a co-conspirator, and if I ever told anyone or went to the police, I would be in jail for the rest of my life. He said no one would believe that I was not involved since I am the largest investor. He said they would all testify against me and even say that I was the one who thought up the plan. I asked them why me and why my dad, who was such a kind person. They said because he had acquired real wealth where their fathers had either not, as in the case of Paul Chambers, or had put what they had in trust and away from their offspring.

"Molly, you may remember last night when I came home and snapped at you for the first time in our marriage. I know that it hurt you, and I apologize. As you can tell, I was under a great deal of pressure. I am hopeful that this afternoon Howard will deny the whole thing and say it was only to scare me into backing off of my demand for a refund of my investment. If not, it may be a long, hard fight but I will continue until I have avenged my father's death at the hands of these thieves.

"I love you, Molly."

Richard Allen slowly rose from his desk chair and several seconds later the tape showed a time and date stamp of 1:30 p.m., Wednesday, December 19, 1994, then went blank.

Tom Mosley broke the chilling silence. "Rewind the tape, Jake. I'm going to get several blank tapes. We'll make copies, just in case. Fortunately I have a second VCR in my office. These guys are dangerous, and they may be getting desperate. I'm beginning to understand why someone might have tried to dispose of you. You were beginning to unwind their whole scheme, and I guess once you have rationalized killing one person it becomes easier for the next one. I can't believe that they were so greedy and impatient that they did this to their fathers. All were fine old gentlemen who contributed much to Crosswind and deserved to live out their retirement enjoying the fruits of their efforts. You're safe here, for the time being, Jake. I suggest that you not check back into your motel until we can get this sorted out."

"I agree," Jake responded as his mind tried to move logically through all that he had heard. "Because this involved a conspiracy to murder a federal judge, I'm certain that the FBI will assert jurisdiction, and quite frankly I think I would rather have them here than the local police. First thing tomorrow I plan to call a friend of mine in the FBI to sort out how best to proceed. She helped me with another case and seems to know the system pretty well. Unfortunately this tape all by itself is not enough to cause an indictment. Just as Richard was reluctant to go to the police without further verification, I'll bet the FBI will not want to go public just yet."

CHAPTER 31

Martinique Glasseur arrived promptly at 9:30 at the front entrance of Presbyterian Village Estates, an assisted living community for senior citizens that had been built within the last five years in conjunction with the University of Oklahoma and Presbyterian Village International. On the 400-acre parcel of land, the joint venture had built everything from cluster homes to a skilled nursing facility accommodating over 1,000 residents.

The cluster homes were all single-family dwellings occupied by senior citizens who preferred to live in a safe and secure environment with easy access to communal facilities such as the central dining room, community pool and recreation areas. The grounds were patrolled day and night by a private police force, which also manned the gatehouse at the only entrance to the complex. Security was expensive, but it was considered one of the three most important features of Presbyterian Village Estates.

The residents living in the cluster homes purchased the right to live in those homes for as long as they were physically capable and desired to live there, then they could move into the assisted living area, the extended care facility or the nursing home if necessary.

The purchase price for the right to occupy a cluster home ranged from $50,000 for a single-bedroom efficiency duplex to $300,000 for a three-bedroom, two-and-a-half-bath, 2,000 square foot home. When the resident left, either through death or a desire to move into a more secure setting, the purchase price was refunded in its entirety; however, no interest was paid and Presbyterian Village was allowed to keep any gains that may have accrued as a result of the investment. Residents of the cluster homes had no ownership interest and could be expelled if, in the opinion of the Village directors, the residents were no longer capable of maintaining their home.

Molly had moved into the assisted living section of Presbyterian Village under a special program funded by the State of Oklahoma for indigent, single senior citizens who had no alternative but the streets. Her building consisted of a series of four sections, each containing eight separate apartment units all on the same level. Each resident entered through a common entryway into a spacious gathering area. All of the apartments had doors opening onto the common area. From a single, circular nursing station in the middle of the common area, a nurse or trained staff person could observe each of the thirty-two rooms. Each room was equipped with emergency cords and buttons that could be pulled or pushed in the event of an emergency. A light would begin blinking over the doorway into that apartment notifying the staff person on duty that one of the residents was in trouble. It also activated a signal at the central security office. If the alarm was not deactivated within sixty seconds, an emergency team was dispatched to the unit.

The back door to the common area led through a series of enclosed walkways to a central dining room available to all of the residents of the assisted living facility as part of their rent, and to any other residents of Presbyterian Village Estates on a pay-as-you-go basis. For those who were unable to use the common dining facility, food was brought to the room.

Molly had risen early and prepared herself for a trip back to Crosswind. Wearing a blue dress with a single strand of pearls that Dr. Glasseur had loaned her for the occasion, Molly Allen looked like the successful wife of a prominent businessman, just as she had looked prior to the tragic death of her husband.

She had walked the several blocks from her assisted-living apartment complex to the main entrance of Presbyterian Village, and now stood before the large mirror hanging on one wall of the lobby. She admired the change that had overtaken her as a result of the unique therapy treatment provided by Doctors Gupta, Reddy and Glasseur.

She and Jake had spent several evenings talking by telephone and outlining the plan that Jake had conceived for bringing the directors of Red Rock Savings and Loan to their knees. When Jake had told her about Richard's tape and the allegations made against his former friends, Molly listened with disbelief that gradually changed to anger. Her mind had gained a focus that now drove her back to Crosswind to avenge her husband's death and correct this horrible injustice.

Seeing Dr. Glasseur's car pull into the waiting area in front of the Village, Molly signaled the receptionist that she was leaving and quickly stepped out to greet Dr. Glasseur. After retrieving Molly's suitcase from the front hall of her apartment building, the two ladies set out for the Mobley Ranch on the east side of Crosswind and a rendezvous with Jake McCarthy.

Meanwhile, FBI Special Agent Sarah Cantrell, on special assignment from the Terrorist Interdiction Force, and two FBI agents from the Oklahoma City office were preparing for the meeting between Molly Allen and William Hathaway that had been scheduled by Molly for later that afternoon.

The first item of business was testing a new radio transmitter that had been shaped into the form of a small pearl pendant that could be hung from, and appear to be part of, a pearl necklace. Through miniaturization and use of an ultra-thin battery, this amplification device could transmit sound for over a quarter of a mile with digital clarity. Even a trained expert had difficulty noticing that this seemingly innocent piece of jewelry contained such a high-powered listening device.

The FBI had also provided appropriate tape recording machines to record the exchange of information between Molly Allen and her former friends. The paperwork necessary to obtain warrants for the arrest of the co-conspirators was ready to present to Judge Zambricki as soon as they obtained sufficient incriminating evidence.

Each of the FBI agents and Jake McCarthy were concerned about protecting Molly Allen from possible danger resulting from her participation in this plan to incriminate the five remaining directors of Red Rock Savings and Loan. Calmly and with strength of character, Molly had insisted that she be part of this plan in order to redeem her husband's reputation and satisfy her need for revenge against his former friends.

After careful discussion among the therapists, Dr. Glasseur agreed to allow Molly this opportunity, but only if she accompanied Molly on the trip and was available to help in the event of a relapse. Jake was glad that Martinique had volunteered to drive Molly down from Oklahoma City, and he was looking forward to seeing her again.

Tom and Dolores Mobley were enjoying every minute of the activity at their ranch. Jake had been staying there for over a week since his near-fatal run-in with Jim O'Connor, and Sarah Cantrell was staying with Mobley's eldest son and his wife and two children in a large farmhouse about a quarter of a mile from the main ranch house. The two FBI agents were not so fortunate and had to commute back and forth to Crosswind, but they spent most of their time out at the ranch and enjoyed the fresh air and friendliness of the Mobleys.

Two and a half hours after leaving Presbyterian Village, Martinique drove her Peugeot convertible down the long driveway of the Bar M Ranch, admiring as had Jake its rugged beauty. Shortly after greeting all of the members of the family and the three FBI agents that were assembled at the Mobley ranch, Molly asked if she could see the videotape. Knowing that it might cause her to relapse into her post-traumatic stress disorder, but also knowing that she would similarly be subjected to stress in her meeting with Hathaway, Jake and Martinique, after a few minutes of discussion, slid the videotape into Mobley's VCR and began playing once again Richard's final comments before his death.

Jake, Martinique and Sarah Cantrell all watched with concern as Molly studied the tape and listened to her husband's final words. Tears came to Molly's eyes as she recognized the qualities of her husband and his expressed desire to hold his friends accountable for their deeds. Jake noticed a tightening of Molly's jaw as the tape proceeded to its end. By that time the tears were gone and there was a new resoluteness in Molly's countenance that made both Jake and Martinique realize that she now possessed the toughness to go forward and speak with Hathaway or anyone else about the tragic sequence of events over the last several years that had led to her husband's death.

"Jake, what Richard said is horrible. How could those men have been so awful to their fathers and to Richard? Those are not the words of a man intending to commit suicide. What do you think happened to him?"

"We can't be sure, Molly," Jake responded. "We would all like to think that Richard was a man on a mission, not a man intending to take his own life. If what Richard has said is true, then these men are capable of murder. Perhaps they caused Richard's death. We just don't know. We have no proof, and this tape, for all of its incriminating statements, would not be admissible in a court of law. It is not a dying declaration since Richard's death was not imminent at the time he made the tape. A smart defense attorney would portray this as an attempt at revenge by a distraught investor who dreamed up this whole story in a misguided attempt to destroy those who caused his losses. Our hope is that you will be able to extract incriminating evidence from Bill Hathaway, who seems to react poorly to pressure. If you appear to be frail and alone in the world, he may be off guard and relate information to you that will allow us to come back at him and force a confession, or at least the unintentional disclosure of enough facts to bring this matter to the U.S.

Attorney's office for prosecution. You understand, however, that there is significant danger. They think they have gotten rid of me, and they may view you as another problem now that you have come back to Crosswind and are asking questions. If they sense that you know about their past actions, they may get desperate. That could get nasty in a hurry. We'll be close, but you be careful."

"Yes, Jake, we have been over this before," Molly answered. "They are bad, and now, more than ever, I want to avenge my husband's death and put these men where they deserve to be, behind bars in a federal penitentiary. I don't care what happens to me. I have nothing to lose and everything to gain in terms of self-respect and protecting the reputation of my husband."

"If you are ready, Molly," Sarah Cantrell spoke up softly, "then we will brief you on this simple device that we plan to attach to your necklace."

"Oh, what a pretty pendant. Is that a real pearl?" Molly asked.

"No, Molly, that is only synthetic material but it has a high sound transmission coefficient that helps amplify the voices as they are transmitted over a tiny transmitter embedded in the fake pearl. As long as you are wearing this pendant, we will be able to hear everything you say and everything that is said to you with near perfect clarity. All we ask is that you do not handle this pendant with your fingers and that you try not to move so rapidly as to make it swing on your neck. You can't hurt the transmitter, but it will mask any sounds other than your fingers rubbing on the pendant or it rubbing on your neck."

"I understand."

"Molly, we are depending on you to act as frail and helpless as you were when you left Crosswind several months ago. I have described you on several occasions to Hathaway and Stern as under psychiatric care and suffering from severe trauma. We want them to think that you are still suffering. If they think you are not fully competent, they may become sloppy and disclose information that will incriminate them. Do you think you can handle that?" Jake asked.

"I have been rehearsing for the last three days, and I am ready," Molly answered resolutely. She then fixed her gaze on a tree just outside the Mobley's living room window, and said, "I, I, I can't quite figure out where I am or what happened to me. I need help. My attorney is gone, and there is no one here but you to help, Bill. What am I to do?"

"Perfect," Jake responded to Molly's act.

"Well, let's have us some lunch so y'all can do your thing on a full stomach," Dolores Mobley piped up as she invited her guests into the dining room for barbecued ribs, southwestern-style baked beans cooked in an earthen crock, potato salad and iced tea.

That afternoon shortly after two o'clock, Molly Allen slowly and deliberately walked through the front door of the First State Bank of Crosswind and, after staring around the bank's interior, hesitatingly approached one of the teller windows.

"I'm looking for Mr. Hathaway, is he in? My name is Molly Allen, and I have an appointment with him."

"Hello, Molly, it's me, Sarah Jane. Remember me? I used to cash your checks when you came in. How are you? I heard that you had suffered after your husband's tragic death. You look well. I'll see if Mr. Hathaway is available."

"I really don't know how I'm doing, Sarah dear. It's a struggle every day just to get up and face the world. I need to talk to Mr. Hathaway soon before I get tired."

"Yes, yes, of course, I will call him immediately. I'm sure he will want to see you. Did you say you had an appointment?"

"I think so," Molly lied as she continued her act.

Several minutes later Bill Hathaway pushed his rotund body toward Molly, and after the usual pleasantries, invited her to come with him to his office.

Hathaway slowly led Molly Allen back to his wood-paneled office with the bigger-than-life portrait of his grandfather. He closed the door behind her as she moved to sit in one of the green leather chairs that faced his massive desk.

Hathaway started the conversation. "I am so pleased to see that you are back in town and still as beautiful as ever, Molly. I know this has been a horrible ordeal for you, and Jane and I want to do whatever we can to help you."

"You have always been a true friend, Bill, and I know that you helped poor Richard...." Molly appeared to wipe a few tears from her eyes and continued, "...through some pretty tough financial times." Molly stopped talking for nearly two minutes while Hathaway sat patiently waiting for her to gather her thoughts. Little did he know that this was part of the well-orchestrated plan to confuse Hathaway and his friends about the real status of Molly Allen's mental health.

Finally, after staring abjectly at the massive painting of the original William Hathaway that occupied nearly half of one of the office walls, Molly continued. "Richard talked to me the night before he died and told me some terrible things about White Sands and his investments in Red Rock Savings and Loan. He told me that he thought you and his other friends were taking his money and not properly investing it in either the savings and loan or in the White Sands development. Is that true, Bill?" Molly asked in a very soft, grandmotherly tone of voice.

The perspiration that immediately presented itself any time Hathaway came under even the slightest pressure began popping at his temples and streaming down his enormous cheeks. Instinctively he reached for his huge white handkerchief and began mopping as he tried to think of an appropriate response to this straightforward and unexpected question. After a brief pause, Hathaway responded. "We all lost a lot of money on that horrible savings and loan venture and on our investment in White Sands. You know that we would never have taken money from Richard. He was our good friend, an important part of Red Rock, and our leader in the White Sands development."

Molly proceeded in the same quiet, almost melancholy tone. "I know, Bill, you were Richard's best friend and banker, and you never would have taken advantage of him. But sometimes when I am going to sleep at night I wonder about Richard's death and wonder why this all happened. I just need some answers to put my poor, feeble mind at rest. I need to get over the nightmares. Can you tell me why all of this happened to us?"

Hathaway sat motionless in his high-backed leather chair, then as a great drop of sweat left the tip of his chin and dropped onto his portly belly, leaving yet another stain on his crimson and gold tie, he lifted his hand as if to reassure Molly that they were all suffering, but could only manage to mop the perspiration that now covered his entire head. As he attended to that chore, Hathaway had time to think up another response.

"I don't know what Richard may have said to you, Molly, but he was obviously distraught at the time. Whatever he may have said should be discounted as the final flailing of a man who has lost his will to live. Whatever drove Richard to take his own life was also deluding him into thinking it was not his fault, but unfortunately we have all suffered great losses as a result of this investment gone bad. If only we had found that underground river out at White Sands, we would all be enjoying the fruits of a good investment."

With that response, Molly quietly stood, looked Bill Hathaway squarely in the eye, and said, "Richard and I relied on your honesty and the integrity of this bank. I hope for your sake and for the sake of the bank that you are right. I wish I could find my attorney who was looking into these matters for me, but now that he is gone I am the only one left, and I will find out what happened. I have nothing to lose."

She turned and left the office while Bill Hathaway sat impassively mopping his face with a fresh handkerchief pulled from a reserve supply, which he conveniently kept in the top drawer of his desk. Within minutes after her departure, Hathaway was on the phone to Stern calling for another emergency meeting. Sarah Cantrell was already on the way back to the Mobley ranch with Molly Allen sitting next to her in the front seat and, for the first time in what seemed like an eternity, Molly was smiling at the way she had planted the seeds of chaos. Hathaway had been smart enough not to say anything incriminating, but both Molly and Sarah knew that he was worried.

"That last challenge you threw out at Hathaway was a winner," Cantrell said as they drove toward the ranch. "If it didn't scare him into further action, then nothing will. I am worried for your safety, Molly, and I want you to stay near us for the next few days until we have these creeps behind bars. OK?"

"OK," Molly responded, still smiling at her performance.

CHAPTER 32

After a full breakfast as only Dolores Mobley could make, Molly and Jake sat in Tom Mobley's office and placed a telephone call to Howard Stern.

"Hello, Howard," Molly Allen said in a soft and uncertain voice. "I spoke yesterday with Bill at the bank and there were a few unanswered questions about Richard's investments. Are you available for an hour or so?"

Howard Stern had anticipated the call from his former client, and with the concurrence of his partners, had devised a plan to uncover exactly how much information Molly Allen really had and, if necessary, dispose of this last source of incriminating evidence. The plan involved meeting with Molly at his offices that evening with the entire group present. In addition, although unpopular with every one of the partners, a decision had been made to bring Kruger back to Crosswind to deal, if necessary, with Molly Allen. Even Jim O'Connor lacked the toughness that would be necessary to dispose of this frail lady who had done none of them any harm and seemed so unlikely a threat.

"Yes, I spoke with Bill yesterday afternoon, and we agreed that you were entitled to hear from all of us about Red Rock Savings and Loan and why Richard's investments turned out so bad. We are all going to be at my office tonight at 7:30, and if you have the time to come by we will answer all of your questions and try to assure you of our good intentions."

"I'll be there. You were Richard's best friends, and I look forward to seeing you all again." Molly gently replaced the handset of the telephone in its cradle and began smiling again, knowing that neither Stern nor any of the other conspirators knew that this was precisely what she and Jake had hoped would happen. She would not be alone.

Eight hours later, Molly Allen, dressed in one of Dolores Mobley's old housedresses and looking more like a bag lady than the former wife of a prominent auto dealer, knocked on the polished, solid walnut door of the offices of Stern, Foster & Smith at half past the hour of seven and was immediately ushered into the conference room in which Jake McCarthy had sat several weeks before. The sun cast its last rays of light on the giant red rock that was clearly visible through the plate glass window of the conference room.

Molly clutched a small purse that had been given to her by Sarah Cantrell earlier that day, and although it did not exactly match the ill-fitting housedress, it did contain sophisticated microphones sewn into the fabric from which the FBI and Jake McCarthy could overhear all that was being said. The pearl necklace did not fit the bag-lady outfit, so Cantrell had suggested another, more powerful listening device that would pick up all of the discussion. Molly placed the handbag on the conference table in front of her.

After exchanging pleasantries, Stern introduced the lone stranger to the group. "Molly, the gentleman sitting at the end of the table is Herman Kruger, an associate of ours, who is here at our request to listen to your questions and help provide us with solutions. Shall we get started?"

From the interior of a white Ford Econoline van parked several doors down from the office building came a worried groan as Jake recognized the name of the person Richard had indicated was responsible for the deaths. "We've got to go in, now!" Jake said to Sarah Cantrell. He's the creep that was following me, I'm sure of it. He's here to kill Molly, I just know it."

Agent Cantrell activated her two-way radio to alert her team to be on the highest level of readiness and assured Jake that they would move at the first hint of any danger. "This is our chance to nail these bastards, and I just want to give them enough rope so we can hang the bunch of them."

Bill Hathaway was in the midst of a lengthy report on the formation and early goals and objectives of Red Rock Savings & Loan when Molly raised her hand about ten inches off of the tabletop and interjected a question. "I have no interest in what you gentlemen were trying to accomplish and deeply regret your failure, since it caused me to lose my husband and all of my property. I am here because Richard told me some horrible things concerning the death of his father; and your father's terrible accident, Howard; and the death of our crusty but dependable newspaper editor, Paul Chambers; and your father's death, Bill. He said you boys may have had them all murdered."

"Molly, that is preposterous," Stern responded as Hathaway immediately began wiping the perspiration that had sprung from both temples like droplets on a soaker hose and began running down his face. "Have you told this to anyone else, Molly?" Stern asked, continuing with his appearance of complete disbelief in Molly's allegations. "If you did, it would be the worst kind of slander and would subject you to legal action to prevent you from spreading such a vile rumor."

Molly had been coached to expect this question early on in the session. Acting tired and confused, Molly dropped her eyes to the table and softly said, "No, I just don't know where to turn. My attorney was looking into Richard's affairs, but I haven't seen him lately or had the chance to tell him." Her voice was intentionally soft and she appeared immensely vulnerable.

"Where have you been, Molly, for the last several months?" John Chambers asked, trying to divert the conversation into more friendly territory. "We heard that you were having memory problems and were under psychiatric care. From your comments it appears the reports were accurate."

Again, Molly had been prepared and stated, untruthfully, that she had left the psychiatric ward of the hospital in Oklahoma City to ease her mind about Richard's last comments. Although still technically under the care of her physician, she had left without telling anyone because she wanted to come back to Crosswind and find out what happened to her husband.

"I have nowhere to go and no one to take care of me," Molly mumbled. "I can't rest until I know what happened to Richard, and I will keep digging and keep looking until I find out. I have nothing to lose."

By this time Hathaway had regained his composure sufficiently to echo Stern's disavowal of any wrongdoing and then generously offered to help Molly in any way that he could. The other gentlemen around the table, except Kruger, nodded their heads in agreement with this general statement of denial and concern.

In response to this false sincerity, Molly Allen decided to pull the trigger. "Thanks, all of you," Molly responded a little less timidly. "There is one thing that you might do for me. Do you have a VCR here in your offices, Howard?"

Stern looked quickly around the group, and then responded in the affirmative. Walking over to a walnut cabinet that ran across the entire end of the conference room, Stern opened one of the cabinet doors to reveal a thirty-five-inch television set with a VCR conveniently stored underneath. "We use this to view video depositions and can even do teleconferencing. High-tech, but expensive. Why do you need this, Molly?"

"Your offices are very nice, Howard. Would you be so kind as to slip this videotape into the machine? Richard made this just before his horrible death, and I thought you might be interested in seeing it."

As Howard Stern walked slowly over to Molly to take the videotape from her, Eric Beamer asked, "Where did you find this tape, Molly? Have you shown it to anyone else?"

Although Molly Allen was not accustomed to lying to anyone, she again had been well prepared for this question. Jake had advised her against putting herself at risk by misleading the group, but Sarah Cantrell had encouraged Molly to say that this was the only copy and that she had not shown it to others. She had been quite emphatic that the tape would be inadmissible as hearsay and that the only way to flush out the conspirators was a frontal attack with the tape. By showing it there was a good possibility that they would act precipitously and disclose information or take action that would incriminate them. If properly documented, observed and recorded, these statements and actions would be far more compelling than Richard's tape. Even against Jake's advice that this could be extremely dangerous, Molly had understood that she was being used as bait and insisted that she be allowed this opportunity to avenge her husband's death. And so, once again, Molly lied.

"I found this tape at the post office where they were holding mail for me. I tried to play it on the VCR at the public library, but when I saw Richard I began to cry and after a few minutes had to turn it off. I hope I don't cry now." A few tears embellished the lie.

Howard Stern pushed the play button on the VCR, and after a few seconds Richard Allen came into view as he moved to his oak desk chair that now was no more than a pile of ashes. There was dead silence in the room as the VCR played on outlining the conspiracy conceived by Stern, Hathaway and Beamer and joined by Chambers and O'Connor. Kruger, sitting at the end of the long conference table, sat motionless but his muscles began to tense involuntarily at the stupidity of his employers, who had decided to present this information to Richard in a failed attempt to extort another payment from him. It left them no alternative but to eliminate him when he refused. Apparently they had failed to eliminate him before he had committed this information to tape. Already Kruger's mind was focusing on eliminating Molly Allen and the tape and possibly everyone in the room. Survival sometimes required it.

When Richard had completed his monologue, Stern returned to the VCR and ejected the tape without rewinding. Had he and his partners not been so horrified by the contents of the tape and its implications for their future freedom, they might have noticed that Molly Allen was not consumed by tears but rather sitting patiently waiting for the anticipated reaction. She did not wait long as Stern took the first bite at the bait.

"Molly, I'm afraid that I will need to keep this tape," Stern said as he placed the tape back in its protective container. "You know that what Richard has said is highly slanderous, and if this tape were to get into the public domain, you would be subject to legal action for slander."

"Howard, you always had an answer for everything," Molly responded. "I'm not worried about slander. I have nothing, and I think it's important to see whether there is any truth to what Richard says. I want the tape back."

"And what will you do if we keep the tape?" Hathaway interjected. "You are hardly in a position to force us to return it to you."

"Well, I don't know. I guess maybe I will just have to go see Detective Randall. He was a friend of Richard's, and I think he would be wiling to explore what really happened to my poor dead husband, and your father, and poor Judge Stern."

This time it was Jim O'Connor's turn to speak, and his remarks were neither polite nor ambiguous. "We can't let you do that, Molly. We have too much at stake, and we have worked too hard. We cannot allow you to go any further with your investigation of these allegations."

In a shallow voice, Molly responded, "Why did you do this? How could you harm your fathers in this way? Did greed drive you to this? Richard was your friend, how could you have murdered him like that?"

The conference room became silent as each of the men tried to deal with this question. No one responded. Seconds passed as each of the individuals other than Herman Kruger sat impassively.

It was equally quiet inside the Ford Econoline van. Jake began to fear that the small microphones in Molly's handbag had been discovered or that there was a malfunction. As he and Sarah Cantrell considered whether it was now time to intervene, John Chambers coughed one of his loud, deep, emphysemic, coughs that reassured the listeners that all was still in order.

"Well, gentlemen," O'Connor finally spoke up, "we understand what must be done, and I suggest that we get on with it no mater how distasteful it may be. Molly, Richard was a very decent person. He should not have poked his nose into matters about which he had neither the will nor the stomach to understand. Unfortunately for him, he got suspicious and wanted all of his money back. He would have ruined us. When we couldn't convince him not to go to the police, we had to eliminate him. Unfortunately for you, Richard preserved his findings on that tape.

"My father was killed by the Mob when I was seventeen," O'Connor continued, "and I have been getting even ever since. I needed a safe refuge, and chose Crosswind. These gentlemen were willing to help me; however, their hands were tied because their fathers refused to allow them to prosper. What Richard says in this tape is basically true. Richard's father didn't fall from that ugly rock. Our friend at the end of the table helped him fall just after he broke his neck. And if it makes you feel any better even for a short while, Richard didn't commit suicide. He must have suspected that we might come after him, so he had this huge pistol that he had no idea how to use. He tried to pull it on me, but before he could get it out of the fine wooden box that he stored it in, I had disabled him. We had planned another tragic accident, but when I saw the pistol the idea of a suicide just fit right into place."

As O'Connor prepared to continue, Kruger stood at the end of the table and said, "Stop! There is no need to continue with this confession. Mrs. Allen, you look like a very nice old lady, but you now know far too much, and these sorry-ass gentlemen cannot allow you to convey this information to anyone."

Looking around the room at each of the men sitting at the conference table, Kruger hesitated as each of the individuals nodded assent to the predetermined fate of Molly Allen.

"Richard had high hopes for White Sands," Stern explained, "because we told him what a wonderful place it would be for you to retire. We had marvelous pictures of beautiful homes, and Richard poured millions of dollars into that development, which in fact never even got started. He accompanied us on our first tour of the area, but never came on any other visits. He couldn't take the side trips to west Texas where we tasted some of the seamier side of life without fearing repercussions from among Crosswind's moral establishment. It doesn't look good for bankers and lawyers and accountants to be whoring around and spending time in seedy bars and strip joints, but sometimes a man needs a little extra-curricular activity to keep his blood flowing. Richard trusted us to keep him advised of the progress of the project, and we told him some wonderful stories about how it was progressing. Then we would ask him for another capital contribution. He was such a patsy. He'd be here today if he hadn't run out of money and tried to back out. Bill's bank would have extended his line of credit. It was really the bank that was funding the deal, only we needed a respectable businessman to appear to justify the amount of the loan."

"Because he spent so much money on that worthless pile of sand," O'Connor interrupted, "we have decided that it is only fitting that you should visit White Sands and see for yourself what a worthless wasteland it really is. We also think you should plan to stay there, for good."

While O'Connor was informing Molly of their plans for her departure, Stern ripped the videotape from its plastic cartridge and threw the tape into a wastepaper basket half full of paper. "John, lend me your cigarette lighter for a minute, will you? We need to dispose of this tape permanently." Soon, a small blaze arose from the metal wastebasket and the tape was consumed.

"Now, Molly, you must go with Mr. Kruger. Herman, you know what to do. No traces."

"I don't wish to go to White Sands," Molly responded. "White Sands killed my husband. I won't go with Mr. Kruger to White Sands. You can't make me. I don't think I like the looks of Mr. Kruger, and I won't go with him."

O'Connor looked Molly Allen squarely in the face with eyes that were mean and penetrating and said, "You have no choice. Soon you will join your husband."

With that, O'Connor grabbed Molly Allen around her shoulders and lifted her frail body off the chair as if to hand her to Herman Kruger, who was now standing beside her. All of the men were standing and began walking out of the conference room into the main corridor of the office suite. Standing along the walls of the corridor were four agents in bulletproof vests and baseball caps with "FBI" printed in large white letters across the front and back. Sarah Cantrell was the first to speak, announcing who they were and ordering the men to stand still and place their hands behind their heads.

The reaction to this sudden turn of events was predictable. Hathaway burst into sweat, his face crimson as his blood pressure rose well beyond a safe level. His massive body fell to the floor as he fainted from the shock of impending apprehension. His white handkerchief fell across his torso as if in surrender.

Beamer thought for a second about trying to escape, realized it was impossible, calculated whether it made any sense to resist, and did nothing. Stern's immediate reaction was indignation that anyone would enter his law offices without permission. He was about to demand to see a warrant and raise an objection, but in the confusion he couldn't focus on whether this was an illegal search and seizure or an arrest without a warrant. He, too, did nothing.

O'Connor had another idea. He bolted for the rear exit of the suite of offices, but before he got to the end of the corridor two FBI agents tackled him. Handcuffs were immediately applied to the subdued O'Connor as the other FBI agents moved toward the remaining men with similar plans.

Kruger analyzed the situation. When O'Connor ran toward the exit, Kruger quietly removed his 9mm semi-automatic pistol from his shoulder holster, grabbed Molly Allen by the front of Dolores Mobley's old housedress, and held his gun to her head as they moved slowly toward the front entrance to the office. Kruger, standing at his full height of six foot two, would have towered over Molly Allen, giving the FBI ample opportunity to take him down. He used her body as a shield as best he could, bending forward to lower his upper body and hide behind her white hair. She looked even frailer and older, but she was beyond fear.

"Back off or this nice old lady turns into mincemeat!" Kruger shouted. "Let me through. I don't care about the rest, just let me through, and don't give me any reason to pull this trigger. I don't know what this is all about or why you're here, but I ain't taking no chances, so just get out of my way and the old lady doesn't get hurt. Any one of you even thinks about pointing a firearm at me, this woman is dead!"

"Give it up, Kruger," Sarah Cantrell said. "You're outgunned, outsmarted and out of luck."

"Shut up, bitch! You got nothing on me, and I got this old lady. Now move!"

At that command, Cantrell and the other FBI agents stepped slightly aside to allow Kruger and Molly Allen to move down the narrow hallway and into the reception area.

"Now I want all of you to stand right where you are and don't nobody make any quick moves. I don't want to get in a firing contest with you because I'll probably lose, but you can be sure that I will take her and a few of you with me." Kruger continued to hold Molly by her dress, holding his pistol to her forehead as he backed away from the FBI agents and toward the large door that would let him out of the suite. Glancing quickly over his shoulders to make sure there were no FBI agents behind him in the reception area, Kruger moved slowly and deliberately, forcing Molly to walk forward as he walked backward. Molly did not resist. She moved in step with him as if she were dancing, offering almost no resistance as he fought to escape this trap.

As Kruger approached the highly polished, solid walnut door into the suite, he again glanced over his right shoulder looking for the door handle. He had a choice. He could use the hand that held Molly between him and the FBI agents and lose his shield, or keep her in place and use his gun hand to open the door. Kruger hesitated momentarily, and then decided to use his gun hand and keep Molly as his human shield. Having come to this decision, he quickly removed his 9mm pistol that had already created an indentation on Molly's forehead and reached around to open the door. As he began this process he pulled Molly even closer to him to maximize her body as a human shield. She was compliant and allowed her body to be pulled so close to Kruger that her chest and hips were in direct contact with his muscular body now tensed with fear and a desire to survive. Kruger's eyes were focused on the small detail of FBI agents who were now in the reception area but making no move to apprehend or upset him.

As Kruger moved his pistol from Molly's forehead and reached behind him to open the door, Molly suddenly tensed, changing instantly from the compliant, frail old lady to the athletic swimmer fresh from a comprehensive exercise program orchestrated by Dr. Glasseur and her capable therapists. Synchronizing her movements with the brief moment when Kruger's gun was behind him, Molly brought her right knee hard into Kruger's groin, using muscles that had daily propelled her through two hundred laps in the Olympic-size Oklahoma University pool.

Molly's kneecap made contact with both of Kruger's testicles. He immediately bent forward in pain and involuntarily released Molly while struggling to regain his equilibrium. As soon as she felt him release his grip on her dress, Molly dove for the richly carpeted floor as four FBI-issue slugs opened four gaping holes in Kruger's chest. The force of the FBI bullets impacting simultaneously on his chest drove Kruger hard against the very door that he had been trying to open. As his body slid to the floor, splinters from the once-highly-polished solid walnut door grabbed at his now grossly bloodstained and tattered shirt, impeding but not stopping his ultimate fall to the floor of the immaculately maintained law offices of Stern, Foster & Smith. The door had one large gaping hole attesting to the impact power of the 9mm weapons used by the FBI and the accuracy of the men and woman that had just used them.

With the elimination of this threat, Sarah Cantrell moved quickly to Molly Allen, who lay on the floor close to the fallen assassin. Although Dolores Mobley's old housedress was missing several buttons and had been slightly torn by Kruger's manhandling, Molly Allen appeared remarkably unfazed by the attack. Her gray hair, which even in her most disoriented daze was remarkably neat, showed no signs of having been in a tussle. As Sarah approached, Molly sat up on the floor of the office and beamed a victorious smile.

"We nailed them, didn't we?" she said without hesitation. "Did you get a tape recording? Did you hear them boast about killing my poor Richard? These are bad people, and they deserve to be put away for good."

CHAPTER 33

"Tom, I think this celebration calls for a special toast to you and your family. On behalf of my partner, his client and my first love, I wish to thank you and Dolores and your sons for your help." With that toast, Reginald Parker raised his glass of wine to the resounding cheers of Jake, Molly, Marty Glasseur, Judy Falsworth and the Mobley family. "It will take Crosswind a few years to heal from this epidemic of greed, but Molly has already made herself felt in the community as one of its new leaders. Time will overcome the negative impact of these tragic events as younger men and women replace those who will soon be enrolled permanently in the federal penitentiary."

"Reggie, you are a dear friend and my savior. Your generosity in sending Jake down here to help me was about the nicest thing that anyone has ever done for me. The next best thing that happened is my getting to know Tom and Dolores better. They have become such wonderful friends, and I am forever indebted to them for their help."

"We also owe a great debt of gratitude to Dr. Marty Glasseur and her wonderful treatment of you at the OU Medical Center," Parker responded. "You all know the innovative therapy that she successfully tried on Molly, and we are pleased to announce that Molly has agreed to contribute $200,000 to the Medical School to continue these alternative therapy initiatives under Marty's care."

With that announcement, Jake McCarthy raised his wine goblet in toast and said, "To Marty Glasseur. May her psychotherapeutic programs continue to push at the boundaries of healing social and mental disorders." To this toast there was a round of applause as Marty Glasseur's normally fair complexion responded to the accolades.

"Molly," Reginald Parker asked after several more toasts by the Mobleys, who occupied over half of the seats around their massive dining room table, "tell us how you are doing."

"Well, Reggie, I think I had better leave that to Jake, since he seems to know more about me than I do myself. He has been handling most of the details. Jake, tell them how we're doing."

Jake McCarthy, who was sitting at about the middle of the long dining room table, responded to the request of his elderly client. "First and foremost, we are pleased to report that Molly is physically and emotionally healthy and excited to be back in Crosswind. She has purchased a small house several blocks away from her former residence, and she has already reestablished many friendships in the community. Financially she is secure. We were able to demonstrate that Richard's death was not a suicide, and within weeks after the arrest of his partners, the insurance company sent a certified check to her order in the amount of $2,018,000, representing the insurance coverage plus interest since Richard's death. In addition, we have filed a lawsuit in Broken Bow Circuit Court against the assets of Howard Stern, including his interest in Stern, Foster & Smith, which we have claimed as a co-defendant since the firm represented Molly and Richard in all of these transactions. The firm has two million dollars of malpractice insurance, and we should be able to prove damages of at least that amount. We have also sued all of the other members of the conspiracy, but none of them had the insurance coverage. Hathaway has only the money from his father's trust, and now that he is no longer employed by the bank he has no real income. Based on Judy's report that Hathaway handled the loans personally and did not involve any other bank employees, we decided not to sue the bank and have been working on an amicable settlement. Chambers spent his entire inheritance even before the estate was settled. He is broke, and the Gazette will most likely fold unless Crosswind can find someone to take it over and unload its debt. At Molly's insistence and with my support, we have not attempted to bankrupt these individuals since everyone but Eric Beamer has a wife and family that were not responsible for any of the actions of their husbands. For that reason, we have offered to settle with each of the married individuals for an amount equal to half of their net worth. In Beamer's case we are claiming it all since he will never be able to enjoy a penny of his wealth. Our calculations indicate that if we are successful in all of this, Molly should be the recipient of another $3.5 million, plus Stern's malpractice insurer should kick in another two million. Molly will not be in financial need for the rest of her life."

"Tell them about the dealership, Jake," Molly interjected.

"We have filed a separate cause of action against Jim O'Connor alleging that his purchase of the Ford dealership was fraudulent and should be set aside by the court. If we are successful, the dealership will revert to Molly Allen as the sole heir of Richard's estate. She has agreed to assume control of the dealership as Chairman of the Board and to restore the name of Allen Ford to the marquee. Through my contacts at Ford legal, we have obtained the favorable ruling that Ford would approve of the immediate transfer of the dealership to Molly. Ford agreed to file an affidavit with the court encouraging it to return the dealership to its rightful owner. At my suggestion, Molly has agreed to hire Ralph Tyson to manage the dealership. Ralph had been with Allen Ford until several weeks ago when O'Connor fired him for talking to me. He seems to have the greatest knowledge of the dealership and, according to Molly, was one of Richard's most loyal employees.

"And speaking of Jim O'Connor, the FBI did a background check on him and his manager, and they are both under indictment for murder in the Commonwealth of Massachusetts. They left Boston because they had crossed the Mafia by trying to take over a section of South Boston without the blessing of the Godfather. They were told to leave and had the choice of leaving either alive or dead. They chose the former, but not before they took vengeance by wiping out two of the Mob's enforcers who had come by O'Connor's house to rough them up as a way of encouraging them to leave more quickly. O'Connor had been warned, and when they showed up at his garage, he and his sidekick, Vincent, shot and killed them. There is an open warrant for O'Connor's arrest in Massachusetts, and he may be sent back there after he stands trial here for murder.

"I guess that pretty well wraps it up. Molly is well, Molly is rich, and Molly is happy. But we have one other bit of news to report. Judy, why don't you tell the group what you're doing now, besides line dancing, of course?"

Judy Falsworth looked appropriately embarrassed, but quickly overcame her discomfort and responded to Jake's invitation. "After Tubby Hathaway was arrested for conspiracy and murder, the Board of Directors of the bank met to remove him from office and elect a new president and CEO. The board had never had to do this in the entire history of the bank since there has always been a Hathaway at the helm. It turns out that there are only 300,000 shares of bank stock outstanding, two-thirds of which are held in trust and the other third I own thanks to the generosity of Mr. Hathaway Sr. The chairman of the board of directors of Crosswind Community Hospital, the beneficiary of the other 200,000 shares following the death of Mr. Hathaway and his mother, is a member of the bank board. He asked me if I would be willing to take on the responsibilities of running the bank. I accepted.

"Tubby was taking over $400,000 a year in salary from the bank even though it was marginally profitable. He put virtually nothing back into refurbishing the hard assets. I agreed to take a smaller salary and have begun the process of restoring what was once a truly great regional bank. We are working with Jake to process a reasonable settlement of

Molly's legitimate claims against the bank for Hathaway's behavior. Fortunately most of the damages are covered by insurance."

"Let's all move out to the front porch," Dolores invited after everyone had congratulated Molly on her restoration. "I have coffee and apple pie waiting, and we can enjoy watching a fantastic Oklahoma sunset." As the guests followed her invitation and walked out to the large front porch of the ranch house, the setting sun reflected brightly off the giant red rock easily visible on the western horizon. It shone with an intensity of color and light that demonstrated once again the importance of this great landmark as a beacon guiding weary travelers in covered wagons across the Great Plains.

About the Author

The author is a practicing attorney and a managing director of a mid-sized law firm located in Troy, Michigan, a suburb of Detroit. A graduate of Princeton University and the University of Michigan Law School, the author is married, has three adult children, is a retired Air Force Colonel and lives in Bloomfield Hills, Michigan.

9 780595 192496